BEASTS FROM HELL

Braldt slammed his blade down with all his force, striking the wolf. Its head flew through the air, tongue lolling between snarling jaws, amazed eyes still staring in furious disbelief, and landed at the feet of the bear. Braldt stepped back, readying himself for the bear's attack, feeling the weakness in his arms as the blood continued to drain from his body . . .

But as Braldt watched, the skull of the wolf began to move, and its edges rippled, re-forming into the features of a man. The bear shimmered, as though obscured by a cloud.

Braldt blinked, wondering if this was an apparition caused by his pain. When he opened his eyes, the bear . . . was a man.

Stars swam above Braldt in a sickening circle, then darkness swallowed the stars . . .

THE HUNTER VICTORIOUS

ALSO BY ROSE ESTES

THE HUNTER
THE HUNTER ON ARENA

Published by
WARNER BOOKS

THE HUNTER VICTORIOUS

BY ROSE ESTES

A Time Warner Company

WARNER BOOKS EDITION

Cover design by Don Puckey
Cover illustration by Larry Elmore

Warner Books, Inc.
1271 Avenue of the Americas
New York, NY 10020

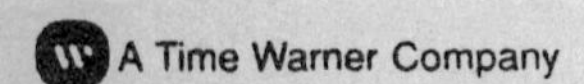

A Time Warner Company

Printed in the United States of America

First Printing: March, 1992

10 9 8 7 6 5 4 3 2 1

They were gaining on him. Braldt's breath came raggedly as he dodged behind a clump of gorse and slithered beneath an overhanging rock ledge. He pressed his forehead against his knees, shutting his eyes against the cold blue glare of the daylight, and tried to regain his breath and his composure.

They had been following him all morning since he had left the settlement, that architectural wonder of proud, soaring towers and cantilevered stairs that seemed to float on the cold air. At first there was nothing in the pale empty sky. Despite the fact that he had been here on Valhalla for more than two months, he had never grown accustomed to the absence of animal life. Valhalla was an empty planet and other than the earthling colonists who had claimed it for their own, it had no natural life other than flora.

Which made it all the more obvious when he spotted the first raven hovering above him on the rising wind currents. Not being of the planet, the raven could only have come from the king Otir Vaeng, he who was the enemy. In time, the black bird was joined by three others of its kind and throughout the morning they followed Braldt as he wandered over the steep, barren hillsides.

Only after he had crossed the sharp, serrated edge of the mountain range upon which the city was built had the others appeared, stepping out from the shadows of the rocks and matching their pace to his.

He had tried to ignore them at first, telling himself there was no law that said he was the only one allowed to walk outside the city walls. But they did not have the appearance of men out for a casual stroll. He was the object of their interest. Not even the king would dare to kill him so close to the city . . . but who was to know? queried his inner voice. He would simply meet with a mysterious accident, tumble off a ledge and fall to his death. Brandtson, his grandfather, and Keri, the woman he loved, might suspect foul play, but they would never be able to prove it. Then, with Braldt out of the way, it would be all too easy to dispatch the aging statesman and the helpless girl.

The men—there were six of them—increased their speed, gaining rapidly on Braldt and drawing their swords as they came, dispelling any lingering doubts that Braldt might have had about their intentions. Dropping his knapsack of provisions and his cloak, Braldt had begun to run at top speed, wending his way through the treacherous landscape with all the agility he had acquired through years of rigorous training. The followers had increased their speed as well. They plunged down the slope, their passage made all the more dangerous by a stretch of loose scree that made sure footing impossible.

The chase had gone on throughout the day and now, as the day approached its end, they were with him still and closing fast. It was apparent from their grim silence and their tenacity that they would be content with nothing less than his death. Six against one—not impossible odds, but difficult.

The days ended abruptly on this world, and the sun, always dim and casting little joy, slid quickly from view each night as though begrudging the colonists what meager warmth it had to offer. The shadows lengthened farther, magnifying each object as it was thrown into dark contrast against the cold, stony ground.

Huddled beneath his rock ledge, grasping for breath and for some plan that would save him, Braldt heard a chorus of eerie screams rising into the chilly air. The hair on the back of his neck rose up at the ghastly sound, human voices wailing and screaming, growing ever more agitated. There were no words as such, just unintelligible sounds, all the more terrifying for their lack of intelligence. The screams increased in volume and frenzy until it seemed that they could go no further without lapsing into insanity. Braldt gripped the hilt of his sword, guessing that the men were working themselves into a killing rage before they rushed him. Abruptly, the ululations turned to howls, long, drawn-out moaning bays that had never been uttered by a human throat. These horrible sounds were accompanied by fierce growls and throaty, raspy roars, equally inhuman. Braldt was shaken; he stared into the growing darkness, wondering what was happening beyond his vision.

Suddenly he heard something, a scrabbling of rock just beyond the entrance to his hiding place. He started to draw his sword from its scabbard, but before it cleared the mouth, a long, dark snout forced its way into the narrow space and wuffed a quiet greeting.

Relief flooded over Braldt. He was no longer alone; Beast had arrived! He had ordered the lupebeast, his loyal and constant companion, to stay with Keri until he returned. Braldt knew that she did not like to be left alone.

But Beast had a mind of his own and, while he had a certain fondness for Keri, his heart belonged to Braldt. Somehow he had snuck out of the city and trailed Braldt to this place. Braldt smiled grimly as he hugged the coarse-furred lupebeast to him. The odds had just gotten better.

His enemies circled the rock where he was hiding, uttering their unnerving cacophony of shrieks and howls and roars, never silent, never in the same place. It was impossible to sleep and, as the chill of the long night settled in around him like an old, familiar ache, he considered his options.

One, he could remain where he was and force them to come to him. There was a certain wisdom in this method, for he was well placed with rock at his back and sides, and he could only be reached by his opponents placing themselves in danger. But if he could not be reached, he would also find it difficult to inflict damage without showing himself. Stalemate.

Two, he could take the offensive and attack. Thinking themselves in a position of greater strength and knowing little of his mind-set, they would not think him likely to choose this option.

Three, he could try to create a diversion, sneak past them and return to the city, leaving them to circle an abandoned rock.

Somehow none of his choices appealed to him; but maybe a combination of tactics . . . Braldt pondered his fledgling plan from a variety of angles and thought that with a degree of well-deserved luck, it might succeed.

The rock beneath which he sheltered was like many of those that littered the mountainside, fractured and porous, brittle as well as unstable in nature. A large buildup of rocky detritus was poised on the lip of the overhang, it would require little to set it in motion. He studied the movement of the shadows. So far it appeared that his enemies were avoiding a direct approach, but they would soon gain confidence and close in on him. He would have to act before they did.

He signaled Beast to remain in place and worked his way to the mouth of the opening. A thin cover of scrubby brush lent scant camouflage, but it was adequate for his purposes. He sliced the edge of his tunic with his knife and tore a long strip of fabric free. This he tied to a bit of brush, which he then buried carefully in the rock debris poised above him. Beast growled, impatient with the enforced silence. Braldt knew that he would gain little advantage by waiting. Giving Beast a hand signal, he flattened himself against the frigid ground and began to inch his way forward. Beast knew the command well and obeyed without a sound, trailing Braldt like a shadow.

Braldt went no farther than the next outcrop, this a mere sliver of rock thrust sideways through the hard earth, but it would do. Braldt freed his sword, taking care to muffle the metal against sound and hide it from the reflection of the rising moon. His short sword and the unraveled bit of fabric he held in the other hand. He waited until Beast had fitted himself into the last bit of shadow and then pulled the long strip of fabric.

The resulting clatter of falling rock was everything he could have hoped for and more. Evidently his small maneuver had triggered a larger rock slide and the dark night reverberated with the sounds of stones and boulders plummeting down the steep mountainside. At the first sound of movement, Braldt let loose a terrible shriek, as though grievously injured and in mortal pain. This he followed with ever-weakening groans and cries for help.

For a time nothing happened. Then the first of his enemies circled in. Even though Braldt had suspected what he now saw, he could scarcely believe his own vision. It was a wolf! Sleek and silent as the night, the others drifted in toward the abandoned hiding hole, their sensitive nostrils casting about for the scent of their prey. Then, even as Braldt readied himself for their discovery, the wolves parted to make way for an enormous black bear, who batted aside the rocks as though they were no more than the weightless heads of flowers. His snuffling growls could be plainly heard by the astounded Braldt and Beast, and his rank scent hung heavy on the chill air.

Their trick would be discovered soon. Still uncertain about the true nature of his enemy, Braldt knew that he had to seize the initiative while it lasted. Uttering a fierce clan call, he hurled himself from hiding, with Beast beside him, and flung himself into the midst of the wolves, his great sword swinging.

One fell instantly, the sword slicing through the back of its neck, all but severing its head from its shoulders. A second was skewered through the chest and shaken loose to writhe its final death agonies under the feet of its astonished companions. A third, taken entirely by surprise, was seized in Beast's powerful jaws, its throat spewing hot blood. Then the moment of surprise passed and they were on him. The two remaining wolves immediately separated, spreading out to flank him on either side. The bear, slower to turn and comprehend the situation, reared up on its massive hind legs, towering above them, jaws agape and dripping with foaming slaver.

Beast dropped the lifeless body and launched himself immediately, again seizing his chosen target by the throat and wrestling it to the ground. The wolf was the larger of the two remaining, outweighing Beast by a third of his body weight, but Beast did not fight by ordinary methods. Lupebeasts were known for their strange habit of rising up on their hind legs to do battle. It made them an even more dangerous adversary when facing humans, for it placed the double rows of serrated fangs and powerful jaws at face level.

Braldt had never understood the technique's value when fighting creatures of its own size until now. After a short scuffle, Beast succeeded in locking his jaws around the throat of his opponent. This in itself might not have been fatal, for the wolf had merely to fall on the ground and twist its body, allowing its weight to break Beast's grip. But even as the wolf carried out this ploy, Beast rose on his hind legs and the abrupt, full-weighted drop tore the throat out of his opponent. The wolf fell to the ground, scrabbling in frantic circles, silent, unable to voice its agony, as its lifeblood gushed away.

The last wolf stood transfixed by the fate of its comrades. Its eyes glistened with hatred in the pale light of the rising moon as it crouched at the feet of the bear, choosing its moment carefully. Braldt and the wolf began a curious ballet, sidestepping in a wide circle, with the bear lumbering between them, its powerful paws outstretched—dancers in a macabre ballet, their only music the keening of the wind and the pulse of blood in their ears. Beast stood over the body of his fallen foe, gore dripping from his muzzle, his eyes glittering madly with bloodlust.

It was the bear who broke the rhythm, darting forward with incredible speed for one so large, its great paw slicing through the air, a fetid stink rolling from its open jaws. Braldt leapt aside unharmed and managed to slash his blade into the side of the immense creature as it rushed past, a glancing blow that drew blood but did little damage.

The wolf acted in concert with its larger ally and lunged forward, catching Braldt off balance and unprepared, its teeth locking on his left leg, throwing him to the ground. It was on him in an instant, straddling his body, its jaws open wide and surging toward his unprotected throat.

Braldt attempted to roll, but the wolf's legs blocked the move and he felt its jaws scissor shut, the teeth slicing through the flesh at the base of his jaw and the blood pouring down his chin as jagged points of fiery pain ripped down to his throat. Bright crimson lights flashed behind his eyes, the hot burning pain the color of blood to his mind's eye. He cried out then in fear and pain and rage, and struck out blindly with his sword, feeling it bite deep into an unseen target. The wolf staggered, falling heavily onto Braldt, its teeth rending his flesh further, matching Braldt's pain with an agonized cry of its own sounding in Braldt's ear.

Braldt rolled, closing his mind against the pain, and felt himself fall clear of the wolf. He struggled to his feet, feeling the steady flow of blood drenching his tunic, its heat turning chill against his body in the cruel wind. He wiped the blood from his eyes and saw the wolf hobbling toward him, its right front leg nearly severed halfway down its length. Never taking its maddened eyes from Braldt, it placed its weight on the mutilated leg and stumbled forward, head and neck outthrust, unprotected for one brief instant. It was all that Braldt needed, and he slammed his blade down with all his force, striking the wolf cleanly, feeling the steel slide between the vertebrae and lopping its head from its neck.

The head flew through the air, tongue lolling between snarling jaws, crazed eyes still staring in furious disbelief, and landed at the feet of the bear. It rolled a short distance before coming to rest, and the bear, still bleeding from its side, dropped to all fours and snuffled at the dismembered skull. Braldt stepped back, raising the sword, readying himself for the bear's attack, feeling the shivering in the back of his knees and the weakness in his arms as the blood continued to drain from his body. He wondered if he would have the strength to fend off the bear and seek the shelter of his rock before he lost consciousness.

Even as he struggled to hold his blade aloft, he felt his strength slipping away, and he struck the ground with his knees and then toppled over, unable to stand, though he knew that falling meant his death. He was filled with a great weariness and the sudden realization that he was very cold. A stone loomed before his eyes, immense, although in truth it was really quite small. He wanted to call out, to say something before he died, but he was very tired and it seemed much too difficult a task to accomplish.

The night swam into focus then and he became aware of Beast pressed against his side, growling, his double rows of teeth glinting in the cold light of the rising moon. The bear . . . The bear crouched down a short distance away, bent over its fallen comrades. And as Braldt watched, incapable of blinking, of shutting the scene from his mind, it seemed to him that the skull of the wolf began to move; its edges rippled, moved in the dark night, re-forming themselves until the features were those of a man instead of a beast. The bear shimmered and dropped to all fours.

As Braldt watched in disbelief, the figure of the bear wavered as though obscured by a cloud. Braldt blinked hard, wondering if it was his vision or an apparition caused by his pain. When he opened his eyes, the bear appeared before him, but it was a bear no longer . . . it was a man. The stars swam above Braldt in a sickening circle, the darkness swallowed the stars, and there was no more.

2

"Berserkers. Shape-changers," Brandtson said in a grim tone as he swabbed his grandson's torn flesh with a healing antiseptic that would bond the torn edges, leaving no sign of injury.

"What are these . . . these things?" asked Braldt, grimacing at the sharp stinging that assailed his flesh, yet marveling that such a miraculous healing potion existed. "Are they men or gods? How can they change their form?"

"They are men, not gods," Brandtson replied heavily as he finished his work and sat back, studying Braldt with a critical, yet caring eye, noting with satisfaction that the mangled flesh had already begun to heal. His large, gnarled hands rested on his thighs and he raised one hand and touched the tip of Braldt's chin gently. "They are men, but they use the same sort of magic that is at work here. But instead of using it for good, rebuilding what has been destroyed, they have turned their gift to evil."

"I do not understand," said Braldt, trying to follow his grandfather's words. But as he had found with so much else on this new world, the words frequently imparted no real meaning. Nothing he had ever experienced had prepared him for the world he found waiting for him on Valhalla. His strength and his wits had always been his salvation. On Valhalla young children rivaled his knowledge and even surpassed him in many areas, and most able-bodied men were his equal in strength.

Brandtson sighed. "And why should you understand? It is a confusing concept. But I will do my best to explain." He studied his grandson for a moment as he considered his words, noting with pleasure the clean, sharp lines of the young man's profile—the high, sharply edged cheekbones, the strong chin, and the bright blue eyes—a younger version of himself. There were differences, to be sure: Braldt's hair was full and thick, so blond as to appear white in strong sunlight, and he was clean-shaven. Brandtson's hair, while still thick, was as white as the snow on the surrounding mountain peaks, as was his beard. There were other similarities as well. Both men were tall, well over six feet, and broad of shoulder. Brandtson carried more weight than Braldt, but still, he was powerfully built, with massive arms and thighs, the corded muscles that rested beneath his darkly tanned skin giving testament to the fact that he was indeed ancestor to the young warrior who sat before him.

"In the old days—and I am speaking of days that no man remembers, before books or written word—there were such men as these who serve Otir Vaeng. They served other kings in those days, but their loyalties were fierce and unswayable. Then, as now, they would have given their lives for their allegiance. They were known as berserkers, a sort of elite bodyguard who protected the king and did his bidding in times of danger or war.

"Before battle, they would work themselves into a frenzy, screaming and yelling, making all manner of frightening noises. This served two purposes. One, it heightened their own rage to a near manic level, turning them into unstoppable killing machines that could only be halted by death. And two, the sound of their screams was often enough to vanquish their foes without a blade being lifted, for their reputations preceded them and they were greatly feared.

"But at such times that battle was met, these men were said to have the ability to turn themselves into wolves and bears that would tear their enemies limb from limb and devour their very flesh."

"But Grandfather, how can this be?" Braldt persisted. "Were they gods that they could do such a thing?"

"They say that there were gods in those days, Odin and Thor and Freya, but these Berserkers were not gods, only men who understood the mysteries of magic. There have always been such men. At times their gifts were scorned and they were reviled as evil and hunted from the face of the earth, but always they have been with us. And they are with us still, even here on Valhalla.

"I had thought that we had come too far for such men to exist, but I was wrong. It seems that such men and such mysteries always appeal to certain minds and in times of trouble when solutions cannot be found by rational means, they reappear to work their mischief."

"Do you understand how it is that they do this thing, this shape changing?" Braldt asked.

"No," Brandtson answered simply, "but neither do I doubt the fact that they exist."

Braldt shook his head and sighed, wincing slightly as the newly formed tender flesh was stretched taut. "But that does not explain why they sought me out, why they attempted to kill me. What possible danger can I be to Otir Vaeng? I am but one man, alone, without any who owe me allegiance. How can I be a threat to one so powerful?"

"You are a threat not so much for yourself as for what you symbolize," said Brandtson. "Otir Vaeng is a rogue, operating outside the laws that govern the known universe. He has broken many laws, spilled blood, and defied the Whole

World Council. But everything that he has done was done with one purpose in mind: the survival of the Scandi nation. It is because he was so strong, so willing to risk the wrath of the rest of the universe, that we have survived and thrived as well. In doing so, he captured the hearts and the loyalties of the masses.

"Some will argue that Otir Vaeng was a man of vision who single-handedly saved our race, but the days for such headstrong actions are long past and there are those among us who believe that he must step aside in order for us to progress. Otir Vaeng has no place in this new world. He and his followers would see a return to the old ways, using the old gods as a means of retaining their hold.

"You, coming as you do from a world he destroyed, are a living symbol of his wrongdoing. Your mere presence is a constant reminder of his misdeeds. He is fearful that you will ally yourself with your father's old friends, those who were opposed to his plans in the past."

"But I do not understand what he has to fear," Braldt persisted. "I am but one man. What can I do to harm a king?"

"You need do nothing but exist," replied Brandtson, "for him to try to kill you, as this day's work has clearly proved. He cannot allow you to live, but he cannot kill you outright, for your death would bring into question the very issues he wishes to avoid."

"Is there no solution, then, other than my death?"

"You are not without friends here, as Otir Vaeng knows well. We must seek them out. I am an old man and I have supported Otir Vaeng in his endeavors, and it will be hard to turn my back on him, but I can see no other way to protect you. Now that I have found you, I will not have you taken from me, as was your father. But you must not complicate the task by placing yourself directly in harm's way," Brandtson chided gently.

"I'm sorry. I had no idea. . . . The city, it closes in around me. I am not accustomed to spending my days encased in stone and the time we spent imprisoned on Rototara makes freedom all the more precious."

"Be patient, Braldt. If all goes well, Otir Vaeng will be removed from power and you will be free to roam wherever you wish."

"The one place I wish to roam no longer exists," Braldt said softly. "Otir Vaeng has seen to that by destroying my world. How can I ever forgive him? It does not matter if he takes my life, but to kill an entire world . . . that I can never forget. Nor will I sit by patiently while others fight my battles for me. By destroying my world and those I loved, Otir Vaeng has added me to the list of those who seek his downfall."

"You have not lost everyone you love," Brandtson replied, feeling the depth of the young man's anguish. "There is still Keri."

Braldt nodded and raised a hand to his chin, which was smooth and soft with tender new tissue. "I thank you for your healing skills. I did not want her to see me as I was. She pretends that all is well, but she carries the hurt of Rototara in her heart still. Does she know what happened?"

Brandtson nodded. "I don't think you give her enough credit. Keri is strong in spirit as well as in her love for you. She is scarred but not irreparably damaged. It is better for her to be involved than for you to treat her like an invalid and pretend that nothing has happened. She is tending Beast's wounds. The creature trusts her and I am too attached to my hands after all these years to trust them within reach of his jaws."

"I feel that I am besieged on all sides," Braldt muttered. "Otir Vaeng and those who follow him on one hand, and Carn, who bears little or no resemblance to the brother I once knew, on the other. All of them would like to see me dead."

"Yes," agreed Brandtson. "You have more enemies than any man deserves. Never have I seen any man, Scandi or otherwise, embrace the old gods the way Carn has done."

"The old gods' thirst for blood fits his mood these days," Braldt said grimly. "His mind has come unhinged. No man valued the price of a flagon and a good time more than Carn. Now all he thinks about is religion and death."

Braldt turned to his grandfather and said, "I wish I could turn back time, undo all the damage that has been done. I am glad that we have found each other, but I would give anything to have things as they used to be."

Brandtson studied the young man, who was the last of his line and his hope for the future, and the depth of Braldt's pain touched his heart. Nor was his conscience eased by knowing that he too had played a role in the destruction of Braldt's life.

"All may not be lost," he said at length. "There are things at work, both good and bad, that you should know about. But I beg you, remain calm. No matter how upsetting you find the things you see and hear, I ask you to hold your tongue. Say nothing, no matter what happens, for our lives may depend upon your silence."

It was after nightfall when Brandtson came for Braldt. He was clad in a long black cloak with a hood that completely covered his white hair; even his silvery beard had been muted to a dull grayish brown. He handed Braldt an identical cloak, which swathed him from head to toe. Braldt opened his mouth to speak, to ask Brandtson where they were going and why disguises were necessary, but something in the old man's demeanor caused him to hold his tongue.

Beast had remained with Keri, gently sedated to keep him still while his flesh mended. His wounds were deeper than Braldt's and he was bruised and sore as well. It was decided that it would be wiser to leave him than to have him accompany them.

Brandtson stepped outside first, holding Braldt back until he was certain that the way was clear. The hour was late, well after starfall, but time mattered little to Valhallans and it was not uncommon to find the streets and corridors nearly as crowded at midnight as they were at midday.

Brandtson led Braldt out along the high, curving edge of the outer balustrade, the exterior walkway that circled the entire perimeter of the mountain that served as the central city of Valhalla, curling around the mountain like some giant snake from base to peak. Popular during clement weather both for the ease it provided in reaching one's destination as well as a place to see and be seen, it was all but deserted now in the frigid depths of winterfall. The icy winds swept down from the peak which hovered above them, clad in a mantle of ice and snow which glimmered blue-white in the reflection of the distant stars.

Braldt wrapped the thick folds of the cloak around him, swirling the bottom edge over his shoulder as Brandtson had done, and burrowed his tender chin down into the folds of the material, grateful for the protection it provided. He had been cold before. He thought back to the many nights he had stood guard at home, protecting his tribe against wild animals, slavers, or whatever dangers might appear. The cold winds had swept in off the desert, chilling the unfortunate guards to the marrow. But the cold on Valhalla was a different sort.

The Scandis had left old earth, their home planet, congested, polluted, and dying of its inhabitants' excesses, and had colonized the planet they named Valhalla. According to their ancient legends, Valhalla was the abode of the gods and the final resting place of all worthy warriors. They had begun their world anew with only their strength, determination, and what little they were able to salvage from earth. Those were difficult times and there had been many setbacks. But the Scandis succeeded and Valhalla took its place among the handful of established earth colonies and other civilizations that made up the Whole World Federation.

They had overcome many problems: the fact that Valhalla had no life-forms other than vegetation, the absence of most raw materials necessary for self-sustenance, and the growth of dissident political factions among their youth. They dealt with these problems as best they could, but the single problem that had no solution was one which they could not have anticipated. The sun that shone on Valhalla was dying.

The problem had become apparent a decade ago. The sun had emitted a furious burst of solar energy which had caused incredible damage on the planet. Hundreds of colonists had been fatally burned, as well as most of the animals that they had brought with them from earth and nurtured at great cost. When the flares diminished, it was apparent that the sun's light was greatly dimmed. There had been numerous flares, accompanied by an equal number of dimmings, in the years that followed. Now the cold was ever-present, bearable during the all too short daylight hours but bone-piercing and mind-numbing in the long, long nights.

Much to Braldt's amazement, Brandtson turned aside after a short time and slid into a niche in the side of the mountain, all but disappearing from sight, thanks to his dark garb. Braldt followed his lead and tucked himself into the shadows as well. He started to speak, but Brandtson gripped his wrist tightly and Braldt saw the sudden glint of starlight on metal. A dagger? Then he heard it, the sound his grandfather had been listening for, the furtive slip of footleather on stone, silent, hurried steps and anxious whispers: "Where are they? Where did they go?"

Brandtson answered the question by slipping silently out of his hiding place and confronting the followers. There was a sudden gasp of surprise, a grunt, the briefest of curses, and then a sigh as a body hit the cold ground. The second of the pair backed away, wielding a blade of his own, longer by far than Brandtson's, but he had forgotten about Braldt and backed up, placing himself almost directly in front of Braldt's hiding place. A bent elbow, the crack of bones, and the man hung heavy and motionless from Braldt's grip. Brandtson did not hesitate for a minute but seized the second would-be assailant and flung him over the balustrade after his associate.

"Who—" Braldt whispered. But Brandtson held his hand up for silence and, after satisfying himself that there were no more where the first had come from, doubled back on their track and swiftly made his way up the mountain.

It was dark on the higher reaches of the slope, with nothing but starlight to illuminate the way. But the path was smooth and girded by the broad stone balustrade which protected them from the sheer drop if they had been foolish enough to venture near the edge. But ice and snow lay thick on the path and as they approached the upper elevations it became increasingly difficult to advance. For every two steps forward, they slid one foot back. The higher they climbed, the more vindictive the wind which tore at their cloaks and attacked their extremities as though it had a personal vendetta against them.

The craggy edge of the plateau was in sight before Brandtson hesitated and looked back the way they had come, studying the path carefully and listening closely. At last he was satisfied that they had not been followed and, signaling to Braldt, edged into a narrow crevice. Braldt was perplexed but followed his grandfather's lead and felt his way into the inky darkness. With nothing to guide him other than a sense of the older man's presence and his fingertips trailing across the rock, he crept inch by inch into what appeared to be a narrow fissure that doubled back on itself several times. Suddenly light appeared before them, softly illuminating the way ahead of them. It was apparent that they were in a narrow passageway of sorts; the rock walls met overhead and flanked them closely on either side.

They came to another switchback and as they turned the sharp corner, Braldt was all but blinded by the flood of light that assaulted his unprepared senses. He threw an arm up over his eyes and at the same time sensed as much as heard a sudden intake of breath and knew that they were not alone. He felt Brandtson's hand upon his arm, a single tight squeeze of reassurance as well as warning. Slowly, blinking against the harsh light, Braldt lowered his arm and stared in shock and disbelief at the sight that met his eyes.

3

They were in a large cavern that rose high above them till it met in a sharp peak. The walls were rough and craggy and held blazing torches set at regular intervals. The thick black smoke that curled away from the flaming brands filled the cavern with a dense haze that blurred the edges of everything in the huge hall. But no amount of softening could lessen the shock of the sight before them.

The enormous space was filled with many hundreds of black-robed figures, their features obscured by the enveloping cloaks, which lent an ominous air to what was already a frightening scene. Somewhere to the front and left, an unseen drummer beat out a constant tattoo that underlaid the scene like the pounding of blood in one's ears. Their silent arrival had elicited a moment of close scrutiny by those standing nearest the entrance, but this was short-lived, as Brandtson's imposing figure met with recognition. Braldt was careful to remain behind Brandtson, for he himself was viewed with distrust by nearly everyone on Valhalla.

Brandtson directed Braldt to an irregularity in the rock wall which, due to its configuration, was wrapped in shadows. Braldt eased into the darkness and Brandtson positioned himself before his grandson, shielding him from sight but allowing Braldt to see all that transpired.

The cavern sloped upward at its farthest end, and situated against the back wall was an immense thronelike chair carved from the rock and ornately ornamented with a tangle of hieroglyphics and the figures of wild animals—bears, wolves, boars, and horses, their eyes set with precious red stones that glittered in the torchlight, and with ivory fangs, tusks, and claws. The interstices between the designs had been rubbed with a black substance so that the raised figures stood out in sharp relief, the animals seeming almost ready to take life and leap from the stone.

Set before the throne was a stone altar chiseled from the same rock, rising from the floor in a single block. Its sides were rough-cut, but the top surface was smooth and had been polished to a high gloss. Along the edge of each of the four sides a deep trough had been cut into the stone and the sight sent a cold chill of premonition up Braldt's spine.

But even more frightening than the stone altar or its throne was the figure that pranced between them. It was a woman, or so it seemed. The woman wore a costume fashioned from a multitude of animal skins, their fur a contrasting mélange of different colors, lengths, and textures. Upon her head she wore the head of a wolf, its skull and upper jaw fitting down over her own, the pelt trailing down her back, the tail brushing the ground behind her. Her features were hidden, for directly beneath the shadow of the muzzle was the face of a bird. Braldt stared in shock until he was able to understand that it was merely the skin of a bird removed whole, the feathers and beak still attached and fashioned into a grotesque mask. Its feathers were glossy black with a blue-green sheen, its beak the cruel curved curl of a bird of prey. The eyes were mere slits that revealed little other than a bright glitter; breasts and loins were clad in drapes of fur.

The shaman, if that was what she was, strode back and forth between the altar and the throne. In her hand she held a carved staff which she brandished as she spoke. Her words were barely understandable; Braldt was able to catch a word here and there, but even though the sounds were familiar, they were somehow strange. It was as though the woman were using a more ancient form of language, the roots from which their present language had sprung. But if Braldt had difficulty understanding her, he was alone, for the gathering of robed figures followed her impassioned words intently and roared back their response at appropriate intervals.

To the right of the altar stood a broad circular stone basin set upon a carved stone base. The figure of a snake wound its way around the pillar, its head resting, mouth agape, on the rim of the basin. Its eyes were also set with glittering red stones, its long curved fangs fashioned of ivory or bone, and between the open jaws gushed a steady flow of fire which fed a pyre contained within the stone basin.

The shaman approached the conflagration, her words growing more and more frenzied, a bit of slaver appearing unnoticed at the corner of her mouth. As she neared the fire, she took from her garments a fur pouch which Braldt had not noticed before. Her hand dipped inside the sack and withdrew, holding several small items which she dropped into the fire one at a time, muttering incantations that seemed ritualistic from the tone of her voice as well as the echoed response from her rapt audience.

A twig was dropped. The fire shot blue sparks; the crowd roared its response. A bit of moss fell and the fire burned yellow. The crowd yelled louder. A stone plummeted into the heart of the pyre and the flames turned green. The black-robed throng shrieked their answer. And then the woman turned to one side, her arm outstretched, pale white, slender, a delicate tracery of blue veins visible beneath the skin, the first sign of vulnerability, of humanness, about the terrifying figure.

Even as Braldt was contemplating this small bit of evidence that the creature was a woman, she turned back to the fire and in her outstretched hand there was a rabbit. It was a large rabbit, white in color, with red eyes that shone bright with terror. It hung suspended from her closed fist, its weight borne fully by its ears. It struggled in the woman's grasp, fighting against some sensed danger. A high, thin squeal burst from its mouth, startling in its resemblance to the cry of a child.

The shaman spoke, the crowd answered, and even as Braldt watched in disbelief and horror, the woman opened her hand and released the rabbit, dropping it into the heart of the flames. The rabbit screamed and twisted in midair, clawing helplessly, and then it was gone, swallowed whole by the flames, which seemed to reach out for it, bulging as they wrapped themselves around its plump body. The flames grew dark, black as night, though the core was visible still, white-hot and pulsing like a living heart.

The mass of robed figures roared loudly, the sound filling the stone chamber and echoing back and forth against the walls till it seemed that he could feel the reverberation in his bones. The shaman raised her staff above her head and screamed. The crowd screamed back. And then it was done. The woman lowered her arm and as the last whisper of sound drained away, she staggered and then fell into the waiting arms of the throne.

Braldt watched in stunned silence, not even needing the cautionary touch from Brandtson to remind him to hold his tongue. The crowd stirred expectantly; a sense of anticipation could clearly be felt in the air.

There was a stir of movement in the front of the hall and a murmur of voices; Braldt strained to see. Carved wooden staffs could be seen rising above the heads of the crowd, and as they passed, the robed figures bowed low in obeisance. There could only be one person on Valhalla who would exact such subservience. Braldt felt suddenly cold. It could be no one but Otir Vaeng, the king.

Braldt could see him clearly now. Otir Vaeng, king of Valhalla. He was a tall man, taller than Braldt himself, with broad shoulders and narrow waist and hips, lean to the point of emaciation. His hair was the bright yellow gold of the sun, as was the beard, which followed the line of his jaw and ended in a sharp, forward jutting point. He was in the habit of stroking this beard often, perhaps unaware of his obsession, and it was due to his constant ministrations that the beard preceded him like the prow of a ship. His nose was narrow and pinched, beaked at the bridge and turned down like a bird of prey. His cheekbones were slanted and angular, rising sharply as though they might slice through the skin that was stretched taut over them. His eyes were a cold, brilliant shade of pale blue, like precious gems. His eyebrows and lashes were so pale as to be invisible, and this made his eyes appear even more piercing and demanding.

He stared out at the silent crowd, stroking his beard, saying nothing until the silence grew so intense as to be discomforting. Only when it had stretched to a breaking point, when Braldt's nerves cried for some action, some word, did the king speak.

"You have heard the volva," he said in a low voice which required utter silence so that he could be heard. "The gods have spoken. Freya herself has told the volva what must be done if we are to save ourselves from doom.

"We have brought the wrath of the gods down upon ourselves because we have failed to honor them. We chose to walk apart from them, placing our faith in new gods, science and technology, and those gods and their followers were what killed the earth. We too will perish and vanish forever if we do not return to the old ways and honor the old gods, as is their due."

"What . . . what would the gods have us do?" asked an

older man situated in the front of the crowd, his quavering voice betraying his nervousness.

"The volva has told us what must be done," replied a second voice, a voice all too familiar to Braldt. He straightened with shock and leaned forward to see what he could scarcely believe. A second figure moved to stand at the king's side and Braldt stumbled back against the wall, weak with shock. Carn! What mischief was this that allied his adopted brother with the king of Valhalla, he who had caused the death of their planet and everyone and everything that had been dear to them? Carn spoke.

"The volva has spoken; the seidr, the divination ceremony, has told us what we needed to know. The gods have spoken through her to us and told us their wishes."

"We must kill the outsiders, kill the unbelievers," said the king, his voice a mere whisper of sound, but clearly heard in the silent hall. "The unbelievers must die. Only then will the gods return their favor to we who have believed in them and been faithful down through the long centuries when the false gods ruled the earth. The sun will shine on us once more and we will thrive and prosper only if our belief is strong."

"Is he serious?" Braldt whispered. Brandtson made an abrupt cutting motion, signaling him to silence. Braldt frowned and settled back into the shadows to listen.

"But this one, this Carn, is an outsider," cried a voice from the midst of the crowd. The crowd pulled aside as though unwilling to be singled out by the king, to be suspected of disagreeing with him.

But Otir Vaeng merely smiled, a grimace that held no intent of humor. "Carn is an outsider, that is true, but his belief in the old gods is strong and true."

"How can this be so?" challenged the voice from the crowd. The king turned to see who had dared to defy him and his eyes glittered as the crowd drew back, revealing a heavyset older man, white-haired and bent in stature but not in resolve. He took no notice of the crowd's fear, but leaned on a stout cane and stared at the king. "How can this Carn believe in our gods?" he questioned in a reasonable tone. "He is not even from our world. One can scarcely imagine as to how he knows of our gods, much less puts his faith in them."

"Do you challenge my word, Saxo? I am your king; if I tell you something is so . . . it is so."

"You are my king, this I do not deny," replied the old man. "And I have followed you these many years even when my heart and mind were troubled by our course of action. But what we have done in the past was necessary for our survival. This . . . this superstitious claptrap that you are reviving, setting in motion, is dangerous and I urge you to think about what it is that you are doing."

The mass of dark-robed figures pulled back farther, widening the gap between themselves and the old man, not wanting to seem as though they were any part of what he was saying. All eyes focused on the king, who stroked his beard and smiled coldly.

"Superstitious claptrap, you say, Saxo? Do you then not believe in Odin and Freya and Thor? Do you dare to deny their existence?"

"Come, come, Otir. Do not think that you can frighten me with that tone of voice," Saxo said with a wearied motion of his hand. "You forget that I have known you since you crawled on the floor, your diaper dragging behind you. You cut your teeth on the hilt of my sword. Your father and I were lifelong friends and I his counsel general. You think to threaten me? I am too old for such threats and too old for this religious nonsense. What do you hope to accomplish with it? You have the loyalty of the people, although whether from fear or from lack of other options, I cannot say. Why do you need to implement this foolishness and what role does this outsider play in your game?"

A vein throbbed at the corner of Otir Vaeng's temple and his teeth were bared as he tugged fiercely on his beard. For a moment it seemed that he would strike the old man down or run him through with his sword, so great was his anger. Then Carn stepped forward and placed his hand on the king's arm, shaking him slightly as he whispered in his ear. Otir Vaeng shook his head, and Carn continued to speak with urgency. Finally the king nodded and stepped back. Carn stepped forward and addressed Saxo as well as the rest of the gathering.

"It is true, I am not one of you. I am an outsider. Until recently, I did not even know of your existence, much less the existence of your gods. I come from a world that is far away in distance as well as in knowledge. All my life I have searched for a greater meaning for my life . . . for all life. I thought I had found it on my own world, but all it brought me was pain and suffering." He gestured toward his horribly scarred face and hands, which had been burned by exposure to the intense heat of a volcano.

"I came to Valhalla by accident, or so I believed, but now I know that it was fate that delivered me here, fate that has brought me knowledge of Odin and Freya, Loki and Thor. These are the truths I have been searching for all my life.

"I have learned that a man cannot live without the guidance of the gods and disaster waits for those who are godless. Nor will the gods hesitate to strike down those who do not believe in them. The gods saved me and destroyed my world because I was the only true believer. You *must* follow your gods and obey their wishes or you and your world will meet the same fate as my world. I may be an outsider, but I am a believer."

Carn's mutilated face was crimson with the passion of his words and his eyes glittered with feverish intensity. His hands opened and closed into fists as he spoke, and it was clear that he believed every word he uttered.

"Would that your faith was so strong, Saxo," Otir Vaeng said softly as he placed his arm around Carn's shoulders and shook him gently, a gesture that spoke of friendship and trust and more. "Take care that you do not bring the wrath of the gods down upon yourself." The threat was implicit and the old man said nothing more, merely stared sadly at the man who was his king.

"The volva has spoken," said Otir Vaeng, his hand sweeping toward the woman on the throne. "The wishes of the gods are clear. We must rid ourselves of outsiders, of disbelievers, of those who are not worthy of Valhalla. Hunt them out from among us. Only then will we and our world be safe."

Braldt started suddenly as Brandtson gripped his hand and silently drew him out and away, back the way they had come, unseen by those around them who pressed forward and were voicing their agreement in loud tones, anxious to prove their loyalty to their king.

Once they had turned the corner of the narrow corridor, Brandtson gripped Braldt even more tightly and together they fled from the madness behind them.

4

Braldt and Brandtson hurried down the side of the moun-tain, anxious to be gone before the gathering broke up. Although it was almost a certainty that everyone would use the interior path to avoid the bitter cold, it was possible that some would choose the outer balustrade. Brandtson had taken a great risk in bringing Braldt with him, for Braldt was the one who Otir Vaeng most wanted dead. Brandtson did not think that Braldt would accept the seriousness of the situation unless he heard the king's words with his own ears.

Braldt followed his grandfather, all but oblivious to the bone-biting cold and the driving sleet which made the slippery path all the more dangerous. He had known that Otir Vaeng was his enemy, but this madness was beyond belief. Men who changed their shape at will and became wild animals, priestesses sacrificing animals to fire, and now an exhortation to kill all those who did not believe as they did! What it amounted to was the open sanction of murder of hundreds, perhaps thousands of innocent people.

Braldt's mind was awhirl with confusion, but one thing he was sure was that if there really were gods, it seemed oddly providential that their wishes always seemed to coincide with the desires of those in power. He had seen it on his own world, the manipulation of the people by the priests, and on Rototara, where the numerous gods belonging to various civilizations often clashed in their desires. And now here again on Valhalla.

Perhaps there were a multitude of gods who belonged to the multitudes of races, but if that were so, the religious netherworld must be a crowded place, and how did those gods interact with each other? The Duroni believed in the gods of nature, believing that each natural element was controlled by its own deity.

The Rototarans, a reptilian race who spent the greater portion of their lives in hibernation, believed in a shadowy deity whom they referred to as "the True God." Braldt had little or no understanding of the Rototaran god, but from what little he did know, he was certain that it was not the same god as the Duroni worshiped.

Another race of beings from some distant point in the galaxy believed in a god by the name of Yantra, whose long list of musings guided the lives and actions of its followers.

But, according to Otir Vaeng, it was Freya, Thor, Loki, and Odin who were the only true gods and he would use them to incite his people to bloodshed and wholesale massacre of those he had deemed the enemy.

Braldt and Keri were at risk, that much was obvious. It would be wise to leave Valhalla before they were killed. But how? Where could they go? Their own world had been destroyed by the Valhallans and Rototara was now firmly held by its own people, who would surely kill Braldt and Keri if they were foolish enough to return. Braldt now knew that there were many other worlds in the universe, but even if there had been a way to get there, who was to say that they would not be exchanging one set of dangerous circumstances for another?

Furthermore, even though Braldt was but the rankest novice in the matters of science and technology, it seemed highly unlikely that murdering any number of people, sacrificing them to the whim of gods whose very existence was doubtful, would alter the fact that Valhalla's sun was dying. Even to his unschooled mind it did not seem logical that one action would have any affect on the other.

Braldt had assumed that they were returning to their own apartments, but to his surprise Brandtson turned aside long before they reached the lower slopes. Fumbling beneath his cloak, he unlocked and then flung open a heavy door that was fitted flush with the smooth flank of the mountain.

It was warm and dry inside the dark corridor and blissfully silent after the howling assault of the weather. Braldt sagged gratefully against the wall, only then aware of the fact that the blood was pounding in his face, and his extremities were numb and unfeeling.

Brandtson did not hesitate but made his way through the narrow chamber, and Braldt stumbled after, wondering where they were. The entranceway ended before still another door, which hissed with the release of pressurized air as it was opened.

Braldt shut his eyes against the bright glare that greeted them. Tears poured down his face as he blinked, adjusting himself to the light. Brandtson led him to a chair which was softly cushioned. To his wearied body it felt like sinking into a mound of feathers.

When at last he was able to make out the details of his surroundings, he saw that he was in an astonishing room unlike anything he had ever seen before. Brandtson handed him a heavy earthenware mug filled with a thick brown liquid that emitted a curl of delicious-smelling steam.

Braldt sipped gratefully at the hot brew and his senses were instantly flooded with delight. The brew was unlike anything he had ever tasted. It was sweet and thick and somehow conveyed a feeling of comfort, a sense of well-being. Braldt wondered if it was magical. "What is this?" he asked.

"Good, isn't it?" Brandtson replied with a smile as he hoisted his own mug in a toast. "It's called cocoa, comes from earth. Saxo's addicted to the stuff, his only real vice. He has enough to last him for the rest of his life. He spent a fortune on it, but then why shouldn't he? All his children are dead, killed by Otir Vaeng. He has no one else to spend his marks on but himself."

"Will he not mind that we are helping ourselves to his supplies?" Braldt asked. "If it is that precious, I would not want—"

Brandtson waved him to silence. "I added my marks to Saxo's. Perhaps it is childish, but I find it oddly comforting myself. . . . Reminds me of my youth. You know I was raised on old earth. Valhalla has its merits, but it will never be home." Brandtson cradled his mug in his gnarled hands and savored the aroma of the rising vapor, his eyes gazing into the distance, viewing the memories of the distant past.

Braldt was quiet, drawing pleasure from the warmth of the room, the soft comfort of the chair, and the newly discovered taste treat of the oddly named "co-co." He was curious as to why they were here in Saxo's quarters and other questions rose to his mind as well, but he knew that Brandtson must have had his reasons for coming to this place, and when he was ready to share those reasons with Braldt, he would. Braldt closed his mind to the questions that rose unbidden and allowed his eyes to wander around the amazing room.

There were six chairs in all, and all of them were thick of cushion, soft and inviting and covered with natural fabric as opposed to man-made synthetics, in colors that had once been bright and cheerful but had worn with age to muted shades of burgundy and blue and green. Several were ornamented with bits of carved wood that served no real purpose other than to enhance their beauty. Here on Valhalla, where stark utilitarianism was the norm, the furniture—the entire room, for that matter—was very unusual.

The floor beneath their feet was covered with numerous rugs, both large and small, cushioning the hard stone floor. These were a wide variety of colors and patterns which should have produced a feeling of discord but somehow seemed appropriate.

There were no lights such as Braldt had seen elsewhere in the city, cold globes of white light that Brandtson had labeled electricity. Saxo's chambers were illuminated by numerous lamps of a type familiar to Braldt, filled with oil, the flaming wick contained within a glass chimney which imparted a warm, ruddy glow over all.

There were numerous other pieces of furniture scattered around the room: tables, shelves, hassocks, desks, even some manner of musical instrument, large and bulky and strangely shaped. All of these items were made of wood, also unusual on a world that seemed to value articles made out of hard, cold, unnatural materials. The wood was dark and gleaming and it was obvious that it had been lovingly tended for many, many years.

Every flat surface was covered with objects, Braldt guessed the collection of a lifetime of mementos. There were pictures of people dressed in odd clothing smiling out at a room on a world whose soil they had never trod. There were bits of rock and shining crystalline formations, a glass globe the size of Braldt's fist filled with water and containing a tiny house, people and green triangular trees dotted with snow.

There were many objects whose use or meaning Braldt could not comprehend, but the most amazing items in the room were things that Brandtson called books. According to Brandtson, no one used books anymore, for they were considered obsolete, replaced by computers, holograms, word-speak, and several other use-specific items. But Brandtson still possessed a small number of books and Braldt was fascinated by the pictures and the idea that the small peculiar marks could convey meaning. Saxo's shelves were lined with books, many of them covered with leather and imprinted with ornate gold letters.

As Braldt's eyes traveled over the room, he was startled by a sudden heavy presence landing in his lap. He half rose, his hand going for his blade, the cup of cocoa nearly spilling. He looked down and saw a furred creature with huge green eyes struggling to keep its balance by the painful use of numerous hooked claws.

"Sit! Sit!" Brandtson chuckled loudly and, realizing that he was in no danger and feeling rather foolish, Braldt settled back in his chair, grimacing as he tried to remove the claws from his flesh.

"What, what is it?" he asked as he and the furry thing regarded each other with wary mutual distrust.

"A real live Norwegian Forest cat," Brandtson said with a chuckle. "Sorry, forgot to warn you about him. His name's Thorwald Trokenheim, or Thunder for short."

The animal stared at Braldt blandly, its lids half closed, hooding the startling green eyes, allowing him to manipulate its paws without comment. Now that he realized that he was not under attack and that the animal had meant no harm, Braldt was able to study it with a bit more objectivity. It was a handsome animal, nearly three feet long from the tip of its pink triangular nose to the end of its huge, plumelike tail. It was thickly furred, the coat heavy enough to keep it warm even in this cold climate. The head was broad and heavy, with clumps of long, fine whiskers at the side of the muzzle that reminded Braldt of a mustache. The upright ears were guarded by tufts of fur which would guard them from the elements. There was a thick, heavy ruff of fur around the animal's neck and tufts of fur stuck up between its toes. The fur itself was most unusual, striped gray, silver, and black on the surface and more than two inches in length, it was underlaid by a second shorter coat, which was fine, soft, and downy in texture, almost impenetrable.

The creature had endured Braldt's examination stoicly and now, seeming almost to smile to itself, settled down on Braldt's lap, tucking its feet beneath it, and as its eyes closed, it began to emit a deep, contented rumbling sound. Once again Braldt was startled and drew back slightly. The creature opened one eye briefly and gave Braldt a sideways glance that all but said, *Oh, be still and let me sleep.*

Brandtson had been watching the silent exchange with a wide grin and regarded his grandson, who was still viewing Thunder with goodly amount of ginger apprehension.

"Quite a compliment. Thunder doesn't take to just anyone," he observed.

"Wonderful," Braldt replied dubiously. "What did you say it is?"

"A cat. A Norwegian Forest cat. Do you not have cats on your world?"

"We *had* many cats on our world," Braldt said sadly, his hand rising to stroke the cat almost without realizing what he was doing. "But none quite like this, none that lived in our homes. Is this common to your people?"

"At one time, no home was complete without a cat or a dog," replied Brandtson, "but as earth began to die, there were too many people and too little food to sustain all the mouths. The pets were among the last to go in the more civilized nations, but when people were forced to decide between their pets and their children, cats and dogs joined the long list of animals that had already been driven to extinction.

There are probably no more than a score of these cats left in the world. Thunder has been with Saxo for more than a decade. In his way he can be as fierce as your lupebeast."

"Why does Saxo have him?" asked Braldt.

"Ask him yourself," replied Brandtson as a door swung open on the far side of the room and Saxo entered. Instantly Thunder leapt gracefully from Braldt's lap and strode to the old man, winding back and forth between his feet, rubbing his head against his legs with the plumelike tail erect, the rumbling sound now greatly amplified. Saxo set aside his cloak, bent down, and scooped the animal into his arms. For a long moment, man and animal butted heads with gentle affection and communed quietly. Braldt had no need to ask why Saxo would want such an animal. The love and loyalty between the two was clearly evident and its own ample reward.

"Well, Braldt, what did you make of that bit of nonsense?" asked Saxo as he sank into a chair and gratefully acknowledged Brandtson as he handed him a steaming cup of cocoa. Thunder curled into a huge furry ball in the middle of Saxo's lap, wrapped his tail over his head, and promptly went to sleep, his contented rumbling undiminished.

"It . . . it was frightening, if he truly meant what he said," Braldt replied slowly. "Would Otir Vaeng really set such a thing in motion?"

"Certainly. Have no doubt about that. Otir Vaeng has ruled for many, many years, and he has not done so because he hesitated to act."

"But I don't understand," Braldt argued. "The majority of those who will die will be your own people. I am an outsider, as are Keri and Uba Mintch, and there may be others whose presence I am unaware of, but we are but a small minority."

"You don't understand," Saxo said patiently, looking

down at Thunder and stroking the soft fur reflectively. "This return to the old ways is nothing but a ploy. If it were not religion, it would be something else. This just happens to suit his needs."

"You see, Braldt," said Brandtson, "our sun in dying. Sooner or later, but most probably sooner, this world will die just as surely as old earth did."

"Yes, I understand that much," said Braldt. "But why is it necessary to kill large numbers of people? It seems to me that everyone will be needed to find a solution to the problem."

"It doesn't work that way," Saxo said with a sigh. "You see, there are *too many* people. Once again, we must leave our world behind, find another planet to call home. There are many, many planets in the universe, but few of them possess the qualities which we require to sustain life. We are already strained to the limit, trying to produce enough food for those who exist on Valhalla. If we are to migrate to another world and survive, it will not be possible, or even desirable, to take everyone."

Braldt stared at the two old men, hearing but scarcely believing the words. "Do you mean to say that Otir Vaeng is using this religion as a cover for eliminating all of those people he does not wish to take to the new world?"

"That is precisely what we are saying," said Brandtson.

"But that is ridiculous!"

Saxo and Brandtson stared at him without comment.

"Otir Vaeng has been reviving the old gods for just that purpose," Saxo said at length. "It is a test, of sorts. All those who follow it are in essence paying him allegiance, accepting his guidance. Those who oppose the gods are declaring themselves against him."

"But that is not what it means," cried Braldt. "It merely means that they do not agree with his choice of religion. What or whom did they worship before Otir Vaeng brought back the old gods?''

"Most worshiped and believed in little," replied Brandtson, "although there were those who still clung to a number of more established earth religions. Technology and science were the death knell of most organized religions after the year 2000. The more we learned about the universe and the more difficult life became on earth, the easier it was to disbelieve in the old gods, for what merciful and all loving god would allow his followers to die in such agonizing ways?"

"The unanswerable question of the centuries," murmured Saxo.

"But it makes no sense," Braldt protested. "The sun will not die for many years to come. Nor has Otir Vaeng found another planet to migrate to. Why, he could use every single pair of hands. It is insanity to even think of killing so many people!"

"You do not understand the logistics of such a move," Saxo said patiently. "It is not like moving a family or a village or even an entire city from one location to another. When one leaves a planet and colonizes another, each person has been carefully chosen for the skills he or she possesses. There is slim margin for error. Who knows what the conditions of the new world will be? Who knows how long it will take to set up a food chain that will provide for all? Every mouth is a liability."

"But there is so much time!" Braldt said vehemently. "I have heard it said that this sun will not fade for many thousands of years. Is it not possible to send everyone? The most important workers go first and then the others in turn according to the needs of the world! Would that not work?"

"If indeed we had the amount of time that you are suggesting," said Saxo, "such a thing would indeed be possible.

But we are working against a much more difficult time frame."

"I do not understand." Braldt frowned.

"The solar flares," said Brandtson. "Yes, the sun will most likely exist for many thousands of years to come, but all life will have been extinguished long before that time, quite possibly in the next few years . . . or months."

"What do you mean?" Braldt asked, leaning forward and staring intently at the two old men.

"The solar flares," Brandtson repeated. "We still have no reliable method of predicting when a solar flare will erupt. Even worse than the flares are the solar storms. The level of radiation and ultraviolet rays that bathe the planet during those times are lethal. Those who are not fortunate to be killed instantly die hideous, painful, lingering deaths. We do not have the luxury of time on our side."

Braldt stared at the two men, absorbing their words, seeing that they were utterly convinced as to the truth of their words. "Who will be chosen?" he asked at last.

"All those who are willing to commit to Otir Vaeng heart and soul," replied Saxo. "It is from their numbers that he will choose his vanguard. We will not be among them."

"Why not?" Braldt asked in astonishment. "You are two of the highest ranking members of the Council of Thanes, as well as the most respected!"

"That is precisely why we will not be chosen," said Saxo, his fingers tugging gently at Thunder's thick fur. "He cannot risk having loyalties divided. He cannot be certain of retaining control unless his is the strongest voice."

"But you were both at the meeting tonight. He saw you; surely he does not question your loyalty!"

"No, he does not question our loyalty," Brandtson replied with an ironic grin as he looked over at Saxo. "He knows all too well that we have minds of our own and are not afraid to speak out against him if we are so moved. Saxo and I are undoubtedly at the top of his death list.''

Braldt was horrified. From all that he had observed during his time on Valhalla, it had seemed that his grandfather was much loved and respected and held a position of honor in the council of his peers. And Saxo . . . he sat at the king's right hand and opened and closed every council meeting. Surely he was untouchable! ''Are there others like yourselves?'' he asked quietly. ''Others in positions of power whom the king views as the enemy? If so, we must seek them out, tell them what you have told me and—''

Suddenly the calm quietude of the room was shattered by an eerie wolf howl that filled the air and electrified their senses. Thunder leapt to his feet, his ears plastered flat against his head, an impressive mouth full of fangs bared in an angry hiss, green eyes blazing. The three men rose from their chairs, cups and their contents tumbling forgotten to the floor. Saxo and Brandtson stared at one another. ''So soon. . . .'' Saxo murmured softly. Then, even as the howling increased and furious blows rained upon the inner door, Saxo looked around the room in sorrow, seized Thunder and his cloak in one swift motion, and exited by way of the outer door, followed by Brandtson and Braldt. As the door swung shut behind them and a series of bolts thunked into the stone walls, they could hear the crazed baying of wild animals and splintering of wood behind them.

5

The ice storm had increased in its intensity and that was their salvation, for as the three men hurled themselves out of the outer door, they were met by powerful buffeting winds that drove snow and sleet against their unprotected flesh like frozen arrows. To a man they doubled over instinctively, in an attempt to present as small a target as possible to the winds. By doing so, they saved their lives, as several shadowy forms, barely visible in the dense obscurity of the storm, staggered forward and swung their blades. Had they been upright, they would have been cleaved apart.

Steel rang out against stone, sending vibrations traveling up the cold metal and into the attackers' arms. Braldt knew well what that would feel like, for a brief moment vicariously imagining the tingling numbness that inevitably followed such a mistake and left one vulnerable to retaliation, for one's hands and arms were momentarily useless, unable to respond to the brain's shouted commands.

Braldt did not wait for his opponents to recover but flung himself upon them with his own blade hacking and flashing. It was all over in an instant, the three would-be assassins lying dead on the icy path. Braldt knew that he and his companions had been lucky, for the men were undoubtedly chilled to the bone and moving far more slowly than they normally would have.

Saxo laid a hand on Braldt's arm and opened his mouth to

speak, but before he could utter a word, shouts and muted words coming from both above and below them on the steep mountain path, indicated that their attackers had not been acting alone. The three men drew together, hastily donning their cloaks and drawing their weapons. Braldt was at a loss for what to do; their attackers were closing in on both sides and the door behind them shook beneath a heavy battery of blows.

Brandtson and Saxo had grasped the situation as well, and to Braldt's complete amazement, after a brief silent exchange followed by a single nod, they both sheathed their swords, gathered their cloaks around them tightly, and stepped to the balustrade.

"What are you doing?" he asked. "Do you plan to take your own lives? Surely we can make them rue their foolishness in attacking us. If we must die, let us take as many of them with us as possible!"

"We do not mean to die, although that may well be the outcome," Brandtson said as he threw a leg over the stone rail. He looked at Saxo, whose white-bearded features were already beginning to blur in the driving snow, and the two old men grinned at each other, a look that contained a lifetime of memories, bitter as well as sweet.

"We have done this many times before as boys," Saxo said as he struggled to straddle the balustrade while tucking an unhappy Thunder securely inside his garments. "Although I had fewer fears in those days and my bones were less brittle."

"But surely you do not think that we can climb down," Braldt protested even as he heard the first of the enemy approaching, desperately hoping that he could dissuade the two old men from what would surely be suicide.

"Come, Braldt, we know what we are doing," Brandtson

commanded in a tone that brooked no argument. "Follow us. Do exactly as we do."

Braldt hesitated, then threw one last look over his shoulder as a tight group of shadowy figures emerged from above, the steel of their blades catching the dim light. He could hear a steady stream of curses flowing from the other direction, and at that very moment the outer door to Saxo's chambers burst open, revealing a horde of men outlined in the light of the room they had just vacated. The odds were too greatly stacked against them. Feeling a sense of hopelessness, Braldt stepped over the balustrade just as a hand darted forward and seized his ankle. His sword flashed and was greeted by a horrified shriek and a hot stream of gushing blood as the hand released its grip and the arm, greatly shortened, jerked away.

Braldt felt his cloak yanked and he stumbled and nearly lost his balance before sitting down hard on the steeply slanted flank of the mountain. "Wrap your cloak around you as tight as possible," Brandtson whispered harshly. "Lay as flat as possible and keep your feet pointed down. Use your hands if you need to brake, but whatever you do, do it slowly, for sudden moves will break your bones or flip you over."

"How do we avoid hitting rocks?" Braldt asked, the foolhardiness of the scheme seeming only one notch lower than intentional suicide. But if two old men were willing to risk their lives in such a venture, could he do otherwise?

"Pray," Brandtson replied with a short barking laugh, and then, whooping into the wind, he was gone, followed immediately by Saxo, their voices trailing behind them as they descended into the dark night.

Still Braldt hesitated, holding fast to a rough icy outcrop, afraid to let go. Then the attackers were there above him, swords flailing the air in an attempt to reach him. One assailant, bolder than the rest, leaned far out over the edge and struck at Braldt. Braldt could easily have slain him had his blade been drawn, but it was sheathed and pinned beneath his leg. The steel struck the ice beside his head, and a shower of icy chips flew up as the blade clanged off, rebounding and passing so close to Braldt's face that he could feel the wind of its passage.

He could hesitate no longer, yet opening his hand and letting go was one of the most difficult things he had ever done. No sooner had he released his grip than he began to slide. His first, automatic inclination was to sit up and dig his heels in, but Brandtson had specifically cautioned him against doing such a thing.

The angry voices faded behind him as he picked up speed, plummeting down the face of the mountain with dizzying speed. He could see nothing; the world was a blur of blackest night, white snow, and gray ice. He could only begin to guess at the rate of his progress by the feel of the ground passing beneath him. It was a terrifying and rough passage, and yet after the first rush of fear he began to feel a sense of exhilaration, and almost without thinking, he let loose a joyous whoop that was instantly returned to him in the wind, although whether it was an echo or an answer from his companions, he could not have said.

Faster and faster he hurtled down the steep incline, bouncing from one icy projection to another, at times actually leaving the ground and flying through the air before landing heavily and picking up speed once more. He struck no actual rocks and he could only guess that they were safely buried under a layer of snow and ice. The days were warm enough to melt the uppermost surface of the snow layer, which promptly froze again at night, providing them with the means for escape.

The voyage seemed to last forever and he could not help but wonder how it would end. Then suddenly disaster struck;

his feet struck a ridge of snow and ice and he felt himself changing direction, sliding sideways, losing what little control he had possessed. For one frightening moment he was skidding down the mountain sideways. Then his shoulder struck a mound with a jarring blow and he tilted still farther, unable to free his hands from his cloak to try to brake his impetus. Then, somehow—he was never quite certain how it had happened—he flipped over in midair and landed on his stomach, racing down the mountain headfirst!

If the journey had been scary laying on his back, there were literally no words to express the terror of flying forward face-first with his hands pinned beneath him, tangled in his cloak.

He was traveling so fast that he could no longer tell whether it was snowing or whether the flurry of flakes shooting up alongside his head was caused by the speed of his passage. He raised his head as high as it would go in a futile attempt to see what was coming, but obstacles loomed up out of the blurry darkness and were gone almost before his eyes and mind could comprehend them, much less think of a way to avoid them. The night had become oddly clear and he could see the dark night sky sprinkled with glittering stars stretching above, calm and peaceful and still.

The voices of the enemy had long since vanished in the night; he could hear nothing but the whistling wind and the schuss of snow beneath him. Then out of the darkness there arose some sort of barrier stretching before him in an unbroken line. He could not tell what it was, but it was unmoving and it seemed quite likely that he would meet it with great force in the next few seconds if he did not manage to somehow stop his furious descent.

He struggled against the folds of cloth now stiff with cold and an accumulation of ice and snow. He dug his toes into the snow and did his best to drag them, to slow his progress, but they too were numb and stiff with the cold and obeyed his commands sluggishly, only to be battered and bruised by the rough surface and a multitude of unseen obstacles.

The barrier was approaching ever more swiftly and fear rose in his breast as he struggled to free himself and halt his descent, but his clumsy attempts merely sent him spinning ever more swiftly. Fear rose up in his throat like a dark wave. He screamed.

Then, seconds away from disaster, he felt himself seized on either side, stopped with an abrupt finality that was no less shocking than the dizzying descent. His head spun and his senses were awhirl. He thought for a moment that he was going to be sick as his mind and body slowly adjusted to the fact that he was no longer moving, and to the even more remarkable fact that he was still alive and intact.

He felt himself hoisted to his feet and he tried to stand, staggering from side to side on numbed feet and legs that felt as though they belonged to someone else. Slowly, he became aware of the fact that his back was burning and it was painful to move. His cloak hung in tatters around him, the heavy fabric torn and shredded with great gaping holes that let in the cold. One elbow was throbbing insistently and a hip and shoulder felt as though they had lost serious arguments with rocks, although he had no specific memory of such incidents. Slowly, the world stopped revolving around him and the noise that was buzzing in his ears separated into words—words that had meaning.

Someone clapped him on the shoulder and shook him gleefully. He tried to share the joy, but it hurt too much.

"Ha! We did it!" Brandtson chuckled as he hugged first Braldt and then Saxo. Braldt stumbled forward and leaned up against what he was now able to discern was another balustrade, while Saxo and Brandtson clutched each other in a bear hug and hopped up and down, dancing joyously at their successful escape.

"What I wouldn't have given to see the looks on their faces!" Brandtson cried as he shook his old friend gently and smiled at Thunder, who was less than pleased with the antics of the two elder statesmen.

"Remember when we used to do that at home, Brandt?" Saxo said with a chuckle, wiping tears from the corners of his eyes. "Remember how mad our mothers were? As I recall, we both had our bottoms warmed for ruining our storm gear, but it was worth it. None of these youngsters have ever done such a thing, nor would they have expected it of us!"

"Neither did I," Braldt said under his breath, though now that the venture was over and done with and they were still alive, he had to admit a new feeling of respect for the two oldsters.

"Where are we?" he asked, interrupting the cheerful flow of conversation, for he had begun to shake, although whether from the cold or delayed reaction to the experience he could not have said. "Should we not be thinking about leaving before they figure out what we have done and work up the courage to follow us?"

"It'll never happen." Saxo chuckled and the two men burst out laughing anew. "You either have to have one foot in the grave already or be completely crazy to do such a thing. We're quite safe for the moment."

Braldt decided not to mention that he did not possess either quality himself, contenting himself with asking, "How can you know that they will not come at us from another direction?" It was becoming difficult to speak because his teeth insisted on clattering and banging together.

Finally Brandtson seemed to recognize the fact that Braldt was somewhat the worse for wear and, cursing himself and Saxo for ten types of old fools, he helped Braldt over the balustrade and together the three of them broke a trail. It was clear that the path had not been used for some time. The layers of snow and ice had melted and frozen many, many times and as they broke through with every step, the multitude of icy crusts sliced through their leggings until their legs were coated with a chill layer of their own blood.

There was no sheltering bulk of the mountain on either side, only waist-high balustrades which left them totally at the mercy of the freezing winds which battered them from all directions. All sign of levity was gone now as they put their heads down against the wind and forced their way forward. The pitch of the path was extremely steep and, had it not been for the knee-deep drifts which plucked at their legs and seemed most reluctant to let them go, they might have taken several nasty falls.

At long last, the path took a sharp turn, doubling back against itself, and now the wind was at their backs, propelling them forward. It seemed forever before they stumbled against yet another balustrade and the three of them crawled over the wide stone ledge with legs that had lost all feeling and could barely support them. Here was the welcoming bulk of the mountain, and the cruel wind fell away to a whisper.

Both Saxo and Brandtson seemed to know where they were going, to have some destination in mind, for which Braldt was grateful. The sooner they got in out of the cold, the better. They slowed their pace and Saxo ran his fingers over the face of the mountain, searching for something. They crawled along, looking for whatever it was, until Saxo let out a joyful cry and the two men began tugging against something that seemed determined not to move.

It was a door, unused and immobile, fused by the ice and the cold until it was nearly a part of the mountain. Braldt joined in, using the tip of his blade to hack away at the ice, aching in every joint and growing ever more desperate with cold and fatigue. At last, groaning and creaking in icy protest, the door gave way to their blows and opened before them to reveal a velvety darkness and warmth that embraced them like a lover's embrace.

Ragnar Ollesson hurried down the outer trail, wrapping himself warmly in his heavy cloak. He chided himself for being a fool as the bitter wind struck him. It would have been wiser to have taken the inner path, protected from the vagaries of the weather, but he had wanted to be alone, to think about the words he had heard that night. It would be too easy to be swayed by the enthusiasm of his companions. Here, alone, he would be able to think.

Ragnar Ollesson had given Otir Vaeng his pledge of allegiance many years before and although he had often had cause to regret his unswerving loyalty, one had to admit that Otir Vaeng had brought them through some difficult times. They had survived and that was all that really counted. Or was it? There had been times when he had nearly spoken out, cast his vote against Otir Vaeng in the Council of Thanes, but always, in the end, he had voted with the king. And what had happened to those who had opposed him? All were dead, or as good as dead. It always seemed a coincidence, but few would argue that those who defied the king either died or found themselves stationed on remote outposts far from the seat of power.

With the notable exception of Brandt Brandtson. He and his circle of associates had been taking a stand against the king recently and they were still alive. But Brandtson was old and powerful, securely entrenched in the council with his own circle of power; it would be hard to dislodge him and should he die or disappear, none would think it an accident. Otir Vaeng had not achieved the throne by being stupid; he knew that Brandtson was beyond approach and would not attempt to attack him openly.

Ragnar's thoughts circled this evening's business uneasily, remembering the flames as they were mirrored on the seeress's naked flesh. In his mind he knew that she was only a woman like any other, but in his heart the mere thought of her carried a wave of cold fear. She was dangerous, no less dangerous than the king. If she pointed at you with a bone, you might just as well fling yourself off the side of the mountain, for she had marked you for death. All your friends would shun you for fear of being marked as well, and death would come sooner, rather than later. It was rumored that she made use of poison rather than the darker magics as she would have one believe, but what did it really matter? Dead was still dead.

Ragnar Ollesson shivered, and not from the cold, as he hurried down the side of the mountain, longing for the welcome warmth of his fire and the heavy weight of his down-filled blankets. If he allowed himself to think about it, there was much about the king's plan that he did not like. Was it really necessary to slaughter all those who could not be brought to a new world? His mind cringed from the thought of the bloodshed to come. He squirmed uneasily as he realized that he and his family were safe from such a purge. As chief programmer of the interstellar computers, he was far too valuable to discard.

He bit his lip and tried to avoid thinking as the decision was made almost without conscious decision. Really, there had never been any doubt about it; he had little courage and no stomach at all for bloodshed and pain, especially when it was his own. Then there were the children to consider. Was it really fair to even think of opposing the king when there were the children to think of? Immediately he felt better.

He began to chide himself for having taken this cold, dangerous route when he could have been warm and safe inside. He hurried down the treacherous slope, nearly falling on a smooth stretch of ice. Then it happened; his feet slid out from under him and he fell heavily to the ground and slid a short way, coming to rest against a strange bulwark of piled snow. He put out a hand to steady himself as he got to his feet, wondering for a moment how and why such an obstacle came to be in the middle of the path. Perhaps it had fallen from the upper slopes. He raised his head to look.

There was a sense of movement, a darkness against the even darker sky, a large shadow that obliterated the sight of the stars and filled him with a sudden sense of unreasoning terror. He felt a hand upon his shoulder and for a brief second he relaxed, thinking that one of his friends had thought to frighten him. He grinned, thinking of the laughter at his expense that would surely follow the telling of this tale and he opened his mouth to speak.

And then, as the hand tightened on his shoulder, he felt another hand seize his chin and a bolt of icy fear lanced through his bowels. He knew then in some intuitive manner that this was no friend and that he would never laugh and joke about what would happen next. He felt a sudden, sharp pang of grief for those he loved and an overwhelming sense of regret that merged neatly with the cold/hot tremor of agony that coursed down through his neck and body.

The body that had been Ragnar Ollesson slumped heavily to the icy ground, the blue eyes open and staring up at the stars, which were once more clearly visible. As he lay there, the life force slipping from his unfeeling body, he was glad that he could see them and he wondered to himself that perhaps the fear of pain and courage was far worse than the actual deed itself. Slowly, the stars dimmed and vanished.

6

Keri sat before the window in the darkened room, strok-ing the sleeping lupebeast and staring out into the dark night. The stars seemed much closer and brighter here. Sometimes it felt as though one could reach out and touch their cold, shimmering brilliance. Perhaps it was because they were different stars, shining down on a different world, so different from the stars she had wished upon as a child.

She smiled ruefully to herself at the thought of the naïve child she had been, such a very short time ago. Never would she have imagined, much less believed, that there were other worlds besides her own—many, many worlds with multitudes of races, all quite different from her own. In her naïveté she had believed her world and her people to be alone in the universe, and the goddess they worshiped to be the one true god. She sighed again, as much in sorrow at the loss of her world as at the loss of her own innocent beliefs. It had been a much simpler, safer life then. Knowledge was painful.

She felt a heavy weight rest gently on her shoulder, then squeeze it with compassion. She covered the hand with her own, feeling the rough coarse hair beneath her fingers, and smiled up into the darkness. "Your hand is cold. Have you been out?"

"Now, what would I be doing out in such weather?" Uba Mintch asked with a throaty chuckle. "This old man feels the chill of this world even indoors. No, I leave the roaming to Braldt and younger bloods."

"You talk as though you are an ancient graybeard," Keri chided with affection as she rose and crossed to the hearth, where a kettle of herb tea was brewing.

She poured two large mugs and moved to turn up the light until Uba Mintch stopped her with a motion of his hand. "Leave it, child, I find the firelight soothing. Sometimes I can almost believe that I am home and convince myself that the baby will soon be tugging on my leg, demanding attention. Did I tell you that she was walking quite well before I left? Getting into everything, she was. . . ."

The sorrow was thick in the old Madrelli's voice and he cleared his throat several times and looked away. Keri moved to his side and settled a heavy blanket around his shoulders, then stroked his head with the tips of her fingers. A heavy weight lay upon her heart, as well as a lump in her throat that refused to be swallowed. Tears sprung to her eyes as she tried resolutely to shut out the painful memory of her own family.

She knew all too well what Uba Mintch was feeling. She and Carn and his band of followers were all that remained of their people, the Duroni. Uba Mintch had fared less well, for no more than a dozen Madrelli had survived the death of their world.

Carn had been accepted with open arms by the king of Valhalla, for Carn was all too ready to believe that Otir Vaeng was some sort of deity. Nothing he had seen had convinced him otherwise, and nothing Keri or Braldt said swayed him from this conviction. Keri and Carn had never been exceptionally close, but now it was as though she were a stranger to him, perhaps even an enemy. Carn avoided her whenever possible and shut his ears to her words when she spoke.

He and Braldt had been raised as brothers, but Keri knew

that while Braldt accepted the younger man and loved him as though they were born of the same flesh, Carn had always harbored a nagging jealousy and steadily growing bitterness. No matter what they undertook, whether it was sports or academics, hunting or merely partying, Braldt was always better than Carn, scoring the highest scores, bagging the best game, winning the most desirable women—it was always Braldt.

To make matters worse, Braldt never seemed to realize what the younger man was feeling. He gladly shared his game and his women and made light of his winning scores, never realizing that the ease with which he shed his prizes merely made the losing more bitter. Keri's love for Braldt had only made matters worse, and now Carn included her in his hatred.

Keri could scarcely even recognize her brother. It was not so much a matter of the ruined skin and deformed features, but the bitter nature contained within the shattered body. He had allowed his hatred of Keri and Braldt and the Madrelli to warp him in some unfixable manner. The skin and the deformities could easily have been reversed, for the Scandis were capable of performing medical miracles, but Carn steadfastly refused to allow them to work their magic. It was almost as though he welcomed the taut, shiny skin that was stretched so tightly over his bones, embraced the pain as a personal stigmata bestowed upon him as a sign of his god's love.

It did not matter that their gods, Mother Moon and all the others, had proved to be but a creation of the Scandis; Carn's religious beliefs were intensely personal and unarguable. He had quite literally been baptized by fire and it would take more than words to sway him from his beliefs.

Keri sighed again and settled next to Uba Mintch in front of the fire. Beast stirred and stretched, his wounds nearly healed. Keri stroked him gently, urging him back to sleep.

"Where are they? What are they doing and what is to

become of us?" she asked. "I cannot stop thinking of home. It is so hard to think that we will never see it again, to think of everyone being . . . being . . . gone."

Uba Mintch covered her small hand with his own immense paw. "There was no time for them to suffer. There was no pain, no fright. It was all over in a heartbeat and they are not gone so long as we remember them; they still live in our hearts."

Keri wanted to cry out that it was not enough to remember. She yearned to hold and be held. But Uba Mintch's pain could be heard in his voice and to indulge her own sorrow would only make his worse.

"What do you think will happen to us?" she asked, in an attempt to take his mind away from his grandchild, that active little minx who had captured her heart as well. But also she asked the question because the worry was never far from her mind. She had never felt safe on this world, despite the fact that she had been welcomed by the king himself and treated exceedingly well. There was an underlying sense of danger that never left her, a need for watchfulness, although she could not have said who or what she was watching for. All she knew was that they were in danger.

"Brandtson enjoys a certain degree of power," Uba Mintch said thoughtfully, his deep, bass rumbling tones filling the small room. "And he has a strong circle of friends among the Council of Thanes. I would like to think that while we are under his protection, we are safe, but I have this terrible suspicion that we have all been marked for death. The king smiles but with only one side of his face."

"I feel it too, this danger," Keri said softly. "What are we to do? How can we protect ourselves?"

"I was at the observatory just now," Uba Mintch said, changing the subject with abrupt suddenness. "The night skies are clear, perfect weather for viewing the heavens."

Keri was startled. "What did you see?" she asked, her heart beating crazily, wondering if they had been somehow mistaken, if their world—

"I have been up there many times, you know," Uba Mintch replied as though he had not heard her question. "At first they did not know what to make of me. They were suspicious, even hostile, but I convinced them of my desire to know, to learn, and now they seem to accept me. I am even welcome." He was silent for a long moment.

"These men are not accorded the proper amount of respect, I think. They understand more miraculous things than any shaman or healer or king, and yet it seems that they are regarded with suspicion and dislike by most of the Scandis."

"I believe that they hold these scientists somehow responsible for the death of their sun," Keri said. "Or at least blame them for not being able to find a solution to the problem."

"I do not think any man has the power to stop death," said Uba Mintch, "whether it be the death of a man or the death of a world."

"But our world was not ready to die!" Keri protested fiercely. "They killed our world! Men did this thing and it should not have happened!"

"Maybe it did not happen," Uba Mintch said slowly.

Wild, unreasonable hope flooded Keri's mind. "What . . . what do you mean?" She clenched her hands around Uba Mintch's arm.

"I do not know for certain. Perhaps I should not have spoken until I know more. . . ."

"What are you saying? Tell me!" Keri cried fiercely.

"Our world is covered with a layer of dark clouds. It is impossible to see what, if anything, lies beneath it. It could be that the cloud of debris is all that remains, but some of the star watchers seem to think otherwise. They say that sometimes when a massive eruption occurs naturally, rock and dust are blown out with great force, a great enough force that it is caught by the winds and will circle the planet for years to come."

"Do they think . . . did you see . . . ?" Keri asked, scarcely daring to hope.

Uba Mintch shook his head. "They are divided in thought. Some say yes, some say no. I could see nothing but the cloud. But even if our world did survive, it would not be as we remember it. The star watchers say that the dark clouds will shield the planet from the sun and it will grow cold—as cold as it is here on Valhalla, perhaps even colder. It will be permanent winter for many, many years to come. Many things will die, among those things that were fortunate enough to survive the initial blast."

"But it will be possible that many would live?"

"Possible," said Uba Mintch, taking her two small hands inside his own. "It is barely possible. You and I, child . . . we must pray to whatever gods we have left that there really is such a thing as a miracle."

Otir Vaeng sat in his high-backed chair staring into the flames that warmed his personal chambers, thinking back over the events of the evening. It was going well, he thought, as well as could be expected. When first he had begun his program to lead the people back to the old gods, he had serious doubts that they would accept the ancient deities. He had been astonished at the ease with which they embraced, even welcomed, the old pantheons.

He had studied all the old masters of manipulation: the Borgias, Machiavelli, Hitler, Mussolini, Churchill, Foster, and most recently Hellserman. All had advocated the use of religion and superstition or its total abolition in order to bind the people to have them obey one's will. Vaeng knew that in times of turmoil and fear, people turned to supernatural deities who might have more control over the fates than mere mortals.

The Scandi nations had been spared many of the horrors that had marched around the globe, perhaps aided by the climate, which, though greatly warmed, was still much cooler than other less fortunate parts of the world. The rising seas had also cut them off and isolated them from easy access except from the desperate hordes to the north. These they had been forced to discourage with lethal measures.

Otir Vaeng had been led by his father, who was king before him, to accept the inevitable conclusion that earth must be abandoned, that they must take to the stars and carve out a new world from the heavens if they were to survive. His father had chosen, then, the best and the brightest among them from all the Scandi nations. The others were to follow in additional crafts. Only Otir Vaeng and his father knew that those ships would never feel the cold breath of space upon their hulls. There was no room for error, no food to be wasted on unnecessary mouths.

It had been hard at first, with angry words and threats of violence when it was realized that no other ships would come, for many loved ones had been left behind. But in the end there was nothing to be done, for it was not possible, in those early years, to make the long voyage back to earth.

They had found the new world and Otir Vaeng's father had named it Valhalla after the old legends, for it was a place of rebirth where their world would live once again. If any still believed in gods—and there were some who still uttered furtive prayers—it was easy to believe that some form of divine intervention had led them to this place. There were tall hills covered with thick stands of trees, lush valleys thick with grasses, and vast bodies of water. The climate was warm—warm enough that they were able to shed their heavy protective clothing. Only later, as the new world continued to cool, did they learn that the sun that shone upon it was dying, that this world had endured a lengthy period of superheating as the dying sun expanded and that now it was contracting and cooling. But even worse was the fact that the planet was barren of life. No fish swam in the waters, no birds winged their way across the vast empty skies, no insect trundled, no snake writhed, no animal trod anywhere on this new earth.

They had brought such things with them, to be sure—a miniature ark, as it were, with all manner of life-forms stored in embryo form. But they had never imagined that it would be necessary to establish an entire food chain. Fish were spawned, birds were hatched, meat animals and beasts of burden were born, but vital links were missing and the newly created creatures either died for lack of sustenance or were fed by human assistance. With the single exception of the grazing animals, none were able to forage for themselves.

As the world grew increasingly colder and snow and ice began to creep down the slopes of the mountains, it had become necessary to abandon their dwellings and colonize the hollow interior of the largest of the mountains, which Otir Vaeng christened Asgard.

A door opened at the far side of the room and Skirnir, Otir Vaeng's prime minister, sidled to the king's side bearing a heated mug of the herbal tea the king drank each night to soothe his nerves and allow him two or three hours of sleep.

"What news, Skirnir?" asked the king as his fingers closed around the steaming mug.

"It is too early to say, sire," Skirnir replied, his narrow eyes darting nervously around the room, never resting for more than a few seconds on any one object, a disconcerting habit that still annoyed the king despite their many years together. "The guards have been sent but as yet have not returned. I anticipate no trouble. What can two old men do against a dozen armed guards?"

"You're a fool to underestimate them, Skirnir, as I have told you a hundred times before. They are clever, resourceful, and bold. Nor are they acting alone. Do not forget Braldt. He has proved himself quite adept at evading our best attempts to dispatch him."

"Skeggi, Mostrarskegg, Thorwald . . . who would have thought that he could have defeated—killed—the very best of my berserkers? I shall miss them." The king fell silent, peering down into the dark swirls of his mug. "Are the burial plans completed?" he asked with a heavy sigh.

"Yes, sire. The funeral will take place six days hence. I have been thinking," Skirnir said quickly. "I have devised a plan that will bind many of our enemies to us, silence their opposition, and still some of the people's concerns. It is a plan that I do not think can fail."

"Come, man, speak out plainly. Let's have none of your self-serving double-talk. What is this clever plan?"

"You must take yourself a bride. . . ." began Skirnir, holding up his hands and backing away, his nervous eyes darting in all directions except toward the king. "Wait, I beg you, hear me out. This is a bride like no other bride. You must wed the Duroni girl, Keri, and you must take her to bride in the old manner as the ancient kings once did, in a ceremony filled with pomp and circumstance and blessed by the gods. It will tie in with the funeral, don't you see, death and rebirth, a promise for the future. It will take the people by surprise and still many of their voices. It will buy you valuable time."

"I have no time for marriage," growled Otir Vaeng, but it was clear that he was intrigued by the idea.

"The people have long wished for you to remarry," Skirnir said persuasively. "It would be a wise move."

"But this Braldt—is she not pledged to him?"

"After tonight, there will be no Braldt. She will be alone and will turn to you as her protector."

"Go," Otir Vaeng said with an abrupt, dismissive gesture. "I will think on it."

Skirnir scurried from the room, all but twisting his hands with glee. He knew the king well and knew that his plan had slithered through the king's vigilant guard and gained a tenuous toehold. It was all he needed. It was as good as done.

7

There was a moment of dangerous confusion inside the dark corridor. The ringing clang of weapons being hastily drawn, the harsh, labored breath of men who fear that death will strike them down within the next few heartbeats. A tremulous, gruff challenge was uttered and Saxo quickly responded with the appropriate words. The sudden relief that filled the air was nearly palpable. A light flared, flooding the narrow stone corridor with a cold brightness.

"Good Lord, man, you nearly got yourselves killed!" said one of the two defenders of the corridor. "Why did you wait so long to speak?"

"Cold," Saxo said between clenched teeth. "Followed." He all but swooned then, bracing himself against the rough wall to keep from falling. The man with the light cursed and leapt to his aid, gripping the older man firmly and leading him toward the door at the far end of the hall. "Brion, help them; be quick about it!"

Braldt shook off the offer of help, for feeling was slowly returning to his numbed limbs. The one called Brion turned then to Brandtson and offered the older man his arm. Brandtson raised his hand to protest as well, but it was easy to see that he was near collapse. His face was as white as his beard and he sagged with fatigue.

"Come, sir, let this fellow lead us to warmth and safety," Braldt said as he took Brandtson's arm and drew him forward, following Saxo's disappearing form. Brandtson was too exhausted to argue and when Brion took his sword from his stiff fingers, he did not protest.

The warmth of the room that lay on the far side of the door assaulted their senses. They all but reeled under the force of the heat and collapsed into waiting chairs.

It was some time before they had recovered enough to speak. Warm drinks were brought to them, their cold wraps removed and replaced with heated blankets, their fatigue and frightening brush with the dangerous elements met with understanding and silent compassion.

Only Thunder had escaped with little or no damage other than to his pride, protected and warmed as he was by Saxo's own body heat and the heavy layering of outer garments. Once Saxo's cloak was removed, Thunder's head popped up, severely startling young Brion. Thunder flattened his ears against his head and hissed nastily as though blaming the young man for all the indignity that he had suffered, then removed himself from Saxo's vest and stalked angrily away to settle in front of the fire and busy himself licking his tail.

Finally they recovered enough to speak and share, with the six men who waited patiently, the events of the night. A moment of heavy silence filled the small room, which Braldt could now see was little more than a barracks room filled with bunks and blankets, a single heavy wooden table, and a number of sturdy chairs.

One of the men shook his head and sighed. "So it has come to this. What can we do to stop him? How can we oppose him? There are so many of them and so few of us."

"We are few, but we are not powerless," said Brandtson. "Those whom Otir Vaeng regards as expendable will surely not agree with his decision, nor will they agree to be killed or left behind to die. They themselves are a weapon which we must use against Otir Vaeng."

"Revolution?" Brion asked in a shocked tone. "You would have the people rise up against the king?"

"Do you like the idea of death better?" Braldt asked harshly. "This man, this king of yours, is a killer, a cold-hearted murderer; even now he is plotting the death of his own people, those who look to him with trust. Has he not caused the death of an entire world and all its people for no reason other than the profit he can extract from its remains? This is not a man who deserves your loyalty."

"But he is the king!" Brion protested.

"He is a murderer who does not deserve the title of king," Braldt said coldly, already tired of the conversation and wondering why Brion could not see the truth of the matter.

"How would we go about reaching the populace, spreading the word of what the king has in mind, without getting ourselves killed? If tonight is any indication, he will not waste any time in searching out those whom he has targeted as his enemies. You are certain that you were pursued? There cannot be any other explanation?"

"None other," Brandtson replied heavily. "They were out to kill us. If we had not remembered the summer road, we would have been dead by now."

"You were lucky that you were not blown off the side of the mountain," said another. "With no protection, out in the open like that . . . it's a miracle you survived."

"Time is of the utmost importance," Braldt muttered, more to himself than to the others. "We must be heard before Otir Vaeng. I know of one who might be of use to us—a dwarf, one Septua by name. He is a clever rascal, a thief by profession and a born survivor. I doubt that he would be included in the king's list of desirables. If the price is right, I'm sure we can recruit him."

"Then there is Jocobe," said another. "He can work from

within the council. Otir Vaeng suspects him but cannot prove anything."

"I can move among the guard," said another. "Many of them are unhappy with the king's rule."

Excited voices filled the room as ideas and plans began to take shape.

As the night wore on, Braldt found himself jerking back to wakefulness, blinking gritty lids to hold back the exhaustion that threatened to overtake him. His brain felt thick and woolly and he could think of nothing more to say.

"You realize, of course, that it is no longer safe for you to remain here," said one of the older men. Braldt was startled out of his slumber.

"It would be better if they thought that you died out there tonight. We could fix it so it appeared that you fell to your deaths, tumbled off the summer road. It is quite believable and it would allow you to vanish and work against them unhampered by pursuit."

"A clever idea!" Brandtson agreed. "Yes! I like it!"

Braldt and Saxo were less enthusiastic. "My books . . . my pictures . . ." Saxo murmured unhappily.

"Keri . . ." Braldt began. "She must be told! It would not be fair to let her think that we are dead."

Brandtson turned to the two dissenters. "Think what you are saying," he said sternly. "If all your favorite books and important possessions disappear and Keri fails to react with the appropriate amount of grief, how well do you think the story of our deaths will be accepted?"

"But Keri . . ." Braldt began.

". . . is young and strong and will survive this momentary cruelty," Brandtson said firmly, and even Braldt was forced to accept the wisdom of his words.

"You cannot stay here; it is too dangerous. If they even

suspected . . . this is one of the first places they would look,'' said one of the older men.

''Then where—'' asked Brion.

''I know a place,'' Braldt said, startling them all, a cocky smile playing on his lips. ''A place that no one would ever dare to think of.''

''What are you saying? Where can we go that would be safe?'' Brandtson asked. ''I can think of nowhere that would be free from their eyes.''

''One cannot live off of this land,'' said Saxo in disgust. ''There are no fish in the waters, no birds in the air, no creatures in the wild. For all of earth's problems, I miss it still.''

''I know a place that would do,'' Braldt insisted. ''A place where we would be safe and well fed for as long as we must stay out of sight.''

All eyes turned to him.

''The burial mound,'' Braldt said in answer to the unspoken question, only to be met with horrified looks and gasps of shock.

''I know what you are thinking, but that's exactly why it is the perfect hiding place,'' he said hurriedly, in an attempt to convince them. ''Think about it for a minute. No one goes there if they can avoid it, there is a large store of food, and it is protected from the elements. Where on Valhalla could possibly be safer?''

The men looked at one another with dismay written on their rugged features, their discomfort obvious.

''Braldt is right,'' Saxo said decisively, raising his hand as a multitude of voices spoke out opposing the plan. ''For all of the reasons you speak of. It is such an outrageous thought, no one would ever suspect that we have dared to shelter there. Come, we must be gone before morning's light. There is no time to lose. Let us be on our way.''

It was decided that they must take the outer path once more, for now more than ever they could not risk being seen. If they vanished without a trace, it was just possible that their enemies would think them dead. None of them wanted to go back out into the cold again, but they dared not risk the inner route, for even at this early hour there was the chance of meeting some wandering soul early to rise or late to bed.

They gathered what supplies they felt would be needed, robbing the beds of their blankets and men of their extra clothing, for even within shelter they would need to conserve their body heat. One of the men left and returned with a compact package of foodstuffs and a gurgling jug of brandy to keep their spirits warm as well.

All too soon their preparations were done and there was nothing left but for Saxo to stuff a growling Thunder back inside his vest and to say their farewells. They clasped hands, murmured words of thanks and pledges of loyalty, and once more slipped out into the howling gale that hurled itself against the mountainside.

The trail down to the base of the mountain was quickly traveled, with the winds buffeting them from all sides and assaulting them with pellets of ice that stung like fire whenever they touched bare skin.

Braldt and Brandtson took turns forcing their way into the wind, breaking the trail through the several feet of snow that covered the ground. Fortunately, their path did not expose them to much open ground, where they would have been all the more in danger from the sheets of hail. They made their way through a narrow gorge which was lined by walls of stone, the bases of cliffs whose peaks could not be seen in the roaring gale. But while they were protected from the driving hail, the high walls channeled the screaming winds, which funneled down upon them with an icy intensity that made all that had gone before seem like a pleasant outing on a summer's day.

Braldt was never able to remember much of that agonizing journey, other than the overwhelming darkness, the howling of the wind, and the deep, bitter, bone-numbing cold. When at last Brandtson shook his arm and tugged him off the trail, he had long since given up any thought other than placing one foot before the other and making certain that he did it again, and again, and again.

He lurched after Brandtson, barely even raising his eyes to see where they were going, for he knew that there would be nothing to see other than the white of snow and dark of night. It came as a shock when he finally realized that they were actually stopping. Wearily, he lifted his head from his chest and wiped the accumulation of snow and ice from his brows and lashes, blinking to bring things into focus.

Everything was dark—there was little or nothing to be seen—and while his ears were still filled with the roaring of the wind, it was no longer beating against his body with the same fierce intensity.

They had entered a narrow defile which branched off the main trail. Here the stone walls were closer, barely wide enough for four men to walk abreast. Dawn was approaching and their way was dimly lit by a pale, watery light which was making slow headway against the heavy darkness. The storm still beat above their heads, but it was distant and could not reach them in this sheltered lee. Before them there rose two immense rock plinths deeply carved with the same figures of animals and sun discs that had adorned the sacrificial altar. Between the two rocks, braced in some unseen manner, was a broad stone lintel, also deeply carved, and hung with a curtain of ice. Beyond the lintel, all was dark.

Now that their goal was in sight, Braldt felt a shiver run down his spine, a shiver that had nothing to do with cold. He had denied his fear and chided the others for theirs, but now that they were here, he felt uncertain and somewhat anxious. What if the old stories were true? Did the spirits of the dead really linger about their final resting place and did they have the power to harm the living? Would the spirits be sympathetic to their plight or ally themselves with their king even in death? Did spirits have the ability to think new thoughts? Braldt's thoughts were jumbled; he had never spoken to a spirit or known anyone who had, although stories of such encounters were legion. Well, they had come this far. There was nothing to do but go on.

It was obvious that Brandtson and Saxo shared his concerns, for their steps slowed as they approached the entrance to the tomb. It was dark beyond the plinths and they could see nothing. They looked at one another and saw their fears reflected in each other's eyes. It was enough to make one smile, and that was almost enough to break the bands of fear.

"I'll go first," said Braldt with a courage that he did not feel. "It was my idea."

"No, we'll all go together," said Brandtson. "Saxo and I are too old to be afraid of ghosts."

"Speak for yourself," grumbled Saxo. "It never hurt anyone to be respectful of that which has yet to be explained."

"Oh, come on, old man—are you saying that you still believe in ghosts and boogies?"

Saxo drew himself upright to his full height, which was still a full head shorter than Brandtson. "I'm just saying that we still don't know all the answers about what happens after death and it cannot hurt to have a little respect for the dead!"

"I agree," Braldt said quickly, not wanting to see dissension among their slim ranks. "The dead are entitled to sleep without being troubled by the disrespect of the living. Nor will we bring them anything but our honor."

His words silenced the two older men, who ceased their quarrel and fell silent as they stepped through the dark portal.

As their eyes grew accustomed to the thick gloom, they were able to make out the features of the place that was to be their hideaway. It was a natural cul-de-sac, a blunt ending of the narrow arroyo, the plinths and lintel creating a narrow neck in the passage. It was no more than thirty yards deep and at the farthest end there was a loose jumble of fallen stone. At its widest point, it was no more than ten yards across. It was hard to judge accurately, for the entire space was filled with large earthenware jugs, literally scores of them with stone lids, piled one on top of the other and rising higher than their heads.

The jars, all deep brown in color, were ornamented with bright symbols, some crude and simplistic, others complex and beautifully executed. There were bright suns and wolves and outlines of long ships equipped with many oars, as well as a variety of symbols which Braldt could not decipher.

"Gunnar Harraldson," said Saxo as he pointed to a jar that stood beside him. "Remember him, Brandt? He died that first winter. Got lost in a snowstorm. We didn't find him till spring thaw."

Braldt could not help but shudder. He took a step forward, his hand outstretched to touch the bright symbols, but Brandtson struck his hand aside before he could do so. "Best not to disturb the sleep of the dead," he said, his eyes averted.

"But sir, there is naught here but empty bones," Braldt protested. "If the dead do indeed slumber, surely it would not be here in this place."

"The dead reside in Valhalla, or so our stories say," Brandtson said, looking to one side, still unwilling to meet Braldt's eyes. "Who can say what is really so? Much of what the legends foretell has already come to pass. I fear that before the story is done, much more will come true."

"Come, old friend," said Saxo, "surely you do not believe that the dead will rise again in Valhalla and come together again at the end of the world. That is a story for children!"

"Do not jest about such things, Saxo," Brandtson growled. "I am no child, far from it. Yet you cannot deny that many things, far too many things that match the old stories, have occurred, to be marked up to mere coincidence. We may be forced to hide here, but I say that we must leave the bones of the dead undisturbed."

"But sir, we will starve to death if we do not freeze first," Braldt protested. "What good will it do to shelter here if we die? Many of these dead were your friends when they walked the earth. Would they deprive you of the means to survive?"

"Braldt is right, old friend," added Saxo, placing his arm around Brandtson's shoulders. "Think for a moment: Gunnar Harraldson was openly declared against Otir Vaeng. In fact, there was some talk that his death was not the accident it was said to be. Gunnar was an experienced survivalist; when did you ever know him to lose his way, even in a snowstorm? He would be the first to urge us to help ourselves."

"There is truth to your words," Brandtson said at last. "I have often pondered the circumstances of his death. He was a good friend and would not begrudge us in our time of need."

Braldt sighed with relief as he wrapped his cloak more tightly around him, for even in this sheltered nook, out of the direct force of the wind, it was still bitterly cold.

The heavy stone lid was removed from the top of the burial urn and the jar gave up its contents. First there was a rich cloak, deep carmine in color and woven of some fine artificial material created for the sole purpose of retaining the body's heat. This Saxo handed to Braldt without even hesitating. Next there was a sack of dried meats and another of mixed, roasted grains, nuts, and dried fruits. There was a layer of reeds and wrapped in pale silks were the bones of Gunnar Harraldson. These were removed with reverence and placed to one side so that the remaining contents could be gathered up. When the jar had been emptied, they had acquired two more warm and weatherproof garments, a silver square no larger than one's smallest finger which produced fire whenever it was needed and would burn forever, and a variety of foodstuffs and serving devices fashioned of precious metals.

Braldt, wearing the warm cloak, began to rearrange the burial urns, stacking them in a semicircle against the wall of the cliff in a way that provided a shelter from the wind. It took some doing to gather enough wood to build a fire. Fortunately, the urns and some of the other materials necessary for the ceremony were carried to the site on long wooden poles, and these provided material for a fire, with a large pile left over for future use.

While he was moving back and forth, Braldt stumbled numerous times over what he took to be stones or boulders. One such misstep sent him sprawling and when he got to his feet, he found that he had uncovered the frozen body of a cock, its bright red and black and green feathers coated with a layer of ice. He stared at it for a long moment and then brushed the snow aside, revealing more than two dozen such pitiful bodies. All had had their necks severed.

He showed one such body to Saxo, who was already busy emptying yet another burial urn. "Oh, yes! Of course!" cried Saxo as he stuffed Thunder's head back inside his vest. "How could I have forgotten? They are cast over the lintel in honor of Odin! There should be enough here to feed us for days. The cold will have kept them fresh." Brandtson shuddered, but Braldt lost no time in erecting a brazier, where a number of the frozen birds were soon dripping and sizzling over the coals.

By the end of the first day, they were well prepared to

survive for an indefinite period of time. The jars had been arranged so that they were sheltered while still exhibiting an untouched outward appearance. A layer of wood and rushes separated them from the cold ground and a raised sleeping platform had been thickly strewn with furs and warm blankets. They had a variety of foodstuffs as well as a goodly number of frozen cocks and rabbits, sacrificed in Odin's name. There was also a pile of gemstones and precious metals, awesome in their beauty but useless for survival. More importantly, there was a large number of weapons, for no man could go to meet the gods without his arms.

These included several gem-encrusted swords and daggers which suited Braldt nicely, but more to Saxo and Brandtson's liking were the laser pistols and stun guns, which displaced air upon emission and sent out powerful shock waves, capable of stunning one's target into instant submission.

These weapons were considered obsolete, having been long surpassed by more advanced technology, but many of the newer weapons were affected by the solar flares and resulting magnetic and electrical disturbances, which often rendered them unreliable.

Unable to depend on their state-of-the-art weaponry, many of the men of Valhalla, including the king's own guard, had returned to weapons such as swords and daggers, which had long served no purpose other than ornamentation and ritual costuming. They soon discovered, much to their amazement, what Braldt had long known—that, wielded competently, swords and daggers were as capable of producing death as any of the sleek, modern weapons.

The use of ancient weapons had staged an astonishing recovery. Now it was considered chic, the in thing to do, and no young warrior would consider being seen in public without a blade gleaming at his side. Braldt was amused by their affectation, but pleased as well, for swords and daggers were weapons he was familiar with as well as highly skilled using. Of the newer weapons, he knew less than nothing. There was so much that he did not know, it was a good feeling to be the Scandis' equal at something.

The three men settled themselves for the night, wrapped snugly in their blankets and furs, watching the flames of the tiny fire, each lost in his own thoughts, wondering what was happening in the world they had left behind.

Keri was wakened from her restless slumber by Beast's throaty growls. His eyes were like two gold beacons gleaming in the early morning light. She started, her head rising from the pillow, knowing that Beast was not prone to casual noise-making; if he growled, it was for a good reason. She felt beneath her pillow for her dagger and clutched the hilt tightly as she silently rose from the bed. Beast pressed against her thigh and stared intently at the door.

She reached for a robe, but even as her hand closed upon the sheer, silky fabric, the door to her room burst open and armed men poured into the small chamber.

She stepped back, but the bed pressed against her legs; there was nowhere to go. She raised the dagger before her, a grim look on her face, her eyes narrowed, her expression giving notice to the slowly advancing men that she would not hesitate to use the weapon. Beast added his ominous growls, revealing his frightening fangs and double rows of teeth.

"Now, now, there is no need for violence." Skirnir sidled into the room, carefully positioning himself behind the armored bulk of a guard. "The king merely wishes your presence and begs you to attend him as soon as is convenient."

"Does the king normally invite people to visit him at this early hour and are his invitations always tendered by armed guards who do not bother to knock on a door before breaking it open?'' Keri asked heatedly, not for a moment fooled by Skirnir, whom she loathed.

''Heh, heh. The king is such a busy man, so very busy, time holds little or no meaning for him as it does for ordinary folk. Surely you understand. Come, my dear, do not be difficult. Come along nicely and present yourself to the king without all this tiresome trouble.''

''This isn't trouble,'' Keri said defiantly, gripping her weapon all the more tightly. ''I'll show you real trouble if you come one step closer. If the king really wants to see me, he can do so in a proper manner.''

''The king is not accustomed to obeying the whims of women,'' Skirnir said with a sneer, daring to venture out from behind the guard. ''You will come with us, now!'' His fingers flicked forward and instantly the guards advanced on Keri and seized her before she could do more than swipe at them with her blade. She nicked the arm of the guard on her right and he cursed as blood flowed, soaking his robes. But he did not release her. She screamed, more in anger and frustration than in fear, and that seemed to trigger Beast, for he launched himself at the injured guard, instinctively going for the most vulnerable prey.

The guard sensed Beast coming toward him, a gray-brown blur of movement streaking through the air. He released Keri and stumbled backward, throwing his hands up in front of him, but it was futile protection against Beast's vicious teeth, designed for ripping, slashing, and tearing. He went down under the weight of Beast's assault and it was over almost before it began as the lupebeast ripped the man's throat out, severing the jugular vein with his saber-sharp teeth.

Before the guard had even realized that he was mortally wounded and his body had ceased its anguished flailing, his companions had surrounded Beast and pointed their swords to his throat and heart.

"No!" Keri screamed, throwing herself at Beast, placing her own body between him and the bristling blades. "Don't kill him. I will go with you if you do not harm him."

"My girl, you have no choice in the matter. You will go with us no matter what we do," Skirnir said grimly. "But in this I will humor you." He paused as the dead man's companions turned to him in protest. "The king," he said sternly, "wishes the animal as well. Slay it if you dare to face his displeasure." The swords lowered with hesitation, the men backing away but still alert, holding Beast at bay. Keri wrenched free and threw her arms around Beast's neck, ready to protect him with her life.

"Can you control the creature?" Skirnir asked, doubt evident in the tone of his voice.

"Yes," Keri replied, although she was far from certain. Beast could be directed and he would obey if he wished, but he was no tame lap creature to obey man's every whim; he obeyed none but his own wild instincts.

"Bring him, then, and prepare yourself to meet the king. But know you that if you seek to deceive us or have any thought of escape, one or both of you will die."

One glance at the man's hard, cold eyes and his thin, cruel lips convinced Keri that he was speaking the truth. She could not bear the thought of losing Beast; she lowered her head to hide the quick tears that came to her eyes. She had no alternative but to do as Skirnir demanded. Where were Braldt and Brandtson and Uba Mintch? She tried to keep her spirits high by telling herself that they would search her out, that they would not allow any harm to come to her, and she tried desperately to believe that it was so.

Barat Krol faced the gathering of Madrelli whom he had awakened from sleep and struggled to control his anger. How could they be so stubborn? Why could they not understand what he was trying to tell them? The message, the words, were certainly simple enough. It was almost as though they chose not to understand. But how could that be? Why would anyone choose to be a slave when they could be free?

"Listen to me," he tried once again. The Madrelli stared back at him with little or no interest in their dull, flat eyes. Several of the males yawned broadly and two of the younger females had already curled themselves into balls and returned to sleep. "It is not right for any man to own another, to enslave him and his children for his own gain. You are not animals to be bought and sold. Your lives belong to you, not to the Scandis. You must join together and defy them, take control of your own destiny!"

He stared at them angrily; they stared back. "But we *are* animals," one large male said slowly. "Why are you so angry with us? Why do you say such things? Who are you? We do not even know you."

"I have told you," he said, breathing deeply and trying to keep control of his considerable temper. "My name is Barat Krol. I am Madrelli, just like you."

"You look like a Madrelli, but we do not know you," a large female with a prominent jutting brow said belligerently. "You do not talk like us. You talk like them." The others began to mutter among themselves and stare at Barat Krol with suspicion.

"I am not one of them; I am one of you, a Madrelli, as you can plainly see. I come from a different world, but that does not change who or what I am."

"You are dumb. There is no other world!" a young Madrelli said, then hooted with laughter, only to be struck across the face by the back of his mother's hand. He whimpered without knowing what he had done.

"Another world?" asked the large male, clearly perplexed.

"I think there are other worlds," an older female, her coat

streaked with gray, said slowly. "I had forgotten about that. I knew about it once."

"There are many other worlds," Barat Krol said quietly, hoping that their attention would hold and wondering why they were so ignorant of themselves and the world they lived in. "There are many Madrelli as well on those other worlds."

"What are they doing there? Why are they not here?" another male asked, curiosity shining brightly in his eyes.

"They have been sent to the other worlds, just as I was, just as all my tribe were, to do the Scandis' work for them."

"The Scandis should do their own work," muttered the sullen youngster.

"I agree, they should do their own work; that is why I am here," said Barat Krol.

"How you gonna make 'em do that?" asked the youngster. "That's what they got us for. Do this! Do that! Makes me mad sometimes!" The female looked aghast and lifted her hand as though to strike him again.

"Good! That's exactly how you should feel!" said Barat Krol. The youngster sat up straight and shot a triumphant look at his mother, who stared at Barat Krol in astonishment.

"You want us to be mad at the Scandis! Why? They take care of us. They give us a place to live and food to eat. They are our masters. Why should we be mad at them?" Many eyes turned to Barat Krol.

"Of course they feed you and give you a place to live," he replied with a sigh. "How could you work for them if they did not provide you with your basic needs? But why should you work for them? Why are they your masters? No one has the right to own another creature. You belong to yourselves and no one else."

One of the males yawned loudly and broke wind at the same time. Many of those around him fell over on their backs laughing and giggling, pointing at the miscreant, who grinned proudly. Barat Krol had lost their attention; no one was even looking at him now. The youngster, the most promising among them, was crossing his eyes and straining in an attempt to imitate his elder.

Barat Krol sighed deeply, wondering whether he should continue to try. What was wrong with these Madrelli? Was it possible that they had not advanced as far as his own tribe? He was deeply depressed and discouraged as he watched their juvenile antics and he wondered whether there was any point in continuing. If he were caught attempting to turn the Madrelli against the Scandis, he knew that he could expect no mercy. But they were his people. How could he do otherwise?

Septua should not have been hard to locate. He lived on the lowest level of the inner concourse amid the crowded stalls of the marketplace. He should not have been hard to find, for how many bald dwarves could there be in Asgard? But he was. It was the third day that Brion had conducted his search, and to be honest, he had begun to lose hope of ever finding the cursed little thief. But knowing how much depended on the finding of the dwarf, Brion had set forth once again, determined to bring him in.

Brion threaded his way through the sleepy shop owners as they rolled up awnings and placed their offerings out for the perusal of the haggling throngs who would fill the narrow corridors in the hours to come.

With nothing native to the planet, it was necessary to import everything from off world, with the single exception of produce, fowl, and grazing animals, which could be raised in small protected holdings at great expense. How and where the merchandise was obtained was never asked and it was taken for granted that most, if not all, of the items offered for sale had a cloudy pedigree.

Unlike old earth, where a vendor and his family might have

specialized in one specific item such as plumbing supplies or garden tools, in Asgard to specialize was to die of starvation. Available merchandise was constantly changing, and to survive one had to be able to adapt to change, to sell anything, whether it was a laser pistol or a bushel of dried fruit. As no one could be expected to be an expert on so many different items, correct information was often impossible to come by. But because a sale might hinge on such information and the ability of the seller to convince the buyer that he did indeed know what he was speaking about, the vendors were, of necessity, skilled prevaricators—or, in a word . . . liars.

When one bought something, anything, caveat emptor was true in Asgard as in no other place in the universe: Let the buyer beware.

But if the inhabitants of Asgard wished to supplement the rigid and boring and unvaried diet of grain, powdered energy drink, protein sticks, and stringy, tasteless, reconstituted fruits, it was necessary to buy, sell, and trade in the marketplace. It was at all times the most crowded place in Asgard, with all segments of the populace mingled together as nowhere else.

While in the marketplace, there was a curious abeyance of the law; most rules concerning position and status were laid aside, for the vendors enjoyed as important a position as the most mighty Thane. The vendors did not fail to exploit the situation, often speaking rudely and insulting the would-be buyers and playing one against the other for the highest possible dollar as they bid for the precious items, knowing that once an item was gone, there might never, ever be another. It was indeed a seller's market.

But while Septua was well known by all, finding him was not an easy matter, for the vendors protected their own and asking after the dwarf earned Brion nothing but blank looks and outright lies. He was told alternately that no such person existed, that the dwarf had died of a contagious disease, and finally that he had died. At each encounter, Brion found himself drawn out as to his purpose in seeking the dwarf thief, to which he replied cryptically that he had been sent by a friend in need.

As before, despite his resolutions, Brion encountered nothing but evasive and misleading information that in the end brought him back to the first person he had spoken to. As he leaned against a stone parapet and sighed at the thought of returning empty-handed yet again, he felt a sharp tug on his tunic. Looking down, he discovered a small, grimy, tousle-headed child with four teeth missing in the front of her mouth. The gamine lisped out that she had a message from Septua, but refused to divulge it until Brion pressed a bronze kroner into her palm. The child grinned with delight, confirming Brion's suspicions that she had already been paid for the task, and directed Brion to a nearby pub with instructions to wait.

Brion did as he was told, collapsing wearily into one of the high-backed booths, and ordered a cup of hot herbal tea from a handsome young woman who was still too sleepy to exhibit any of the exuberant good nature that she would display later in the day. Brion grimaced as he swallowed the hot brew, feeling, as always, somehow unsatisfied with its thin, pallid taste.

As he was mulling over the depressing lack of coffee, wondering how many people remembered it and mourned its loss as he did, he suddenly became aware of the fact that he was no longer alone. Startled, he looked around and saw, much to his amazement, the strangest person he had ever seen sitting quietly at his side and regarding him with obvious amusement.

"S'prized you, huh? Never even 'eard me comin'!"

"Why, yes, that's true," Brion stammered. "Where . . . how . . . ?"

"Like the wind," said the dwarf. "Septua moves like the wind, like a shadow I am . . . never seen, never heard, then gone." He waved his short, stubby fingers through the air, then closed them in a fist in dramatic fashion.

"Yes. Well, um . . ." Brion struggled to keep his expression serious. Did Braldt really think that this odd little fellow could help them? Brion doubted that he could aid them in anything as serious as this life-and-death struggle. But he had his orders and, while he might doubt, he would do as he had been told.

"Now, 'ow does you wants me to 'elp you?" the dwarf asked. "Does you need a key fetched or a lock opened, or be it a weightier matter? An' 'ho be this 'friend,' what sent you, eh? Won't do you no good, 'hoever it be, if you be lookin' for a job on the cheap. I be the best an' I be paid accordin'ly!"

"Braldt sent me," said Brion, and watched as the most amazing array of emotions played across the broad face. Beams of pleasure gave way to confusion, concern, and then fear and outright suspicion. "Braldt, eh? Don't know no Braldt," said the dwarf as he began to sidle from the booth, his short legs not even reaching the floor.

And this is a master thief, Brion thought with an inward groan. *I hope the fellow knows enough to stay out of card games!* "That's too bad. Braldt was certain that you'd be able to handle the job," Brion said as he stared down at his cup, making no attempt whatsoever to stop the dwarf's exit. "I guess he was wrong about you. He seemed to think you were the best man for the job."

Septua hesitated. "'E said that? What 'xactly did 'e say?" Curiosity and vanity fought with the desire to flee as the dwarf hovered at the edge of the booth.

"Well, it's a difficult job, with some danger involved, as well as a good deal of honor and gratitude, and, well, what can I say? Even though some of us disagreed with him, Braldt insisted that you were the only one who could get the job done. He wouldn't even consider letting anyone else do it. 'Septua's our man,' he said. 'No one else will do! If Septua can't do it, the job can't be done!' '' Brion watched the dwarf out of the corner of his eye, noting that his chest swelled visibly with pride and importance.

It was a much chastened Septua who left the inn when he and Brion parted several hours later. There was no sign of the braggadocio that had typified his behavior when first they met. At first he had resisted the idea that the planet was dying, would soon be naught but an icy rock in orbit around a dead sun. But Brion knew his facts and he was a persuasive young man.

Once Septua had accepted the fact that Brion was telling the truth, he had even less difficulty believing that Otir Vaeng would flee the planet leaving the majority of his people behind to die slow and miserable deaths. Nor did he have any delusions about being one of the chosen few; he had ruffled too many feathers to be anywhere but at the bottom of any number of lists.

His emotions had swung from disbelief to rage to depression and then to calm determination. "Braldt was right," he said with a stubborn tilt to his chin as he looked straight into Brion's eyes. "I be your man. Tell me what you would 'ave me do."

9

The blue alien was known by the name Fortran, an eso-teric appellation of an obsolete language which its parents had discovered while doing research on primitive galactic cultures. They had thought the word lovely and in a moment of daring had used it to name their eagerly awaited first offspring. It had caused Fortran no end of difficulty during the first several hundred years of his adolescence, for originality of thought was not a highly valued concept on his world.

Saddled with such a disconcerting name and teased for centuries, some individuals might have withdrawn, become moody or vindictive. But Fortran had received more than just an unusual name; he had inherited his parents' superior intelligence, as well as their zest for life and their sense of curiosity, which led them to explore outside the stringent boundaries that governed their world. Not that Fortran had welcomed these attributes, for it was hard for him to advance within the system, burdened with such disabilities.

Yantrek only knew how hard he had tried to stifle the impulses which had haunted his young life, such as actually daring to question the Grand Yerk as to the meaning of one of Yantrek's more obscure musings. That single blurted question had earned him a thousand days of repentence! His mentors had hoped that the unusually severe penalty would cause him to think before he spoke in the future.

Unfortunately, that had not been the case. Mutar—lovely,

lovely Mutar—was there ever another with quite the same shade of blue? Fortran thought not. He could only hope that Mutar and Fortran's mentors would never learn of this latest indiscretion. Yantrek only knew how many days of penance he would have to serve if they found out.

But still, even if his impulsive act caused him five—no, ten thousand days of penance, it would still have been worth it! Fortran fairly glowed as he remembered the excitement of that day in the ring, the day of their rebellion.

He and five hundred of his brethren had been voyaging to a Yantran retreat to humble themselves and pray to be found worthy of advancing to the next station in life, preparatory to choosing their life mates. It was an important ritual and one that Fortan had waited for with impatience, for not even Mutar could be expected to wait for him forever. She had let him know that he was to make no mistakes this time, that no more impulses were to be allowed. This was his last chance.

He was determined to do the right thing, but he had never gotten the opportunity. Shortly after they offloaded . . . why, they had not been contemplating Yantrek's forty-seventh musing for more than fifty days when an alien ship had descended and taken them all captive!

There had been no resistance, of course, for Yantrek only knew if this was some form of test or not, although personally Fortran doubted it. He doubted it even further when they were offloaded to the surface of a remote planet known as Rototara, where it soon became obvious that they were expected to fight! Actually fight in a physical manner with a wide variety of aliens gathered in a similar manner for the amusement of their captors. It was incomprehensible!

Fortran had become more and more certain that this was no action of Yantra, that there was absolutely no divine hand orchestrating this action, but his companions were not as easily convinced. They would not fight and nothing their captors did could force them to do so. They merely rolled their thin, square bodies into tight cylinders and became inert. Nothing that was done to them caused them pain or discomfort, for their bodies were only the physical manifestation of their true being, which was entirely mental and in no way corporeal.

Fortran had tried to be patient, to give himself up to total trust in Yantra, to place his spirit in abeyance, but it was hard, if not downright impossible. For one thing, abeyance was terribly, terribly boring, all that nothingness. And Yantra never answered, no matter how nicely you implored him to do so. It was far more interesting watching the goings-on of all those different sorts of creatures. Some of them were incredibly ugly, with all sorts of protuberances sticking out of their various bodies. They would never find glory in Yantra's eyes, for none of them had the least amount of patience or humility. Especially the one known as Braldt.

Fortran was most taken with the alien known as Braldt, even though he was incredibly ugly—the only bit of blue anywhere on him were two tiny dots centered in his top lump! But even if he had an embarrassing lack of blueness, he was not the least bit hesitant to act on his impulses, a fact that Fortran admired very, very much. Nor did he seem to spend any amount of time ruing those same impulsive actions, and the others who made up his clique seemed to admire him greatly! It was all very puzzling.

And then one night, just as Fortran was trying to repent yet another impulsive action which he had given way to that very day (he had opened his manifestation and absorbed a being who was most annoying and kept striking at him with a sharp pointed object, even though he had known that it would ultimately solve nothing and be considered a serious breech of conduct). The one known as Braldt had spoken to him, actually addressed him aloud and appealed to him for help! Him! Fortran! It was unimaginable! He had tried to resist, he really had, but in the end it was too hard and he had spoken back, startling the one known as Braldt, which was really quite amusing.

He was astonished to learn that neither Braldt nor any of his clique had ever heard of Yantra, nor was Braldt very interested in learning about his musings, even though he was polite enough to feign interest. It soon became apparent that all Braldt was interested in was for Fortran and his clique to assist them in the use of physical attrition to gain their freedom. Fortran had spent a period of time in vain trying to convince Braldt that violence was not an acceptable method and that it would be wiser to give oneself up to Yantra's will; but Braldt was not convinced.

Fortran tried hard to resist Braldt's importuning, but his own doubts refused to be silenced and he was terribly, terribly afraid that if he stayed gone too long, more than a hundred years, Mutar might actually give up on him and choose another! It was that which ultimately convinced him of the necessity of aiding the one known as Braldt. In fact, he gave in in record time and he experienced a heady rush of euphoria as he agreed to lend his assistance. It had been even less difficult for Fortran to convince his clique, far less difficult than he had imagined. Was it possible that they too were troubled with doubts and impulses?

They had done as Braldt had directed them to do, removing their physical manifestations from the cells where they had been placed, moving through time, space, and bars in a manner which Braldt failed to comprehend, although the principle was really quite simple. They had joined the fray and Fortran had given himself over to impulses that he had never indulged before, quite primitive impulses such as anger and violence and trickery and happiness, positively rejoicing every time he succeeded in absorbing one of those Braldt had identified as the enemy. It was . . . it was—what was that word?—oh, yes, it was fun!

Fortran was enjoying himself immensely, whirling and twirling and floating about, absorbing a guard here, sneaking up on an unsuspecting soldier there, lapping at the edges of a sword arm here, when suddenly he was nearly paralyzed by the voice of the Grand Yerk, which echoed inside him like the fall of darkest night!

That was all that it had taken for the young rebellion to end. It had been a simple matter for the remaining guards and soldiers to approach them with trepidation, then roll them into unresisting cylinders and toss them in this dark cell far beneath the surface of the world in a portion of the dungeon where no one ever went.

Judging from the sounds that reached them, strange things had occurred after they left the arena. There was the continued sound of battle, the sound of retreat, and then, strangely, the tramp of many feet advancing. Then there was much death and afterward, the cells above echoed with the voices of their former captors. It was most confusing.

Fortran had tried to be patient, tried to be silent, tried to still his questions in the long boring days and nights that followed, but it was so very hard to do. He wondered if anyone remembered that they existed. What if the guards who had placed them here had all been killed? What if no one ever found them, ever, ever, ever? Fortran knew in his heart that Mutar would not wait more than a hundred years.

And where was the Grand Yerk? And Yantra? Why did he not speak or act? Was it his will to let them lie here forever? How would that serve any purpose? The more Fortran thought about it, the more angry, impatient, and, yes, it was true, impulsive, he became until at last he could contain himself no longer. One hundred and twenty-seven days and nights after they had been tossed in this dark cell, Fortran gathered his impulsiveness to him and burst into impetuous action!

Carn was a happy man, although the use of the word *happy* seemed too childish to apply to the complex emotions that filled him during his every waking moment. All his life he had felt unimportant, had suffered in daily comparison to Braldt and searched without hope for some meaning to his existence.

He thought that he had found the answer inside the mountain when Mother Moon, the goddess he had worshiped all his life, revealed herself to him as she had revealed herself to no other. It had nearly cost him his life, that revelation, and he wore the scars still like a badge of honor. But now he knew that what he had experienced had not been the true goddess but merely a test for what was to come.

He had passed that painful initiation and now he had been accepted into the highest ranks of the honored few, those who were permitted to know the true gods.

There was still much that he did not understand, but Otir Vaeng assured him that all would be made clear to him soon. And as a sign of the gods' favor, the volva had taken him to her bed and joined with him, imparting ecstasy such as he had never known before.

The names of the gods were strangely different, Thor and Odin and Freya foremost among them, but their roles were much the same as the gods he had always known. And here, as on his own world, the gods were responsible for everything, including the fates of men. Men's actions or the lack of them and the proper reverence toward the gods dictated the events that followed. It was the role of those such as he and Otir Vaeng and the volva to convey and interpret the will of the gods to men, their humble servants. It was a grave responsibility, but one that Carn bore with willing reverence.

Otir Vaeng had requested his presence at first light and Carn made his way to the king's chambers, pretending not to notice the averted eyes of those he met along the way. Fools! Could they not see beyond the shiny, disfigured flesh? Could they not see that he wore the mark of the gods?

Carn flushed with pride as the guards stood aside and admitted him to the king's inner chambers without hesitation. They knew!

Otir Vaeng was seated as always in his high-backed carved chair, his chin resting on his fist, staring into the flames of the fire pit, which he did not appear to see. The prime minister, a bent, wizened gnome of a creature who clearly distrusted and disliked Carn and guarded his time with the king jealously, stood as always at the king's left hand. Carn barely glanced at the man but was well aware of him and was determined that when Otir Vaeng entrusted him with the power that had been promised, Skirnir would be the first of many changes he would implement.

Silence weighed heavily in the room as the king continued to gaze into the fire as though seeking an answer in the dancing flames. From time to time he would nod as if in response to some comment that only he could hear. Skirnir's narrow, pointy face and ferretlike eyes were focused intently on the king, waiting in attendance for whatever it was that was happening.

The silence was disconcerting and, as the minutes stretched longer and longer, Carn began to wonder what it was that was occurring and why he could not understand. Why was he here and what was expected of him? Skirnir seemed to have no difficulty understanding his role and this disturbed Carn even more, for it implied that the prime minister was a part of whatever it was that was occurring. Carn could not allow Skirnir to see how deeply he was disturbed and so he folded his hands and assumed a respectful stance, composing his face with a calmness that he did not feel.

Later—Carn could not have said how much later—the king stirred from his trance, his strangely silent communion, and blinked his eyes and sighed as though waking from sleep. He twisted his head from side to side and stretched his hands and arms out to the heat of the fire pit. He sank back into his chair as though exhausted, his chin resting on his chest. Only then did he seem to take notice of Carn. For a moment his eyes clouded as if he could not remember who Carn was, but it was only for a brief moment, then his eyes focused on Carn with that glittering, unblinking brilliance that Carn found so uncomfortable.

"Ah, brother Carn, so good of you to have come," the king said softly, barely turning his head enough to fix Carn with his gaze. "Come closer, brother. I am weary."

As Carn approached the king, dread seemed to weight his limbs and it took great determination to force himself to close the distance between them. Those bright glittering eyes reminded him of nothing if not a serpent fixing its prey in a hypnotic glance before the fatal strike. He could not help but shudder inwardly and wonder if he were making a terrible mistake. Instantly he rejected the cowardly notion, casting it from his mind, denying it. Surely there was danger when one came so close to raw, naked power, but while the risks were high, so were the rewards. He raised his chin, looked straight into the king's eyes, and advanced until he stood directly before the throne.

Otir Vaeng allowed his gaze to rest on Carn so long that he felt his resolve beginning to shrivel; it felt as though he were being examined both inside as well as out. He could not help but wonder what the king was seeing, and he felt as though he were undergoing some sort of inspection. He hoped—no, prayed—that he was not to be found lacking.

Carn knew that Skirnir was staring at him too and knew without looking that the man would be wearing his usual smirk, taking great pleasure in Carn's discomfort. He was determined not to break and give Skirnir any more reason for pleasure at his expense.

Finally the king seemed to reach some conclusion and he grunted and nodded toward a low chair placed between him and the fire. "Sit yourself down, brother Carn. Skirnir, our hospitality is sorely lacking. Please attend to our guest."

Carn seated himself gingerly, uncomfortably aware that the chair was oddly shortened so that his legs were sprawled awkwardly before him and he was forced to tilt his head backward to meet the king's eyes. He was also closer to the flames than he would have wished and his body, cloaked in heavy garments, was soon drenched in rivulets of perspiration. He took the goblet of amber fluid that Skirnir handed him, and Skirnir released it almost before Carn's scarred, stiff fingers had closed around the stem, causing him to fumble awkwardly, nearly dropping the precious crystal.

The king frowned and then smoothed the expression away with a ready smile that did not touch his cold blue eyes. "I have been communing with the gods, my friend, and they have this night placed a great burden upon my shoulders, as well as charging me with a great honor. You too are to share in the glory."

Carn felt his heart begin to thump within his chest and he felt faint. Yes! It had begun, the march to glory, as he had known that it would if his faith were only strong enough! He stared at the king expectantly with a tentative smile on his scarred lips.

"The gods have decreed that I am to wed. They wish an heir to the throne and a sacrifice as well, a worthy sacrifice to let them know the depth of our gratitude. The wedding will be a celebration such as Valhalla has never known, a feast befitting the gods, one that they will surely remember. Blood and wine shall mingle and flow down the slopes and we shall sing our praises of the gods until the mountains ring. The gods will reward us for our piety and dedication by granting us the gift of life. Immediately following the ceremony and the feasting, those whom the gods have selected as worthy of glory and life everlasting shall depart this world to dwell in the halls of the gods forever.''

Otir Vaeng sat unmoving in his chair, as he had done throughout his entire amazing commentary. Carn stared at him in stunned disbelief. There was a certain logic in Otir Vaeng marrying, for the kingdom certainly needed an heir, although he had entertained some personal notions along those lines himself.

As to the rest of it . . . well, Carn quickly reflected, he had no aversion to bloodshed as long as it was not his own. As for the feast, Carn had little interest in food these days, but a good feast would take the people's minds off the flow of blood that the king had promised; commoners were always weak-hearted when it came to blood.

But what did he mean about leaving this world and dwelling among the halls of the gods? It was that that troubled Carn the most. He could feel the weight of the king's eyes upon him, waiting for his answer, and he knew without looking that Skirnir's gaze was fastened on him as well, waiting, hoping that he would make some unforgivable mistake. Carn intended to make no mistakes.

''Interesting,'' he said smoothly, ''at first hearing. I will be interested in learning the details. When will this take place?''

''Soon.'' The king waved his hand wearily, as though bored with such mundane details and seemingly satisfied with

Carn's response—or rather, the lack of it; he closed his eyes and sighed wearily. "All of it will be worked out in the days to come."

"And Braldt? What of Braldt?" The words were forced out almost against Carn's will. "What role will Braldt play in your plan?"

"Braldt? He will be the sacrifice, offered up for the pleasure of the gods as well as mine, if we ever find him."

Carn tried to hide the smile that came to his lips. It would not be seemly to take pleasure in the death of one's own brother. It took several moments before the rest of Otir Vaeng's words took hold in his mind. "Gone? Braldt's gone?"

"That is of little importance; we will soon have him in hand. There are only so many places to hide on Valhalla," Skirnir said with a dismissive gesture. His eyes shone with malevolence as he said softly, "A better question would have been who the king is going to bring to bed and throne. That is the question you should have asked."

Suddenly Carn's heart began to flutter and his mouth went dry. Both Skirnir and the king were watching him now, waiting for him to speak, to ask the question. But even as they waited, in his heart Carn already knew the answer.

The volva reclined lazily on her chaise longue, rejoicing in the heat of the flames. She drank deeply from the crystal goblet, savoring the smooth, rich bloom of the crimson wine. The volva was many things, but first and foremost she was a sensuous woman who reveled in creature comforts.

A throat was cleared impatiently. The volva smiled to herself and languidly turned her head away from the mesmerizing flames of the open fire pit. It did the king good to wait upon the whims of another; she enjoyed making him wait.

"Impatience does not become you," she said lazily, settling herself against her pillows and taking measure of the man who strode back and forth pacing from one wall to the next and then began again. As always, he was tense and consumed with his own seriousness, drawn so tightly that if he were plucked, he would surely hum. The thought amused her. "It is good that you are so easily entertained," the king said bitterly. "I myself find little to laugh at these days."

The volva did not respond, but merely sipped from her goblet and caressed her inner thigh with long, slender, scarlet-tipped nails.

Otir Vaeng stared at her, his eyes dark with a seething conflict of emotions. The volva saw in his glanced fury, frustration, and violence all competing with desire. That was good; it was as it should be. One could not allow such men to gain the upper hand, feel secure.

"Your plans," she drawled casually, as though barely interested in the topic, "are they taking shape?"

"If you can bring yourself to pay attention, there are some matters we need to discuss," Otir Vaeng said sharply. "You do have a large stake in the outcome, you know."

The volva said nothing, merely smiled and shrugged as though the subject were of little or no interest.

Rage burned brightly in Otir Vaeng's eyes and for a moment the volva wondered if she had perhaps gone too far, for he took a half step forward and it seemed that he was about to strike her. Then apparently he thought better of it, for the light faded from his eyes and he sank into a chair, resting his forehead against his knuckles.

"I don't know why I do this," he said in a low tone, almost as though speaking to himself.

"Of course you do; don't play childish games. You do it because you enjoy having the power to rule men's lives. What other reason is there? Come, now, stop this nonsense. Tell me, what are your plans for the girl? What are you thinking?"

Otir Vaeng was startled from his lethargy. There were few who dared speak to him so frankly, much less women, for whom it was widely known he had little patience. He was a man who sought no counsel but his own and was unaccustomed to explaining his actions. His eyes blazed momentarily as he struggled with his anger, but then his eyes met hers and suddenly, inexplicably, he was gripped by uncertainty. He wavered. His eyes fell.

When he had instituted the return to the old gods, the volva had been but a ploy, a means of swaying the masses with religious fervor. But the volva needed no convincing arguments to aid his efforts, for she had long believed in the old gods and practiced the old arts, as had her mother and her mother before her. She had joined him without a murmur, but at odd moments he had the disconcerting thought that perhaps it was he who had joined her cause.

She was a strange and slightly frightening woman, with few of the graces normally attributed to her gender. He felt fear and a sense of revulsion whenever she turned her sultry eyes upon him, the threat implied in the palpable heated aura of her sexuality. Otir Vaeng repressed a faint shudder; he could no more imagine coupling with the woman than lying down with a sleeping tiger.

Despite his fears and suspicions, the king knew that he could not afford to alienate the seeress. His plans had advanced rapidly and things were beginning to gel. He would need her services to bring them to fruition.

"We have taken her, and the beast. I did not want the creature, but the girl refused to come without it; she might have struggled and caused herself harm. I want no bloodshed. There will be time for that later."

"We can sacrifice the beast before the girl; the sight of blood will rouse and roughen their spirits, and when the knife slices through the girl's throat and we give her to the gods, they will go mad; you can tell them anything and they will obey you."

"I had thought that if we gave the creature to the gods, perhaps they would be satisfied and not require the girl." Otir Vaeng's voice had lost its power and he turned aside as he spoke so that he did not have to look at her.

There was a lengthy silence, during which time the volva fell very still. Her eyes bored into the king, who fidgeted and squirmed like a small child who had done wrong and been called to account. The tension grew till it shivered on the nerves before the seeress spoke.

Her voice was glossy soft, a silky purr as she regarded the

king with hooded eyes, much as a panther regards its prey. "The gods speak directly to me. They whisper in my ear, telling me their needs, charging me to fulfill them. The girl will go as a bride to the gods, untouched, pure, a suitable sacrifice; the blood of a beast will not appease them."

"I do not see how the gods, amorphous, ethereal creatures if they even exist, can desire anything, much less the life and flesh of a young girl!"

The seeress smiled at him. "That is your problem, not mine."

Septua strolled through the crowded marketplace, wending his way through the throngs of sharp-eyed shoppers and those who came as most did, merely to see and be seen. The marketplace was the heart of Valhalla, a promenade of sorts where literally all manner of deals were done, everything from the sale of purloined goods to promises of betrothal. If you could not find what you were looking for in the marketplace, it was not to be found on Valhalla.

It pulsed with an undercurrent of excitement that Septua found as intoxicating as any drug and almost as impossible to be without. When he was separated from the marketplace, he felt incomplete in a way that had nothing to do with the physical inequalities he had been dealt by nature. Here, as nowhere else, he was any man's equal, and in most cases far superior.

Septua stopped at the corner of a display of hardware, a mountain of metallic arms and legs, smooth heads with no eyes, a veritable burial mound of dead and useless robots, their delicate computerized innerworkings slain by the erratic, unpredictable emissions of the dying sun. It warmed his heart just looking upon them lying still and silent, never to move again. The robots had been a bane upon his existence, causing him no end of problems for more years than he could count.

Silent, predatory, never sleeping. Their demise brought him great pleasure.

He grinned broadly at the vendor who began to sing their praises, thinking that he had found a buyer. Septua entertained the notion of buying one or two, just for laughs, using them to hold mops and brooms and such. But then, he wasn't much for housekeeping.

Once more he set forth upon his way, breathing in the rich scents of the goods offered for sale: lush, golden pomonas, dripping with juice, imported at great cost from far-off Galardia; pungent sacks of stick cinnamon, worth their weight in gold, plucked from the last few precious trees of old earth; glittering arrays of weaponry, swords and daggers and all manner of deadly honed items forged and fashioned on the hearths of Rototara.

Septua loved daggers and swords and the like. None was happier over the demise of such state-of-the-art weapons as laser pistols, stunners and beamers than he. He rejoiced over the deadly solar flares that disrupted everything that depended on computer chips and solid state circuitry to function. He had never been adept at the more sophisticated weaponry, but swords and daggers—ah, now, that was another matter. Give him a dagger, and his own natural gift of stealth and size was no longer a factor; he could compete against the largest of men and emerge the victor.

Stealth and speed were Septua's finest attributes, along with a shrewd and crafty mind that was capable of interpreting seemingly unrelated facts and discovering cleverly disguised schemes. This was just the sort of puzzle he was working on now. He turned over what young Brion had told him, the bare facts: the sun was dying, Otir Vaeng was assembling a core group of those who would be chosen to populate the new world, and Septua would not be among those chosen.

The dwarf shrugged his broad shoulders, a grimace on his

expressive face. He had not been among those chosen the last time they had immigrated to a new world; he would have been astonished had it been otherwise this time. All those who remained on Valhalla would die. Well, where there was a will, there was a way. When Valhalla's sun finally winked out, he would not be among those left to freeze in the darkness.

He mulled over the tasks that young Brion had set before him, simple enough on the surface, little challenge for one as clever as he. But there had to be more to it; it just took some figuring to find out what was the true, hidden agenda.

Brion had said that Septua would be well paid for his services. He just didn't know how right he was. Septua hefted the heavy pouch of coins that he had liberated from the young warrior's possession, calculating how many of the kroner he would have to spend to find out what he needed to know. Whatever it was, the cost meant nothing in the long run, for if he did not succeed and there was no world, what need would there be for money?

The snow had fallen without cease for two days and nights, burying what few indications of trespass there had been beneath a thick blanket of snow. It draped over the burial urns and packed solidly upon the roof of the fugitives' lair. They were surrounded by snow on all sides and Braldt found it unnerving, for there was no definition of any sort and it almost felt as though he were adrift in a sea of smoke.

The falling snow imparted several benefits that he had not anticipated. It served as insulation, keeping them warmer than they had been before, and the constant fall of flakes concealed the rising wisps of smoke from their tiny fire.

The fire was not really necessary, but all of them felt the need, for there was something cheery, alive, in the crackling flames that drove away the silence and the isolation that threatened to overwhelm them. They spoke more often than usual, repeating old tales and sharing more recent memories, just so that there would be something to listen to besides the howl of the wind and the slithery swirl of snow. It was the silence, the isolation, and the fear of what was happening at home that threatened their equanimity. They were brave and courageous men, but they were men of action, unaccustomed to silence and waiting, and they fretted under the burden of forced inactivity. Thunder had no such difficulty and was content to spend most of his time wrapped deep in slumber. Braldt envied him.

They saw no more of Skirnir, although Braldt found himself almost wishing that the grave robber would work up the courage to return, simply to break the monotony. Neither had they seen or heard from Brion or any of the others. Secretly Braldt began to wonder if something had gone wrong, if they had been found out.

Thus, when loud and colorful curses were heard on the morning of the seventh day, Braldt was first out of the tiny shelter, hand on the hilt of his sword, ruing the stiffness that seemed to have settled permanently between his shoulder blades. Saxo and Brandtson were behind him, peering into the driving snow.

"It's like trying to breathe water," Saxo grumbled in a low voice. "And I can't see a damn thing."

Neither, it appeared, could the unseen traveler, whose impossible obscenities could be plainly heard nonetheless. Listening intently, Braldt realized with a shock of recognition that he knew that voice, had heard those same physically impossible curses before!

"Septua! Septua, is that you?"

"Better my mother 'ad become a nun than I be fool enough to come out in weather like this for any man!" came the heated reply. "Where are you? Show yourself, send up a flare, wave yer arms! Not that any of it will do any good; like as not they'll find my poor frozen corpse someday, or—ooops!"

There was a solid thumping noise and then silence; everything was still. "Septua?" Braldt said tentatively, taking several steps forward into the blizzard, wondering what had happened. Where had the dwarf gone? He heard a low moan somewhere off to his right and, with Saxo and Brandtson following close behind him, he waded through the deep drifts which had piled high against the wall of urns. He took another step forward and felt his footing give way as he stepped on something soft that twisted beneath him. Taken by surprise, he tried to save himself but could not and tumbled forward, sprawling facefirst in the snow.

The snow erupted beneath him in a flurry of arms and legs and glaring eyes. It was several moments before Braldt could separate himself and the dwarf and extract them both from the clinging snow. Once Septua was righted, it was easy to see why they had caught no glimpse of him, for the snow was higher than the little man himself!

"It weren't so bad when I first started out," Septua explained when at last they had carried him back to the shelter, outfitted him with dry clothes, and placed a steaming mug into his stiff fingers. "Thought I could make it, no trouble a-tall, but it kept gettin' deeper an' deeper till pretty soon it were 'igher than me 'ead! Kept 'avin' to jump up like, to get me bearins, an' even then it were a close thing! I were like some kind of mole, burrowin' through the snow!" The dwarf chuckled at the rueful image and honked his nose loudly into a bright square of cloth.

"No mole would have been so clever as to have found his way here to us," Brandtson said. "It could not have been an easy task!"

"Phoo! No self-respectin' mole would 'ave been so stupid,

neither, to come out in weather like this!'' Septua said, adding a few colorful curses on the subject of his own stupidity.

''How is it that you did find us? Why is it that you have come?'' Brandtson asked, and alerted by the steely tone in his voice, Braldt realized that he and Saxo were viewing the dwarf with hostility and distrust. Septua was at best not the most reassuring of figures, but while Braldt might question the little man's commitment to ethics, he had no reason to question his loyalty. Still, he too was interested in learning what had brought the dwarf, who was no lover of physical discomfort, out in such a terrible storm.

''Didn't see no way around it,'' Septua said, bathing his face in the warmth of the steaming mug, seemingly unaware of their suspicions. ''I 'ad to come. It were me or no one to tell you what be 'appenin'. 'Tis nothin' good.'' His mobile features—the large, woeful eyes, the bulbous nose, wide mouth, and pointy little chin—were almost comical, but Braldt felt his mouth go dry at the dwarf's words and his heart began to hammer in his chest.

''What's happening? Keri? Is she all right?'' He grabbed the dwarf by the front of his garments and half raised him from the ground.

'' 'Ere, 'ere, let me be,'' whined Septua, scrambling to save his tea. ''It weren't my doin'!''

''Tell me,'' Braldt commanded.

Septua made a great fuss of being offended, all but pouting as he straightened his robes, rearranged himself, and sipped his tea before he would speak. It was all that Braldt could do to keep from throttling him.

''Went to meet Brion, but 'e weren't there! 'Ung around an' 'eard some worrisome rumors about this one an' that bein' arrested. 'Ole battalions be disappearin' just like that!'' He snapped his fingers. ''An' there be all sorts o' ugly rumors floatin' 'round the marketplace 'bout 'ow they was traitors an' such like." He raised a wide, stubby hand with fat little sausage fingers. "I know, I know, Keri." He looked off into the whirling snow, unwilling or unable to meet Braldt's eyes. "She be taken by the king. 'E intends to marry 'er, or so I 'ear."

Braldt uttered a curse and rose to his feet as though intending to rush out into the storm, and fought off the hands that reached to restrain him. He strode out into the snow and then reappeared, lifting Septua under the arms and raising him up to look him in the eye. "Is this some sort of joke?" He shook the dwarf back and forth till Septua's head rattled and his eyes watered. The precious mug lay unnoticed, spilling its contents into the snow.

" 'Ey! 'Ey! 'Tis no joke. Lemme be!" shouted the dwarf, pummeling Braldt with his fists. "Why would I come all this way to tell you a bad joke? You think I be crazy? But I knew it be worse if I din't come, an' let you find out on yer own!"

Braldt scanned Septua with a searching gaze and the dwarf met his eyes with no difficulty. Slowly, Braldt lowered him to the ground and once again Septua made a great show of rearranging his clothes and shaking his head and arms as though checking to make certain that everything was still attached. "Shouldn't ought to do that. I thought we be friends!"

Braldt did not respond, but merely stood staring into the white distance, his thoughts clearly elsewhere. Then he turned abruptly and began gathering up his weapons. Saxo was the first to realize what Braldt was up to and placed a hand on his arm. Braldt shook it off without comment. Brandtson and Septua quickly grasped what was happening and both of them moved in to dissuade Braldt.

"You cannot return. It would be like signing your death warrant," argued Brandtson. "They are looking for us—all of us. Have you forgotten? There is no place that is safe in Valhalla, nowhere that you could hide where they could not find you. Once they found you, you would be unable to save Keri, much less yourself, and they would force you to tell them everything you know about our plans."

"I wouldn't tell them anything," Braldt said between clenched teeth as he continued to gather up his few posessions.

"I do not doubt your courage or your strength," said Brandtson. "Otir Vaeng would not use weapons or the threat of pain against you, but drugs that would cause you to repeat everything you know. You would be powerless to resist. Would you jeopardize all of our lives, our only hope, on this foolish venture?"

Braldt dropped his hands to his sides and turned to face his grandfather. "I cannot let him take Keri, and do nothing to save her. Would you have me sacrifice her? Is she to be the cost of our venture? I will not buy my life with hers."

"She is not giving up her life, merely marrying," Saxo said, attempting to reason with Braldt. "Despite my own personal opinions, not everyone considers marriage to be tantamount to death."

Braldt was not amused. "Why would Otir Vaeng want to marry her?" he demanded of the dwarf.

"Don't know," Septua replied with widespread hands. "Don't know what's goin' on. No one seems to know nothin'. It's like them murders. Otir Vaeng says it be you, but how can that be if you be stuck way out 'ere in the snow?"

"What murders?" demanded Brandtson.

"Dunno. Bunch o' dead guys. All o' 'em 'ad somethin' or other to do with the launch, space an' all. All of 'em dead— five, I think."

"And they think we're responsible?" Braldt asked.

Septua nodded. "That be what the king be sayin'. An'

since yer not there to say no, he ain't 'ad no trouble pinnin' it on you.''

''Maybe he's taken Keri to force our return,'' Braldt muttered as he began to pace back and forth in the small enclosure.

''Mebbe,'' agreed Septua, ''but still an' all, I think 'e plans to take 'er to wife. There be all manner of fixins goin' on.''

''Then he can't be meaning to harm her,'' Braldt said, the tension easing somewhat.

Saxo and Brandtson looked at each other with alarm—a look which Braldt was quick to notice. ''What? What is it? Tell me!''

''A wedding is not necessarily a good thing,'' replied Saxo. ''You see''—he cleared his throat—''in the old religion, in times of great trouble, the kings were known to petition the gods for favors—bribing them, you might say—with precious gifts, gold and fine weapons and . . . and . . .''

''. . . and a beautiful young woman as their bride,'' Brandtson finished for his friend. ''The delegation, consisting of the king, his bride, the volva, and a mass of commoners will come here to this place bearing food and gifts. The bride will be adorned with fine clothes and bedecked with gold and precious gemstones. Amid great pomp and ceremony, they will be wed. Then a cock will be slain, a knife drawn across its throat, and its body flung across the lintel to announce the coming of the bride. Then the bride will willingly bare her breast and the volva will plunge a blade into her heart. Her body will be carried into the burial mound and given unto the keeping of the gods. If she is found to the liking of the gods, they may choose to grant the king's petition.''

Braldt stared at them in disbelief. ''This is nonsense,'' he said at length. ''This whole religion is nonsense. How can anyone believe it? And Keri will never give herself willingly! We must do something to stop this!''

"Whether the religion is nonsense or not has no real bearing," Brandtson said heavily. "People believe what they need to believe in order to live. They are frightened. Their world is dying and they are afraid that they will die as well. If it eases their fears to believe that someone or something can be persuaded to help them, to change the future, can you blame them for wanting to believe that it is true?"

"I can blame them if the cost is Keri's life!" Braldt said heatedly. "And you can believe this: I will not allow it to happen!"

Otir Vaeng was worried. Too many things were going wrong.

First and foremost there was the matter of Braldt and the two old men, Saxo and Brandtson. How could they have disappeared so completely? There was an entire world to hide in, that was true, but they had had no advance warning and no time to gather the necessary provisions that would enable them to remain at large. He tried, as Skirnir suggested, to imagine them lying cold and stiff beneath the blowing snows, but an alternate picture kept imposing itself—that of the three of them sitting warm and snug around a roaring campfire, lifting mugs of wine, toasting their success and laughing at him. It ate at him constantly, chewed at his innards like a paranoid tapeworm.

When he could make himself think of anything else, he was confronted by other bleak thoughts. The murders. Someone was methodically killing those most vital to the upcoming launch. To date, five—no, now it was six specialists had been slain. The flight was still possible—others would take their place—but the flight would be far more dangerous without the benefit of the senior technicians' expertise.

The remaining experts had been sequestered in safe quarters under heavy guard and were escorted to and from their work.

It would take an army to break down the defenses guarding

the remaining technicians. But still, he would feel much better if the maniac could be found. Skirnir was in charge of ferreting out the assassin and the man had ways that had always proved effective in the past.

Then there was the girl, Keri, and her brother Carn. Both had proved difficult. Otir Vaeng had expected the girl to protest, but he had thought that Carn would be more amenable even though he did not know the complete scenario.

Otir Vaeng closed his eyes and sighed, realizing that Carn would eventually have to be eliminated. His head throbbed. There was a deep ache behind his eyes and he was tired all the time. The weariness was bone deep and had nothing at all to do with sleep. Would there ever be an end to this business? It had been such a long time since anything was simple.

For the first time, Otir Vaeng wondered if it was all too much . . . if it was worth it. It was a startling thought. He had been reared to be king, had lived all his life with intrigue, deception, and death, and never had he questioned or even doubted the means to the end, much less whether or not the goal was worth achieving. Now, for the first time, Otir Vaeng was consumed with doubts.

Then there was the girl. Keri. He sighed again and looked at his hand, which he had done a hundred times in the last hour. He had gone to speak to the girl—to calm her fears. But before he could speak, the cursed lupebeast had attacked him. He had thrown his arm across his face and throat, and had been badly bitten, chewing and tearing at his hand like a chunk of meat. Keri had pulled the beast away as his other hand clawed at his sword. But the damage had already been done. No amount of medication seemed to halt the infection or reverse the damage. In fact, the hand looked worse than it had only an hour ago. The entire hand was swelled to three times its normal size, the skin stretched taut and shiny over the swollen flesh. He could feel it throb with every pulse of his heart and it ached damnably no matter how he positioned it. The flesh surrounding the wound itself was ragged and torn and had turned black around the edges. Yellow pus oozed from it and soaked the bandages. Angry red lines radiated up his wrist and streaked his arm.

The doctors had little to offer except more antibiotics that seemed to do little or no good and the ridiculous suggestion that he soak his hand and arm in very, very hot water to draw the poison out.

The situation was absurd. They had made so many miraculous advances in medicine and healing, yet they were helpless to halt a simple infection. A fever raged in his body as his immune system attempted to fight the invading organisms. It was almost enough to make him laugh, if it hadn't hurt to do so—the thought that a primitive animal from a conquered world could accomplish what a lifetime of enemies had been powerless to accomplish: his death.

Skirnir and the doctors had been quick to deny that this was even a possibility, but he had seen the gleam of fear in their eyes and the furtive glances when they thought he did not notice. The bacteria contained in the beast's mouth, coating its jagged double rows of fangs, was virulent in the extreme and did not seem to respond to the strongest of vaccines. Despite their bluff assurances, the doctors were very worried.

It was easy to see that what they were afraid of was what he might do to them; none of them really cared about he himself, despite their lip service to the contrary. More and more, Otir Vaeng had come to realize as never before just how alone he really was. His wife had died long ago. Theirs had been a loveless, political marriage and she had not chosen to extend her life artificially as he had done.

Only recently had he begun to brood, wondering if life with him had made her so unhappy that death seemed preferable. Now, years and years after her bones had turned to dust on old earth, he found himself wishing that he had it to do over again. Despite their efforts, they had had no children. Early in the marriage she had loved him, but he had been far too busy with his various intrigues to devote any real amount of time and caring and eventually her love had died.

Oddly, the girl, Keri, was the only one who really seemed to care, and the wound had been her fault in the first place. He tried hard to conjure up a rage, but could not. He found himself wishing, not for the first time, that there was some way to circumvent the volva's plans. There was something about the girl that appealed to him, caused him to look at things as he had not seen them in many a long year. For all of her brave exterior, Keri was so fresh and clean and innocent of the horrors of life that he found himself wanting to protect her, to spare her from the harsh realities.

Ah. Otir Vaeng shook his head and grinned in wry amusement. It was certainly a sign of age, this feeling of an old man for a young woman. Otir Vaeng cradled his hand against his chest and sat down in his chair to rest—*Just for a minute*, he thought, *just for a few minutes*.

Keri paced back and forth in the chambers where she was now sequestered. They were plush and comfortable, outfitted with everything she might have wanted, including a closet full of magnificent clothes, far more beautiful than any she had ever owned. But the luxuries that surrounded her were not enough to keep her mind off her problems.

Back and forth she paced, with Beast lying in front of the fireplace, muzzle resting on his outstretched paws, following her with his eyes.

"You miss him too, don't you?" she said, and Beast whined as though he had understood her words. "Where do you suppose they are? Are they all right?" Beast looked at her with soulful eyes and whined again. There was a sudden commotion at the door and it swung open, then slammed abruptly shut as Uba Mintch stumbled across the threshold, barely catching himself from falling.

Keri hurried across the room and threw herself into the old Madrelli's arms, holding onto him tightly. He placed his huge shaggy arms around her and gently smoothed her dark curls away from her forehead with an immense black paw.

At one time—not so long ago, actually—Keri would have considered Uba Mintch an animal and cringed from his touch, but now he and Beast were her only comfort in this frightening world. She permitted herself the luxury of a few tears and just for a moment allowed herself to feel safe. There was something about the great bulk of the old Madrelli that generated a feeling of safety and protection. At last she placed a hand on his chest and drew away, wiping her eyes and sniffling a little. She gave him a wan smile.

Uba Mintch chucked her under the chin much as her own father might have done, and this threatened to start the tears flowing again. "No time for tears, child. There is much to be done, much to be said. Dry your eyes and sit by me, here by the fire. These old bones cannot get enough heat to keep them warm on this cold world. Here, sit here by me." He patted the thick shag rug located directly in front of the fire.

Before Uba Mintch seated himself, he gave the room a cursory search, peering behind pictures and feeling the undersides of furniture. Keri knew that he believed the room and their conversation was under constant surveillance, although she found it hard to believe that anyone would be interested in what she might say or do. Uba Mintch had never found anything to support his belief, but he remained convinced that it was true, and all of their conversations took place in front of the fireplace after an armload of wood had been added. The resulting crackling and spitting as the fire reached the tiny pockets of water contained in the wood were enough to muddle the most sensitive monitoring.

"I believe them to be alive," the Madrelli said in a very low voice, and grabbed Keri's hands before she could react. "I talked to young Brion not ten minutes before the king's guards came for him. We can only hope that he is strong enough to resist them."

"But I **have** heard that . . ." Keri's voice dwindled away and Uba Mintch knew that she was referring to the fact that no one could stand up to the king's interrogation, for it was done with drugs that extracted all knowledge despite a man's best resolve.

"I too have heard the stories," Uba Mintch said heavily, "but there are other ways of keeping one's silence if the stakes are high enough." Keri looked at him with horrified understanding.

"Where are they? Are they truly safe?"

"The less you know, the safer you'll be. You cannot relate what you do not know. I will tell you only that they were able to get away from the city and that they are safe and well provisioned. There was a plan, but now that Brion and the others have been taken, I do not know what will happen."

"Can we not do something to help?"

Uba Mintch looked at her with fondness. "My dear, you seem to forget that we are little better than prisoners ourselves. We would never be able to leave this place, and even if we were able to do so, our presence would bring nothing but danger down upon those we wish to protect. The best thing we can do for them is keep our distance."

"Then, how—"

"I had thought that perhaps that dwarf, or maybe Barat Krol. But both of them seem to have disappeared. I cannot find either of them."

"Septua, yes, he would do it if the price was right,"

Keri said, twisting a heavy gold bracelet set with rubies and emeralds that Otir Vaeng had given her. Such a thing would certainly catch the dwarf's fancy and she would part with it without a moment's hesitation.

"They say the king is in a fury about Braldt and the others. He has turned the place upside down looking for them; not one chamber has escaped search. The volva has accompanied the guard and has pointed her bone at more than a few who were not even suspect."

"Pointed her bone?"

Uba Mintch took her hands in his as he explained. "If the volva points her bone at you, you are as good as dead. It means you're guilty of whatever she chooses to accuse you of. They take you away and, often as not, you are the sacrifice at the next paean to the gods.

"I *hate* that woman," Keri said vehemently. "Why does Carn allow her to use him? Can he not see what she is doing?"

"I do not understand your brother; he is a very angry young man and much of what he does is not predicated on reason, but emotion."

"It is as though he has turned his back upon us. Braldt was a brother to him—they laughed and fought and played together since they were children. They loved each other. How can he forget that?"

"There is a sickness inside your brother, a disease that no medicine can put right. He is jealous of Braldt and I imagine that he has been jealous all his life. You may be right: It is possible to love and hate someone at the same time. But something has tipped the balance. At this moment he hates Braldt, and any love he may have felt has been overwhelmed by this black jealousy."

"It's my fault. If I had not fallen in love with Braldt and then forced them to take me with them, none of this would ever have happened. They would still be friends."

"Don't take this burden of guilt onto yourself," cautioned Uba Mintch. "Your feelings for Braldt may well have had something to do with Carn's emotions, but I suspect it had more to do with the fact that Auslic, your high chief, chose Braldt to succeed him as ruler, rather than Carn."

Keri looked into his eyes and nodded. "You are probably right. Carn has always thought that it would be he who was chosen, for the position was his by birthright. Braldt was not even one of us; it must have been a terrible blow. I never really thought about it."

"You can be certain that Carn has thought about little else."

"But why the volva? She is a terrible woman. What can she possibly want with Carn?"

Uba Mintch replied dryly, "I'm certain that Carn views his being chosen by her as an honor. As to what she wants of him, well, we will just have to wait and see. I admit, I have no more understanding of her motives than you do."

"Beast bit the king, you know," Keri said, changing the subject abruptly.

"What? No, I had not heard. How? Why?"

"I don't know. Perhaps he thought that the king was trying to hurt me, he's been on edge ever since they brought us here. He's obeyed me, but barely. In truth, I'm surprised that he hasn't gone for someone before this."

"I suppose it was not fatal," Uba Mintch said in a hopeful voice that was a feeble attempt at humor.

Keri stared at him with her huge brown eyes magnified by tears.

"What have I said, my dear? I did not mean to upset you. It was but a poor joke!"

"It was a terrible bite. The king reached out to give me this"—she raised her arm so that the Madrelli could see the jeweled bracelet—"and before I could stop him, Beast went for him— If he hadn't thrown his hand up— Oh— it was horrible! I could hear the bones snap, and the blood! Oh! There was blood everywhere!"

Uba Mintch stared down at Beast, who looked up and met his gaze with a self-satisfied quirk to his muzzle as though he understood full well the subject under discussion. The fearsome double rows of jagged teeth which had caused so much damage were easily viewed, for as the lupebeast had matured, the double rows of fangs had grown as well. Now, just short of maturity, the beast had reached his full size and his teeth, always impressive, extended slightly beyond the jaws in a ferocious overbite, meshing in a manner that could not be unlocked by any amount of struggling. Uba Mintch thought the king lucky that he had come away with his hand still attached to his body. "I am surprised that he did not kill Beast."

"He could have done so," Keri agreed, "but I clung to his arm and begged him not to. Had the guards been in the room, I do not think Beast would be alive today. As it was, I persuaded him to release the king. I did my best to stop the bleeding, but it was very bad. I have not seen him since and I have heard that he is very ill."

"It could not have happened to a more deserving soul," Uba Mintch said with satisfaction, despite Keri's grief.

"He has always been very nice to me," she said in defense of the injured king.

"Then, my dear, from what I hear, you are the only person on several worlds who is able to say that. Should he indeed die, you will be the only one to mourn him."

The Madrelli crept toward the great silver vessel, slipping from one bit of cover to the next. For all his great size, he was very agile and could move like a shadow if it was necessary.

The snow still swept down with great force, scouring everything that dared exposure with flakes that burned and stung upon contact. He was close enough that he could hear the slithery whispers as the snow struck the sleek hull of the spacecraft and caressed the metallic skin.

Huge arc vapor lights shed pools of bright bluish white light on the craft and all around the perimeter. Barat Krol halted at the very edge, studying the scene, taking in the huddled forms of the guards crouched over a small fire at the far edge of the area, trying to stay warm rather than walk the perimeter as they had been charged to do.

He could sympathize with them, for it was wicked weather, a deeper, more bitter cold than he had ever experienced. It had been necessary for him to don one of the survival suits that the guards wore to protect them from the cold.

It had been difficult finding a suit large enough to fit him and even harder still persuading the man inside to part with it. At this moment, that man lay staring up at the dark sky, his neck tilted at a strange angle, a puzzled look still clouding his unseeing eyes.

The king had finally acknowledged that they were under attack and had thrown a cordon of protection around the remaining technicians. Barat Krol would have preferred to eliminate them all, but one did what one could. He was surprised that there were so few guards stationed around the vessel. Were they really so confident of their own power that they could ignore the fact that there were those who opposed them? If so, all the better for his purposes.

He studied the snow-swept landscape and moved to a point opposite the guards' shelter, where the spacecraft itself blocked their line of view. Here would be his best approach. He had watched the guards' careful promenade on nights when the snow had not beat down with such relentless force and saw that they were most careful to walk only the outermost perimeter. From this he deduced that there were traps or pressure points to be avoided.

There were also a number of laser beams lacing the open space, but the dead guard had thoughtfully provided him with a pair of night vision goggles that enabled him to see the deadly beams of light that could now be carefully avoided. The goggles were far too small and squeezed his head like a vise, but he endured the discomfort, knowing that it was necessary.

Barat Krol was not accustomed to dealing with such advanced weaponry, but sabotage was another matter. He had been part of the original party and one of the three survivors of those who had sabotaged and brought a halt to the Scandis' mining of his world. That had been his first lesson in the fine art of sabotage, and since then he had grown even more adept.

He had gathered an armload of ice chunks. One at a time he fashioned large, heavy snowballs, each with a lump of ice buried in its center. These he carefully lobbed, tossing them over the dangerous beams on a zigzag course which he had chosen. If even one of the beams were broken or a single pressure point activated, the game would be over. It seemed as though the gods were watching over his actions, for not once did his missiles touch down on a pressure point.

The tension was beginning to take its toll as his snowballs fell closer and closer to the ship. Then, just as he had feared, one of his projectiles fell short and clipped the edge of a laser beam. Instantly there was a sizzling crackle and a whole field came alive with high-intensity beams glowing blue and red, and the guards began racing this way and that.

Barat Krol fell back into the shadows and buried himself in a mound of snow, with only his goggles remaining uncovered, and watched as the guards suddenly assumed the state of alertness that they should have exhibited all along.

The driving snow had obliterated most of his footprints and

he had dragged a cape behind him, sweeping away whatever evidence remained. They did not find his trail, but they did locate the blob of snow and ice that had triggered the alarm. To enter the area, it was necessary for them to shut down the laser beams and Barat Krol watched them carefully as they picked their way through the field, noting and memorizing where they placed their feet.

The snowball had fallen quite close to the base of the ship's gantry and they lifted what remained and studied it with great interest. He was not close enough to hear all of what they said, but the wind carried bits and pieces of their conversation to him, enough for him to learn that it was not the first time that chunks of storm-driven snow had been blown onto the area, setting off the alarms. They tossed the snowball aside with disgust and carefully made their way back to the outer perimeter.

They stamped around for a bit, taking a final look around the area, and then, confident that security had not been breached, they hurried back to their hut.

Barat Krol lost no time either, throwing aside the snow that had shielded him and hurrying toward the ship, placing his feet in the guards' exact footprints, thus eliminating any guesswork as to where the pressure points might be. He was a good deal heavier than his snowballs and, where they might not weigh enough to set the pressure points off, his greater bulk certainly would. He reached the gantry just as the guards entered the hut. Seconds later, a millisecond after he gained the first level of crossbars, the laser beams switched on.

The Scandis had placed all their faith in their guards and their sensory devices and had not taken more than the most simple precautions with the gantry itself. It was an easy matter for Barat Krol to avoid tripping those few alarms, quickly scaling the heights until he reached the entrance to the ship itself.

He had not hoped to gain entry to the vessel, thinking that it would be heavily guarded, or locked at the very least. But once he reached the catwalk that spanned the distance between the gantry and the ship, he slipped under a heavy fold of some transparent material and found himself making his way through a series of airlocks and then entering the hold of the ship itself.

Barat Krol was not a complete novice, having traveled from Rototara to Valhalla on a spacecraft, but it was not an experience one grew accustomed to easily. The interior of the great ship was bathed in a soft blue light that made everything appear strange and otherworldly. He could not even begin to guess at the purpose of most things, but he knew what it was that he was looking for.

He had worked for the Scandis on his own world and lived on Valhalla long enough to know that the most complex mechanisms often needed only the smallest of spaces, for their information was contained in almost infinitesimal chips. He intended no obvious acts of sabotage, no wide swath of destruction that would alert the enemy that their ranks had been breached. Instead he would search out places where he might snap a wire, loosen a bolt, scratch a computer chip, and otherwise harm the vast and mighty ship.

He worked long and hard throughout the night, weaseling his way into the heart of the vessel, wreaking havoc in minuscule ways that would not easily be detected and, if then, making it appear that the damage was accidental rather than intentional. He was careful to cover his tracks, to leave no evidence that he had been there, for he did not want them to grow alarmed enough to institute a widespread search that might uncover his malfeasance.

He finished the last bit of mischief, fraying several relay wires that were part of an immense trunk of colorful threads more than two feet in diameter that snaked beneath one of the floor panels. He was delighted with this fortuitous find, even though he had not the slightest idea what its purpose was, and after a moment's thought he severed and pulled free a goodly number of the wires, burying the damage deep within the multitude. With any luck at all, it would prove to be something important, and with so many wires, it would be difficult to find the exact location of the breaks. Even if the breaks were found, they would mean hours and hours of tedious splicing and testing. The thought was enough to make him smile.

Wan glimmers of pale daylight were stretching tentative fingers over the jagged horizon when Barat Krol finished the last of his work. He could feel the exhaustion in his muscles and he stretched wide before he began the long, cautious crawl down the gantry. But it was a good tired, with the sense of satisfaction one got after a hard night's work.

Carn struggled to hold on to his fading strength. He gasped with exhaustion as well as fear. Never had he felt less in charge of his own existence than when he was with the volva. She was unlike any other woman he had ever known. Always before, he had been in control of his relationships, deciding when and how often he would see a woman, and always it was he who initiated sexual encounters.

But with this woman, the volva—if she had a name, he did not know it—it was not like any relationship he had ever known. He was no neophyte, no rank beginner, he had made love before, but this was not love, nor anything that resembled it. It was lust and pure physical passion, and love was only noticed because of its absence.

This woman had him completely in her thrall. At silent moments, alone in his chambers, he asked himself time and again why he would allow anyone, much less a woman, to subject him to such degradation. But every time he attempted to break away, she bent him to her will again, and each time it was harder and harder to oppose her. He wondered if, as she had said, the blood of witches ran in her veins.

He gasped again and groaned, his entire body sheathed in sweat, his senses reeling on a tightrope of sensation that was neither pain nor ecstasy but a combination of both. The volva leaned over him and peered into his eyes, a question in her own, waiting for him to speak, to beg her to stop. He closed his eyes and turned aside, wanting the torment to stop, but unwilling to relinquish the rapture that accompanied it. He groaned again and knew without looking that she was smiling.

There was a sudden jolt of pain and his eyes fluttered open in shock, his heart hammering hard against his ribs. The volva was laying across his body, her flesh plastered to his with a layer of perspiration, her sharpened teeth fastened in the flesh at the side of his neck. The pain grew more intense as her teeth sliced through the thick, shiny scar tissue; he could feel the rivulets of blood coursing down his flesh, hear the drops as they fell onto the cushions. He cried out despite his resolve not to let her know that she had hurt him, and he heard her low chuckle of amusement.

Rage fought with pain and humiliation, the knowledge that he was little more than this woman's plaything, a toy that might be easily discarded if it ceased to amuse . . . or if it were broken.

As the various emotions warred inside him, he felt a sensation almost akin to a tingle of electricity shoot through his body, lifting him higher and higher till he crested on a wave of sheer exultation so intense that he thought his heart would burst apart under the strain. His body arched time and again as the volva drew the strength from him, squeezing him between her powerful loins, touching, caressing him, her every touch leaving shivery, burning trails on his body.

He had reached a point that was almost unbearable. He

hovered on the verge of unconsciousness and wondered if he might die, although if it had been his decision whether or not to stop, even he could not have said what he would do. He recognized at some distant point in his fevered brain that he had pushed his poor, damaged body to its very limits. A man was not like a machine, but somehow he knew that if he continued, some part of him would burn out and he would never be the same again.

The volva pulled back, leaned away from him, and the cessation of sensation was as great a shock as the infliction. He was like an addict in the final throes of addiction, where reality, a return to normalcy, was unable to be borne. He reached for her and pulled her to him. She laughed aloud, a cry of victory, and thrust her body full upon his, driving him, forcing him, driving him up, up, up and over the edge . . . into the waiting darkness.

12

Fortran was confused. He had flung himself into action, unfurling his blue form from the tight roll he had assumed for the past 127 days and nights. Although he was not capable of feeling true physical sensations, just the mere act of unfolding was exhilarating! Fortran had, in a true manner of speaking, burst forth, opening himself up to life and all that it had to offer.

Impressive as that was, it was not the best part. No sooner had he unfurled himself than all around him there were mutterings and stirrings and emanations of energy. His brothers were coming to life as well. Fortran could scarcely believe that such a thing was happening, unless . . . A chilling thought came to him: Perhaps they were not joining him, as he had first thought, but, realizing that he was about to do something, sought to stop him! Perhaps they viewed him and his impetuous actions as a threat to their own progress. After all, one could not help but be contaminated, tainted, by the mere association with the rebel Fortran! One would always be remembered that way. "Oh, yes, the class of 7983. That means you were one of those rebels . . ." The shame would follow one for the rest of one's life.

For a brief moment, Fortran was cowed by the specter of his peers' contempt as well as the possible—no, be honest, the probable—loss of the lovely Mutar, but then his mythic backbone stiffened as he further contemplated the probability of all the years of boredom stretching before him, just lying here forgotten in the darkness of this distant planet.

In a mind-wrenching, stretching moment of courage and personal growth, Fortran dared to doubt, even reject the existence of the supreme deity known as Yantra. It was a terrifying as well as an exhilarating moment, heart- and breath-stopping—that is, it would have been if he had had a heart or the need to breathe.

And at that very moment, as he began to blur into the transitional phase that took him and his kind from one place to another, he heard a voice echo inside him—many voices, really, that of the Grand Yerk as well as a number of the Triune of Yerkels. And there . . . there were his mother and father! And—was it really possible?—they were congratulating him and praising his courage and strength of vision! His mother was sobbing softly, although with pride and happiness. The Grand Yerk, however, was muttering to one of his associates.

Fortran, although he should have been paying attention to the speech the Most Eminent Bezir was beginning, replete with flowery terms, could not help but focus on what the Grand Yerk was saying: "Why is it the troublemakers who always realize it first? Fortran! Of all of them, why did it have to be Fortran?"

His associate replied, "Do you think there is some correlation between rebellion and intelligence? It is a most troubling thought. I am quite certain that we ourselves were never so difficult. Intelligent, certainly; but rebellious, never. Well, we might as well get on with it. Fortran was the first, but others will follow, it's always the way. Fortran," he said with a sigh. "If only it had been Vexlur."

"The wedding, Majesty." Skirnir was doing his best to keep the king's attention focused on the matter at hand. A bad choice of words. Skirnir did his best to avoid looking at the king's hand, that grossly deformed object that the king kept cradled in a lamb's-wool sling on his chest. But it was difficult to avoid—the thing was like a magnet that drew his attention. It was hideous, shiny and swollen like a cartoon caricature of a hand. It was a mélange of colors, black and blue and yellowish green, with streaks of red lancing up the arm and now advancing well past the elbow.

The healers had done everything within their power, desperate to heal their leader, whom they depended on for continued life. If they failed to heal him, they would not live long enough to view the final moments of the dying sun.

None of their efforts had been effective. The hideous wound continued to suppurate and worsen rather than improve. In desperation, they had suggested—no, urged—that the king let them remove the arm. It would save his life and with the marvelous advances in cybernetic prosthetics . . . But the king had resolutely dismissed the possibility. What was infinitely worse, he no longer seemed to care. He seemed deadened by apathy and inertia and merely stared at them without speaking most of the time, no matter what they said.

Skirnir had asked the volva to join him, hoping that she could add her voice to his, to persuade the king to marry the girl, sooner rather than later. There might not be a later if the wound did not improve. They needed the wedding to reassure the people and they needed the sacrifice to whip them into doing their bidding, wiping out all of those who had been deemed as undesirable, those for whom there was no space on the shuttles.

They were attempting to create a gulf between the chosen and those who were not chosen by the gods. If they could convince the people that it was the will of the gods, so much the better, for killings justified by feelings of righteousness left the fewest scars on a populace. And, as it had been proved many times before, such killings actually drew the survivors together with a sense of attenuated pride, almost like a team spirit, a patriotism.

Such thinking was far more preferable to the only other alternative, that the Scandis participate in some vile, degenerate act that would mark them with shame for the rest of their days.

This phenomenon had been thoroughly researched in the years following the great earth war of 1939–1945 when the German nation had systematically eliminated a population of "undesirables," millions and millions of them. The Germans had lost the war in the end and the condemnation of the world was focused on them for decades.

But for the Scandis the greatest lesson that had come out of the earth's last great war was that people could be manipulated, could be persuaded to do anything, no matter how horrendous, if they could be convinced that they were in the right. More specifically, if they could believe that their actions were sanctioned by the gods and that—and this was most important—they would benefit from their sanctions, while other unfortunates would suffer a well-deserved fate. Under those conditions, there was no destructive and time-consuming drain of self-guilt and breast-thumping. The people were bound together by the sense of having accomplished something difficult but worthwhile, and if the job was done right, there would be no one left to argue otherwise.

The plan could not be implemented without the king's cooperation. Only he could wed the girl, and due to the feelings of hatred and guilt that so many Scandis were feeling for the Duroni these days, what more logical a sacrifice?

There were those who argued that they should not have broken Federated laws and colonized an inhabited planet, but those voices would be among the first to vanish. If the king would only agree to wed! Skirnir began to lose patience; he could feel his carefully erected facade beginning to crack under the strain.

"Is the boat finished?" Otir Vaeng asked suddenly. It took Skirnir a moment to regroup his thinking. "The boat? Uh, yes, Majesty. It is all but finished and lies waiting for your direction," Skirnir said smoothly, inwardly seething at the waste of man-hours. The very best of artisans had been necessary for the construction of the high-prowed, high-sterned vessel that the king had demanded be built at the edge of the great dead sea. Complete with mast and sail, round shields painted with the emblems of prominent Scandi families hung along the sides above the oarlocks and a great pile of kindling was stacked on the varnished deck. A total waste of time, but Skirnir knew that he dared not defy the king . . . yet.

The king seemed to settle deeper into his lethargy. Skirnir pressed on. "Majesty, the wedding?" The king opened his eyes, which were bloodshot, the corneas yellowed. He waved his hand in a gesture of dismissal. "Whenever," he said with difficulty. "Whenever you think the time is right, but I have decided that I do not want the girl to be harmed. She is innocent of any wrongdoing and there has been too much death already. That is my decision."

"Sir!" Skirnir drew his breath in sharply and glanced at the volva, whose eyes narrowed at the king's words. "Everything depends upon the girl. Alive, she means nothing, but her death will unite the people!"

The king gestured again, an indication of his waning interest. "Yes, yes, but heed me, Skirnir. No harm is to come to the girl."

"Majesty," Skirnir said with bowed head and knee, hiding his rage from his king. He shot a sidelong look at the volva, who had said nothing at all during the entire audience. The volva met his eyes, a chilly glance that extinguished the fire that burned in his belly like a bucket of icy water. She met and held his gaze and although no word was spoken, no sign exchanged, he knew with sudden certainty that her goals were the same as his. Despite the king's wishes, the girl was as good as dead.

"At the next full moon," the king said suddenly. "That is in four days' time. The ceremony will be held on board the ship."

"But sir, I had thought that the burial mound would be a more appropriate site. Even if the girl is to be spared, we must slice the throat of a cock and throw it over the lintel to the gods. There are certain rites that must be followed!"

"The ship," Otir Vaeng said wearily, shutting his eyes and resting his head against the back of his throne. There was a sense of finality in his words that Skirnir did not dare defy. "The ship, Majesty. Indeed, the ship."

The sun that shone on Valhalla was nearing the end of its long life. For countless millions of years it had blazed, feeding upon a seemingly infinite supply of volatile gases. But nothing is truely infinite, and in time the fiery star began to ebb as the gases that fed the massive inferno diminished.

It did not die quietly, this huge flaming mass, but made its might felt through spectacular solar flares that lashed out at the cold, dark skies of space as though protesting its fate.

The resulting magnetic disturbances were felt throughout the galaxy, creating havoc with ships and other space installations when precisely calibrated computer settings and radio frequencies were altered. Fortunately, all but one of the ships affected discovered the changes and were able to reset their equipment. The one ship whose navigator was not quite so alert blundered far off course and was never heard from again.

This was, of course, long before the Scandis found the planet and colonized it. In those early years when the sun first began to wane, most of the damage was inflicted upon the satellite planet that depended on it for light and life.

First to die were the microscopic algae that lived in the oceans and inland waters. Irradiated by massive jolts of ultraviolet rays, they vanished and were not reborn. Those who fed upon them were the next to die, and so it went in relentless domino fashion up and down the food chain until all forms of life save those that burrowed deep beneath the surface were dead.

Much of the plant life was affected as well. The more delicate, specialized forms, those that required the narrowest margin of circumstances to survive, died first as the temperatures rose higher and higher and the ultraviolet rays bombarded the surface of the planet. Finally, only those plants and trees which were capable of taking the most severe abuse were left alive.

When the Scandis found the planet, the worst of the solar flares were over. The great heat that had seared the planet had vanished, leaving only barren deserts of shifting sands and bleached lifeless mountains as testament to the violent destruction that had occurred.

Exhausted both mentally and physically, and having found nowhere else to go, to the Scandis, Valhalla, despite its emptiness and lack of life, had appeared as a godsend. The Scandis had lost no time in claiming it for their own and set about building their homes and cities.

It was not until a sudden burst of solar storms erupted on the surface of the sun and long fingers of solar energy arced across the sky that they began to realize the seriousness of the problem. They were taught this lesson in a manner that they would not soon forget. Fully half of their people would die from the effects of radiation poisoning received during that brief burst of energy. Every single animal that was not fortunate enough to be sheltered underground or similarly protected either contracted some form of radiation sickness or was rendered sterile.

In one single stroke of random fate, nearly half of the life on the planet was killed and the future of the fledgling colony was thrown in deepest doubt.

It was impossible to leave the surface of the planet, for the raging solar flares were impossible to predict and the Scandis had far too few ships to sacrifice even one. The method of travel that they had pioneered for short distances between worlds was completely dependent on the transmission of electronic waves; the solar disturbances made the contemplation of such travel only slightly better than suicide. For similar reasons, they could not transmit off planet.

The ship bearing Braldt and his companions had been the last to arrive before the space surrounding the planet became deadly, and the gods must truly have been smiling on them, for even then flight was considered far too dangerous to attempt.

It was hoped that the flares would diminish, and this was even before the Scandis realized the degree of damage that had been inflicted on both humans and animals. Their scientists had hoped to report that the flares were an isolated incident, unlikely to happen again, but their findings proved just the opposite.

Now they knew what they were looking for. There was ample evidence that such flares had been occurring for eons. It also explained the fact that Valhalla had once supported native life-forms which had mysteriously ceased to exist. It became increasingly obvious that they could not expect anything but more of the same.

The Scandis had not managed to survive on their own ravaged earth without learning a few tricks. Shortly after colonizing the planet, they had discovered a natural marvel:

Many of the peaks in a range of mountains that formed a major spine of the world were hollow, perhaps emptied out by rivers of molten rock during the formation of the planet. The Scandis were not about to waste time questioning the whys and wherefors of what appeared to be their salvation from the deadly solar flares. What they could not have known was that the worst of the flares was over and that the dying sun had entered the final phase of its death throes.

As the gases began to diminish, the sun began to actively die, shrinking almost visibly before the eyes of the horrified astronomers. The Scandis had taken shelter in the largest of the hollow mountains, setting up their city and calling it Aasgard.

There was a certain amount of irony in the name which none could escape, for Aasgard was the final resting place of the gods, a reward for a job well done. At first it had carried a sense of hope, a feeling that anything was possible if only one strove hard enough. Now mention of the name left only a taste of bitter irony and few could ignore that, according to the old myths, Valhalla and Aasgard could only be reached by dying, a state they themselves might easily achieve without even trying.

Despite the drawbacks, the Scandis might have attempted to remain on Valhalla locked safely within their hollow mountain, but it was not possible. Long before the sun shed its last feeble ray of light, the planet would have become buried beneath a thick sheath of snow and ice. Not only would they lack a sun, but an atmosphere as well. Life would be impossible to sustain. If they were to survive, they had no choice but to leave Valhalla.

Where to go, assuming they could escape the fickle flares. There were those among the Council of Thanes who favored a return to earth; after all, those ills were well understood and it was always easier to deal with known evils than new, uncertain problems. That suggestion was finally defeated by the mention of some of the ruthless methods which the Scandis had used to facilitate their departure from earth. They had left many enemies behind and all too few friends. They would not be welcomed on earth.

Rototara was another option; but then, they had ruthlessly exploited the planet, eliminating or imprisoning the native population. Unfortunately, they had not realized that, periodically, the majority of the reptilian population went into deep hibernation, awakening and emerging with the arrival of semi-decadential rains.

The awakened reptiles were massive, powerful, and militant, determined to take back their world from those who had defiled it. Not all of the Scandis had been fortunate enough to escape the awakening rampage. No one knew how long the reptiles were likely to remain out of hibernation; little was known about their life cycle. There were those who argued that they merely mated and then either died off or returned to a state of hibernation until the next rains. But it was all theory; no one could say for certain what they would find if they returned to Rototara, and none of those who had actually been there and witnessed the reptilian wrath were anxious to risk it a second time.

There were other inhabited planets and artificial life stations to choose from, but these were Federation-controlled and no matter what their choice, they would be governed by the rules and rulers of others; it was not a pleasant thought.

Their options had appeared to be limited in number and all of them bleak when the astronomers first came up with their startling discovery; it had seemed impossible, at first, that Braldt's planet, known on the star charts as K7, had somehow survived the explosion that was to have blown it to bits. The cloud of debris, which they had hoped to mine of its valuable rhodium, filled the space that the planet had once occupied. Only recently, readings and subsequent calculations had seemed to indicate that the planet still existed! It had not been possible to actually view the planet, for it was effectively shielded by a dense, dark cloud.

How was such a thing possible? On the face of it, it seemed most unlikely, but then a number of theories—wildly hopeful, even absurd theories—were advanced. Among the least ridiculous was the possibility that the charges Leif Arndtson, the leader of the expedition to destroy the planet, had (1) failed to detonate or (2) been consumed by the volcano itself. Poor Leif Arndtson, who had wanted nothing more than to succeed in his mission, was now torn between defending the success of his mission and praying that it had failed.

A second, more logical theory, which was gaining support as the data became available between solar flares, seemed to indicate a massive volcanic eruption. There were those, of course, who doubted that any act of nature could do such an immense amount of damage, but those who knew their ancient history pointed to the legendary eruption in the Mediterranean Sea which had totally destroyed an island and gave rise to the persistent myth of Atlantis. There was also the devastating eruption of Mount Vesuvius in Italy, and Krakatau in Java, not to mention Mount St. Helens in 1988 and the final death throes of Vesuvius in 2039, which put an end to all life in southern Italy.

Clouds of volcanic debris circled the globe for years following the worst of those eruptions. So severe was the ultimate destruction of Vesuvius that the temperature of the entire world was lowered for more than ten years, which had played a significant role in the ultimate demise of earth.

Uncertain of their data and torn by internal bickering, the small coterie of scientists were uncertain of what course of action they should follow. A goodly number wanted to inform the king of their findings and urge him to direct their launch efforts to K7.

But an equally large number argued otherwise, for they had experienced the wrath of the king and were not anxious to urge him to a course of action of which they were less than certain. What if there was nothing beneath that cloud of dust but dust? And even if there was a planet, maybe it had survived the initial blast only to die due to lack of sunlight. A terrible bit of irony, to escape one dying planet only to arrive on another.

13

Braldt could stand the inactivity no longer. He was a man of action, accustomed to solving his problems with deeds. He could not envision what good could come of such laying about. Brandtson and Saxo argued that lying low would relieve some of the tension on the city and divert attention from their compatriots. This lessening of hostilities would permit them to continue with their plan.

But Braldt could not ignore the fact that many of their co-conspirators had been arrested and it was quite possible that the plan had already been compromised. Even worse, they had had no communication with the city since Septua's arrival. And what about Keri? That thought, more than any other, worried Braldt constantly. What would she think of him for deserting her, leaving her alone with no friends other than Uba Mintch and Beast?

It was the thought of Keri that decided him at last. He gathered a few weapons and donned the warmest clothes he could find before stroking a watchful Thunder and bidding a silent farewell to the sleeping Saxo and Brandtson. He could only hope they would understand. Septua was a snoring lump huddled under a mound of blankets and furs.

The snow had abated and the night was clear and brittle cold. The stars sparkled in the black sky and truly seemed close enough to touch. There was no sound other than the soft skitter of snow being blown across the tops of the glittering drifts. And the crunch of footsteps. Braldt stopped for a moment and listened. The footsteps stopped as well, yet it seemed that the sound continued for the slightest bit longer than it should have. Braldt walked on until he found what he was looking for, a small arroyo that entered on the left. He stepped into the shadows of the gully and continued to tramp his feet in the deep piled snow, treading ever more softly to simulate distance.

The ploy worked as he had hoped, for a small figure scurried out of the darkness, leaping and hopping to utilize the trail he had broken. The tension faded. Braldt leaned back against the wall of the arroyo and assumed a casual stance. "Looking for me?" he asked softly.

Septua slid to a halt, nearly falling headfirst into a drift. His hand was on his dagger, his lips drawn back in a snarl, when his eyes fixed the location of Braldt's voice and he saw who had spoken. Immediately his posture became humble and apologetic. "Didn't want to get left behind. Thought you might need me. You doesn't know the city like I does."

Braldt thought about it. It was true. Septua knew the ins and outs of the city like the features of his own face, but those facial features were equally well known to those who might be seeking him. Still, there had been no indication that he was being sought. Perhaps the dwarf could be of use.

"Why are you so anxious to return?" Braldt asked, for Septua was not known for his courage or eagerness to face danger.

The dwarf hung his head and looked aside, unwilling to meet Braldt's eyes. He mumbled something under his breath.

Braldt leaned forward, curious now in spite of himself. Gone was the brash, belligerent attitude that typified the little man. Braldt would almost have sworn that he was blushing! Suddenly Braldt understood.

"It's Mirna, isn't it? That double-dealing wench! She's got her hooks into you again."

"It ain't like that, really!" Septua leapt to her defense despite the fact that the self-serving Mirna had betrayed him in the past and would undoubtedly do so again if the circumstances warranted it.

"Right," Braldt said dryly. He studied the dwarf for a long moment. "We take care of business first and then you can attend to personal matters—but no short cuts, no foolish risks. Understood?"

"I don't wanna get caught no more 'n you do," the dwarf muttered, then brightened considerably. "If I help you, you'll come wit' me whilst I talk to Mirna?"

Braldt hesitated, but it seemed only fair, and he had to admit to being curious about a woman who could turn the self-reliant dwarf thief into helpless mush. He nodded his agreement and Septua's face stretched into a wide grin.

The odd pair set off at a brisk pace, Braldt in the lead, breaking a path in the heavy snow, and Septua hopping along behind. Shortly before dawn they reached the base of the mountain that was home to the population of Valhalla. There had been few words exchanged during the long trek, all energy being conserved for the difficult trail. Now that the peak of the mountain was in sight, a huge dark craggy bulk silhouetted against the pale light of the coming dawn, they huddled together for a conference.

"The guard be tightened ever'where," Septua whispered, obviously aware of the fact that voices carry exceptionally well in the silence of the night. "We don't dare try goin' in any o' the main gates."

"Should we try to scale the flank of the mountain and find our way in from one of the outer doors?"

"No, lemmee think a minute." The dwarf chewed his

lower lip and his brow furrowed in concentration. "Sheep pens," he proclaimed after a long moment of troubled thought. "We'll go in through the sheep pens. No one would ever think to watch 'em!"

Braldt was dubious, but held his silence. The little man might have many faults, but stealth and cunning were his stock in trade. In this, Braldt would have to trust him.

The sheep pens announced their presence by smell long before they appeared in sight, a rank, gamy stench that lay on the air like a heavy blanket. The sheep, with their thick, tangled coat of oily wool, were among the few creatures who were able to thrive in Valhalla's arctic cold. As long as their feed held out, they would survive. The fact that they provided meat, milk, and wool and could live in less than ideal conditions also meant that they were valuable enough to be included in future galactic migrations.

They were enclosed in a large circular pen of rough-cut timber abutting the flank of the mountain. A small round opening had been chiseled into the face of the mountain and fitted with a simple wooden swinging door which allowed the sheep to move indoors and out at will. No guards were posted, which Braldt found a strange oversight, but Septua shrugged it off. "What they got to worry 'bout? Ain't no 'uman enemies on this 'ere world an' there be no natural predators left to bother 'em. If there be any guards, they be inside, not standin' out 'ere in the weather like us dummies."

Braldt nodded; the dwarf's words were logical. But still a nagging worry remained. They slipped into the pen and made their way through the flock, frozen dung crunching beneath their boots and the rancid stench thick in their nostrils.

The sheep were nervous and uneasy at their presence, jostling one another and bleating their distress. Wide eyes rolled and heads tossed as they pawed the ground. Braldt could feel their hysteria growing by the second; it gathered in the air like a living thing. He crouched low to the earth without any real thought except that of removing himself from their vision. Septua followed his lead and, strangely enough, the sheep quieted, with only those nearest the human invaders snorting and leaping aside.

"Dumb. They be real dumb," whispered the dwarf. "If they can't see us, it's like we were never here."

On hands and knees they crept through the milling flock. The earth, protected by the tightly packed herd and constantly churned by their sharp hooves, was not completely frozen, and soon Braldt's and Septua's lower extremities were covered with a pungent layer of feces. Oddly, this familiar scent seemed to reassure the sheep and, other than garnering a few suspicious and puzzled glances, the pair was able to make their way to the swinging door without further problem.

Braldt eyed the hinged door with apprehension. If there was a guard posted inside the sheep pens, the door to the outside would be closely watched. He was not anxious to stick his head through to investigate—not if one was as fond of his head as he was.

Septua must have been thinking along similar lines, for he tugged at Braldt's cloak and pointed at the upper rung of the fence, where half a dozen or more pelts were hanging. Braldt understood immediately. Septua scurried over to the side of the pen and pulled down two skins. They were stiff with the cold and bent double. It took a good bit of careful flexing before the frozen fleeces could be draped over their backs. Even then it was necessary to tie the pelts to their arms and legs and around their necks with woolly strips trimmed from the edges; otherwise the pelts fell off after a few steps.

By the time the pelts were secure, the sheep had lost their fear of the strange intruders and merely glanced at them with the disdainful look one reserves for madmen or children who are misbehaving in public. This was all to the good, for when

Braldt and Septua were finally ready to make their move, several sheep decided that going indoors was also a good idea and pushed ahead as well as behind them as they passed through the swinging wooden flap.

Their precautions were well founded, for it was immediately apparent that there was a guard posted over this lowly entrance. Fortunately for them, his intellect was not greatly superior to that of his charges and he barely glanced over at the influx of sheep as the two intruders entered the mountain stronghold.

They found themselves in a pen that was the mirror image of the one outside. Rock walls composed two sides of the pen. The third side was a tall metallic device with numerous dials and levers and a wide trough at the bottom which sheep licked even though it was obviously empty. "Feeder," Septua said cryptically. The feeder formed the third wall of the enclosure, which left them only one possible avenue of exit—the one with the guard.

They wandered around the far edges of the pen, beginning to sweat under the heavy pelts and inhaling their own less than fragrant aroma as they whispered back and forth, trying to decide upon a plan. Septua was all for waiting until the guard fell asleep, as it seemed he might do, before they made their move. Braldt was far too impatient to put his faith in such a vague possibility.

They were still arguing about what to do when a large ewe who had been eyeing them with distrust suddenly decided that she did not like their looks. Emitting a deep *baahh*, she lowered her head and came at them, catching Septua in the ribs and tossing him several feet in the air. Braldt's heart all but stopped and he reached for the hilt of his sword, even though it gave him a most unsheeply profile.

Fortunately, the guard had been busying himself with his

rations and merely looked up with irritation, grunted "Here, stop that, you stupid cow!" and flung a rock, which missed the culprit completely and bounced off Braldt's wool-covered head. All of the sheep began to bleat and mill about aimlessly and Braldt could do little else but scramble along, helping the winded dwarf to his hands and knees. The ewe trotted up for a second bash at Septua, a malevolent look in her large brown eyes. Braldt, still feeling the ache of the well-flung missile, growled at the sheep and fixed her with a look of naked hostility. The sheep bleated and leapt aside, skittering away with head held high as though she had suddenly remembered far better things to do.

The guard, satisfied that his fluffy charges would not attempt to kill or maim each other for the next several minutes, addressed himself to the contents of his meal ration. Braldt and Septua took advantage of the man's interest in his food to draw closer.

He was a large man, taller than Braldt and much heavier. With the guard's attention focused elsewhere, they were able to approach without being noticed. Reaching up, Braldt seized the guard's leg with both hands, pulled him down into the mass of sheep.

Even though he had been taken by surprise, the guard put up a good fight, and if he had not been disadvantaged by Septua's flair for dirty tricks, his strength might have won the day. Just as he was opening his mouth, perhaps to yell for reinforcements, the thief shoved a clod of sheep dung into his mouth, effectively silencing him until Braldt was able to knock him out. They left him among his flock, securely bound and gagged and wrapped in both fleeces. Unless one entered the pen and examined the animals closely, he resembled nothing so much as a slumbering sheep.

Before they bound him, they stripped the guard of his

clothes, which Braldt exchanged for his own. A quick wash in the sheep's water trough and a wipe-down with a handful of rough hay removed most of the stink from him as well. The dwarf was the problem. There was no way he could have worn the guard's immense clothing. He dabbed at the stains on his knees and proclaimed himself fit to travel.

Braldt knew that there was no sense in arguing with the dwarf, who could be as stubborn as he was hardheaded, so he picked him up without comment and stripped the stinking clothes from his flailing limbs as one might strip the husk from an ear of corn. This accomplished, he dropped the struggling dwarf into the water tank and refused to let him out until he had scrubbed himself pink.

The angry thief glowered at Braldt and snarled a wide variety of curses in an even wider number of languages, all of which Braldt ignored. "Get dressed," he said, tossing Septua the guard's voluminous cloak. "We haven't got time for this. Smarten up. They would have smelled you coming long before they saw you."

"What am I supposed to do with this?" Septua asked in barely civil tones.

"We have to assume that they'll be looking for you—Septua, the dwarf thief," Braldt explained patiently. "Every one of the guards will be watching for a dwarf male. The only thing we can do to alter your appearance is make you a woman or a child. You decide."

In the end, much to Septua's disgust, even he had to agree that few children would choose to wear a cloak indoors, and his baldness would give him away immediately. They cut off the excess length of the cape to make a tunic of sorts and wrapped a ruff of sheep pelt around his head so that it peeked out beneath the edges of the cape's hood. Unless one looked very closely, the dwarf could pass for a gray-haired old granny. Satisfied, if not content with their disguises, they left the animal pens and followed a corridor which the dwarf assured Braldt would lead to the main concourse.

No sooner had they turned into the corridor than they came face to face with a contingent of fully armed guards, who challenged them instantly and demanded that they produce their identification.

14

Barat Krol had talked with Uba Mintch at length, telling him of his frustrations, his difficulty in speaking with the resident tribe of Madrelli. "I just don't understand why they can't seem to comprehend the danger they're in," he said as he paced back and forth in the small chamber that had been assigned to them.

Uba Mintch watched the young male and wondered what else was on his mind. He was too agitated; something else was troubling him. He thought about asking Barat Krol directly, but immediately decided against it. Barat Krol was hot-tempered and impetuous, too young for such heavy responsibilities as had been placed upon him. But with Batta Flor's death, there had been no one else. Barat Krol would learn self-restraint in time . . . if they were given the time.

"Do not judge them so harshly," Uba Mintch cautioned. "They have not been given the same opportunities that we have."

"What opportunities do you speak of?" Barat Krol said bitterly. "The opportunity for self-rule until our masters decide to blow us and our world into dust? Sometimes I wonder which of us is more unfortunate. Their ignorance is their protection."

"I know that it is difficult to view the matter without emotion, but try to set aside your anger and view the larger picture," Uba Mintch said when the younger male ran out of words. "We owe the Scandis a great deal." He raised a hand to silence Barat Krol. "From their viewpoint, it is their right to do whatever they choose with us. No! Listen to me! Who is to say where responsibility begins and ends?

"At first we were no more than animals. Our brains were no better developed than those of intelligent dogs. But we had one advantage, one gift of nature that elevated us, separated us from all the other beasts: We had opposable thumbs. It doesn't sound like much, but that single difference was the reason that the Scandi biogenetic engineers chose us and not dogs to bless with the gift of intelligence.

"We were taken from the wild and our genes were manipulated and augmented to produce the beings we have become today. When necessary, our diets were also augmented so that our bodies grew apace with our new intelligence. We were able to think and reason and solve problems whose existence we had never before even imagined. We became the strong right arm and brain of the Scandis, succeeding and failing, living and dying, on hostile planets with deadly environments to accomplish their deeds.

"They learned from our mistakes and altered our genetic makeup still further until we evolved to this point, a species capable of creating their own civilization, independent and self-ruled."

"Don't you understand what you have said?" Barat Krol burst out, unable to hold his tongue any longer. "Think about your words. By your own admission, they have used us like laboratory animals! We're no more than experiments to them, possessions! They don't think of us as living, thinking beings with the right to freely exist. We're possessions that merely happen to be alive!"

"I understand precisely what I have said," Uba Mintch said gently. "Do not allow your emotions to overwhelm you. You are right, they do view us as possessions. But who is to say that they are wrong? One owns pets, does one not? Even we Madrelli have been known to harbor singing birds and small furry creatures in our own homes. In the beginning we were no different. Intelligence, the ability to even imagine the concept of freedom and self-rule, came from the Scandis. They birthed us; they are our creators, our parents. We owe them a great debt for the gift of intelligent life.''

''That debt, if there ever was one, was paid in full with the blood of all those Madrelli who died under their knives in the laboratory, who gasped for clean air on poisonous planets, who were blown to dust with our world. We have paid the price and now we are free. And our less fortunate brothers must be freed as well. We must discover how to share this dubious gift with them. I will not rest until it is done. Nor will the Scandis discard us like cast-off garbage when they take their leave of this world.

''You must decide where your loyalties lie, Uba Mintch—to the Scandis or to your own people. I have revered you and followed you without question all of my life, but here is where we must part. If you are not with me in this, then I have no choice but to consider you the enemy.''

Uba Mintch stared at the young Madrelli as he considered his words. There was much truth in what he said. He thought of all those who had died, including his son and, with the extinction of his world, all those he had personally held dear. The price was indeed dear. He lowered his head. ''I am not the enemy,'' he said softly. ''I am with you. Tell me what you would have me do.''

''. . . make me come lookin' for you like some kind o' child! Keepin' the captain waitin'! What were you thinkin' about?'' Quick as a flash, as soon as Septua caught sight of the approaching guard, he had reached up and seized Braldt by the nose and pulled him down so that his face was hidden from view. He began speaking in a loud, shrill, womanish voice, badgering the astonished Braldt in an unceasing diatribe about his many supposed vices. As they came closer to the equally astonished contingent, Septua twisted Braldt still further till his nose all but touched his knees. Braldt's eyes watered from the pain. When he got his hands on the dwarf . . . !

"What be you lookin' at?" screeched the dwarf, halting directly in front of the sergeant of the guards. Braldt could do nothing but look at the man's shoes and curse silently.

"Identification?" the man said, the word spoken almost apologetically in the face of the dwarf's invective.

"Got no time for such nonsense. This one 'ere be wanted by Captain Bakkstrom hisself! Gone an' wagered an' lost all 'is wages to that worthless lout what minds the sheep. I'd wager them sheep 'as got bigger brains than the two 'o them. What the captain will do ain't 'alf as bad as what I 'as in mind. . . ."

The dwarf rattled on and on, jerking Braldt forward by his nose as he spoke, sounding incredibly like a shrewish wife. Despite himself, Braldt cried out in pain as the sensitive cartilage was bent and pulled. He batted ineffectively at his tormentor. Much to his astonishment, he saw from teary eyes the feet of the guards part before them, shuffling aside to allow the shrill harridan to pass. Braldt felt his face flush with embarrassment and shame even as he told himself that it was but a clever ploy.

Septua kept up the tirade until the guards had been left safely behind. Only then did he release Braldt from the painful position. Braldt staggered about for a moment, wiping his streaming eyes and clutching his throbbing nose. "Wads thad really nedcessary?"

"Got us past 'um, din't it?" the dwarf replied cheerfully. Braldt could only hold his nose and glare. He had to admit, it had been an unusual and effective deceit. "Dodn't eber do thad agaid," he growled.

Septua only smiled, then led the way briskly forward. "Com'mon. Let's get out o' 'ere before they decides to go congratulate the winner!"

It was still early and there were few people up and about other than the vendors who sleepily went about the morning routine of setting out their wares. Since there had been no new shipments in recent months, due to the severity of solar activity, there were fewer commodities offered for sale and prices on available merchandise had risen even higher than usual. The air in the marketplace was grim and few had any interest in the odd pair that hurried past.

Moving swiftly, they made their way up the broad thoroughfare that spiraled up the inner walls of the ancient volcanic cone. The small blue dot that was the open sky was far above them. The marketplace, filling the center of the hollow core, receded as they climbed steadily higher.

Doorways, painted numerous different colors, although red seemed the predominant choice, lined the inner wall. These were the entrances to large apartments, the quarters of persons with some degree of importance. Those of lesser importance were situated along narrow corridors that intersected the rising concourse and were often no more than tiny cubicles carved out of the porous rock. They continued to climb the circular terrace, which grew increasingly steeper the higher one rose.

"Where we be goin'?" Septua panted, hop-skipping to keep up with Braldt's longer stride.

"Keri. I have to see her," Braldt replied tersely.

Septua did his best to convince Braldt that such a thing was foolishness, that the girl would undoubtedly be well guarded by the king's men. But Braldt would not listen. Muttering and cursing about hardheads, the dwarf followed as fast as his short legs could carry him.

Braldt reached the narrow corridor that led to Keri's quarters and without knocking opened the door and stepped through, calling her name softly. He crept to the low couch, which was mounded with blankets, and reached out to gently shake her shoulder. The mound stirred, twisted in the down-filled covers, and turned. Braldt pulled the cover down from her head, murmuring sweet nonsense.

Too late he saw the thatch of blond-white hair, too late he sensed the presence of others in the room. Drawing his sword, he whirled, only to find himself facing six fully armed men with swords at the ready. He spun back toward the bed to discover a large, wide-shouldered, broad-chested man rising with a wide grin on his face. It was the captain of the guards, Gunnar Bakkstrom.

"What's the matter? Don't I appeal to you?" He advanced on Braldt, driving him back against the waiting swords, a mirthless grin spread on his lantern-jawed face. "I told the king that you would come. All we had to do was wait. I thank you for proving me right."

"Where is she?" Braldt asked hoarsely. "What has been done with her?"

"I know, I know, tell you or you'll kill me if it takes the rest of your life." Bakkstrom dismissed Braldt's unsaid words with a flick of his fingers. "Interesting, a product of the Bronze Age spouting B-grade movie material. It would seem that clichés cut across even galactic lines."

Braldt stared at him without comprehending the man's words. He thought about throwing himself at the man; there was a chance that he could seize him and use him as a living shield. But he could feel the prick of swords at his back and even though the man was blathering on nonsensically, he still looked quite capable of wielding his sword. Still, he had to do something. He could not allow himself to be taken without a fight.

"Please, I have no aversion to spilling your blood. It means nothing to me." Gunnar Bakkstrom placed the tip of his sword beneath Braldt's chin and sighed, shaking his head from side to side. "It's amazing, really. I can read the thoughts as they plod through your tiny brain. Do not fight. It is foolish and futile. You may do so if you wish, but I promise you that you will die. Or you may lay down your weapons and I will lead you to your lady. The choice is yours."

The man fixed him with a lazy, bored smile. His eyes were icy cold and spoke eloquently of his indifference. He could kill Braldt with as little thought as one used to kill a fly. Braldt did not fear death, but he had no wish to throw his life away.

Plastered against the corridor wall, Septua heard Braldt's sword clatter to the floor and Bakkstrom's low chuckle of amusement. It twisted in his gut like a sickness as he crept away from the entrance and scuttled into the nearest labyrinth of corridors as quickly as his shaking legs would carry him. That laugh. It echoed in his worst nightmares, although he had heard it often enough in his waking hours.

Bakkstrom had not found it necessary to bring reinforcements when he trapped Septua breaking into the High Thane's apartments. He had laughed then. He had laughed again when Septua was sentenced, banished to the arena on Rototara, stripped nearly naked, and wrapped in metal bands, his arms pinned to his sides, unable to move. Septua had felt the eyes of the curious on him then, staring at his squat, misshapen form, and he had felt the years of hatred well up in him. He hated them all with their smirking faces and tall, straight bodies. He hated red-haired, green-eyed Mirna, who had said that she loved him and then betrayed him to the captain of the guards. And most of all, he hated Gunnar Bakkstrom.

That hatred rose up in him again, along with the fear, as

the dwarf lost himself in the dark corridors, running without thought wherever his feet took him. If Braldt was right, if they were looking for him, it was only a matter of time before they hunted him down and killed him. He stopped then and leaned against a door, gasping for breath. Maybe he would die; it didn't really matter so much. There was no way he could help Braldt now, but he could do one thing. He could make certain that Gunnar Bakkstrom never laughed again.

15

Barat Krol fought to keep the elation from his face. Could it be true? Could he actually be making progress at last? Time and time again he had visited the Madrelli compound, a stinking, crowded dormitory where males and females, adults and young were housed. There was absolutely no privacy. Every function of their lives, from copulating to elimination, was open to view, their own and that of anyone else who cared to watch.

He had tried to make them see the inequity of their lives, but he had never made any headway. They simply did not care to listen. Then he thought about incentives. True, it was a shoddy trick, but there was so little time to spare and so much at stake, at this point he would have seized upon any ploy that would work.

And work it had. He had plundered a storeroom and stolen several sacks of sugar, which the Madrelli loved and seldom received. Using the sweets as an incentive, he had bribed them to listen to him and grudgingly agree to do as he asked, but only after he had promised them a continuing supply of the forbidden sweet.

What he had asked was that they allow him to inject them with the drug that had elevated his own tribe's intelligence to a level equal to that of the Scandis themselves. As yet he had no real idea how he would go about doing such a thing; he had no knowledge of where the drug was kept, nor even if there was an adequate supply on hand to inject everyone. He could only guess at the effect it would have on them, for they had never been given the drug before.

Barat Krol had wrestled with the ethics of what he intended to do, asking himself if his actions would make him no different than the Scandi scientists who had manipulated Madrelli minds and bodies for so many centuries. He did not have the time to give the drug in carefully metered doses, increasing the amounts slowly, allowing the Madrelli days, months, years to adjust to their development.

He was fighting for their very survival, whether they realized it or not. If it earned him their hatred, at least they would be alive to hate. He could only hope that such a large concentrated dose would not have an adverse effect. There was no way of knowing. He had not dared to tell Uba Mintch of his plans, knowing that the old one would never agree.

He handed out the cubes of sugar, smiling at the way the young ones seized it, seeing the naked joy and greed on their faces, and feeling happiness mixed with worry at what he was about to do.

Events began to move with a momentum of their own. Otir Vaeng's doctors had managed to stop the infection from advancing, but they had not been able to destroy it. Although they had not shared their concerns, they feared that it was but a matter of time before the infection overcame their newest drug.

They did not dare inform the king, for he was in no mood to be philosophical or forgiving about their failure. Others had departed this world as well as other worlds for displeasing the king, and failing to save his life was certain to earn his displeasure! Then too there was always hope and prayer. The doctors hoped and prayed harder than ever before in their lives that they were wrong and that the king would somehow miraculously survive.

His hand and arm were a hideous sight of suppurating flesh. Dark blood and thick, yellowish pus mingled and dripped continuously. He could not bear the weight of bandages which would have served no real purpose except to hide the gruesome limb from view. It only took one glance to know how serious the situation really was.

Otir Vaeng was not stupid. He had to realize how grim the outlook. But he was strangely calm; even the frequent outbursts which so terrorized his court had ceased. He was often lost in his thoughts and did not seem to hear when spoken to.

It might be thought that those who attended the king, those who had suffered the most from his unreasonable rages, might have drawn comfort from his strange quietude. Instead, it troubled them; as with a persistent pain that suddenly vanishes, they could not help but wonder when it would return or what would replace it.

Nor would they have been reassured if they could have read his mind, for after a long, long scientifically extended lifetime, Otir Vaeng was tired of his life. As his mind floated on currents of pain that the drugs could not adequately mask, it seemed to him that his rotting arm was a visible symbol of his entire life.

The pain, so clear and sharp that sometimes it quite literally took his breath away, was more real and true than anything he had felt in many a year. As much as it hurt, he savored his agony and wondered when he had ceased to feel. He could not even remember. It had been a very, very long time since he had genuinely loved or felt true happiness. He could not even remember the last time he had felt such an emotion.

There was something very sad in that. Moisture welled in Otir Vaeng's eyes and he realized with a sense of shock that he was crying! He could not even recall the last time in his long, long life that such a thing had happened, and that made him even sadder.

A part of him recognized what was happening and tried to force his mind back into its accustomed grooves. After all, he was the king. There were important matters to be tended to, decisions to be made, plans to be laid. But somehow none of it seemed to matter anymore. He just didn't care.

He wondered if this was how the end would come, awash in a sea of indifference. Strangely, even that did not seem to matter. He found his wandering thoughts focusing in two directions, backward and forward. Memories of his earliest years surfaced most often, for he had been happy then, loved and loving in return, unaware of the long years of intrigue and worry that were soon to come.

He plucked small, shining moments from his memory and held them like a glowing lamp to warm his heart and mind. He conjured up the face of a woman who had genuinely loved him, cared for he himself and not his power or his wealth. He excluded the memory of her expulsion from his court, for she was not suitable for marriage and too great a political liability to remain.

He thought of a young boy, the bright, laughing eyes and squeals of excitement as he first discovered the delicious fear of tempting the curling waves of the ocean. He remembered the tiny arms that had wrapped themselves around his neck, the sticky hands. He remembered the sweet, powdery smell of the child, the whispers of shared secrets, and the looks of trusting love.

He shut his mind against the flood of memories that crowded in, demanding to be heard. Those same trusting eyes had grown calculating and cold; the hands, small no longer, wrapping themselves around the hilt of a blade that the child, now a man, would gladly have thrust into his heart.

He dreamed about earth as it had been before the temperatures and the seas rose, before the dying began. Clean, cold air, so cold it caused one's teeth to ache. The sun glinting off the snow on the peaks of the mountains, shining so brightly that tears came. The fjords, still dark blue, nearly black, pure and freezing cold, lancing between the verdant mountain slopes like probing fingers anxious to feel the land. And the scent of the firs! It was a scent that he would never forget and never cease to yearn for. So sharp and acrid, so pungent and heady, more satisfying than the most expensive perfume.

He shut out the vision of the fjords, thick and brownish yellow with refuse and the corpses of the deepest dwellers who had succumbed at last, their bodies bursting as they rose to the poisoned surface. He refused to remember the naked slopes, rising to the skies, all remnants of green long since vanished, only the bare skeletons of trunks and branches silhouetted against the contaminated earth. These were memories he did not choose to view.

And now as never before, he found himself thinking of what was to come. On earth he, as the majority of others, had rejected formal religion, for it was difficult to believe in gods who would allow such death and utter desolation to befall those who lived their lives according to the proscribed tenets and doctrines.

Yet, voyaging through space, experiencing the immensity of the universe, watching the earth as it grew smaller and smaller and finally vanished, feeling the fear of death and the exhilaration of discovering a new world, it was impossible to believe that all of it was just an accident. It was impossible to believe that it had all just "happened." Yet it was also impossible to believe in the old, established religions, for none of them seemed to have any relevance after experiencing the immensity of the universe.

Strangely, as strongly as they had cast aside their belief in religion on earth, there was now an even stronger compulsion among the Scandis to believe in something other than themselves. It was then that the old gods had reemerged. Otir Vaeng and the volva had recognized the need and resurrected them, Odin and Thor, Freya, Loki, and all the others. And somehow those older, more primitive gods seemed far more appropriate than those that had supplanted them. It was easier to believe in a god who presided over the chaos of the elements than a god who rewarded faithful belief with cruelty and death.

The old gods had foretold of the coming destruction of the world and just such a thing had occurred on earth. They had also foretold the end of an age and the emergence of a new race of men and gods who would repeople the world in the age that would be. It was apparent to Otir Vaeng that that was exactly what was happening. Things were ending, on earth and now here, on Valhalla. Those who survived the death of this age would people the new world that was yet to come.

Now, as he approached his own final ending, Otir Vaeng began to wonder what was to come. He and the volva had resurrected the old gods, it was true, but was it also not true that they had always been there? It could be argued that nature had repaid the people in full, taken its revenge upon them for raping the earth. And Loki, that god of mischief, must be enjoying himself, having a great belly laugh at the mess they had made of their lives and their world.

He wondered if there truly was an afterlife. The thought was comforting, being welcomed into the Great Hall which he now envisioned somewhere in the vast darkness of space, taking his place among all the other warriors and lifting a horn of mead.

If his mind had been clearer, Otir Vaeng might have marveled or at least had a moment of ironic laughter at the ease with which he had discarded three thousand years of established religion, shedding it like a too-small skin. He might also have chuckled at the ease with which he embraced a religion which he himself had reestablished as a mere soporific to satisfy the masses. But he no longer enjoyed that clarity of vision which had enabled him to rule for such a long time. In the end, as he approached his death, Otir Vaeng was not a king, he was merely a man.

Dying though he might be, he had no intention of leaving the world with things undone. The gods wished it so; they whispered in his ear when he slept, and now, more often, when he was awake. Sometimes, when the pain and the drugs wrapped him in their grip and tugged him between them, it was hard to know if he was awake or asleep; things seemed to blur more and more often. But he knew what it was that he had to do. And he would not, could not, die until it was finished.

There was great excitement among the astronomers, those who still remained at the observatory. Using their most powerful telescopes as well as a variety of mass analyzers, they had come to the conclusion that the planet known to them as K7 had not been destroyed as they had first assumed.

There had been a massive explosion—that much was certainly true, for the entire planet was cloaked by a dense cloud of fine particular debris. At first it was thought that the dark clouds were all that remained of the planet, for Leif Arndtson had sworn that he had set all the charges that would bring about its destruction.

But then, amazingly, the spectrographs and other delicate analyzers began chattering out their long lists of figures—figures that were not consistent with total annihilation. Now their readings were conclusive. There had indeed been a dreadful, cataclysmic explosion of epic proportions, but the planet itself was still intact.

Many of them had talked with the old Madrelli Uba Mintch and learned of the existence of the great volcano. Further inquiry had informed them that it was inside the core of this same volcano that young Arndtson had set his explosive charges. Incredible as it might seem, it now appeared that the explosion had merely triggered the eruption of the volcano. While some doubted that a volcano could shroud an entire planet, there were others who had facts to prove that it had happened before on earth.

Now there was no longer any doubt. For the past several days, their spectrographic equations had raised their hopes, and then, this very morning, the clouds had parted briefly and permitted them a glimpse of the world itself.

There had been cheering and laughter and finally tears. There was no way of knowing what the surface of the planet was like and what damage had been done by the explosion. It was possible, even probable, that the cloud of debris had cut the world off from the sun, turning it into a frigid, lifeless world similar to the one they currently inhabited.

But that would be too cruel a joke for even Loki, that god of mischief and deceit, to play upon them. More than likely, the entire planet had not been affected, only parts. Surely the sun had been able to pierce the thick black clouds in some places, allowing life to continue.

The old Madrelli had fallen silent during their speculations and too late they realized that his entire tribe had lived at the base of the volcano. The odds were very much against their survival. He had nothing more to tell them and after a time he left. They had enjoyed him—he was refreshing, quite different than the smelly, raffish creatures they were accustomed to—but they were also relieved to see him go, for his depression threw a pall over their newfound happiness. They would have to tell the king, but for the moment they held the knowledge to themselves.

There were many worlds in the universe, it was true, but those suited to life as they knew it were few and far between and all of them had been colonized long ago. The existence of K7 meant that they had found a world to immigrate to, a world to call their own. They would not die.

It did not occur to those scientists that if the world had survived, so then had the inhabitants who were foolish enough to think of it as their world.

Braldt flexed his arms for the hundredth time and felt the futility of the action in the ache in his muscles. No matter how hard he expanded his muscles, the bands did not loosen the slightest bit. They adjusted to his every move, never growing larger, but shrinking tighter and tighter each time he inhaled or relaxed. It was hard to breathe now, and there was a constant buzzing in his ears, an accompaniment to the burning behind his eyes.

He was not alone. There were others who shared his confinement, a sad assortment of Scandis who for one reason or another had run afoul of the establishment. Most of them had avoided him as though he were contaminated, but one woman had seemed overly curious and even now was leaning casually against the wall, staring at him with speculative eyes.

She seemed to come to some conclusion and strolled over to him. She leaned forward and prodded him with a long, painted fingernail. He met her eyes, which were a deep sea-green, fringed with improbably thick red lashes. There was a light sprinkling of freckles over the bridge of her nose and across her cheeks which might have given her a childish or wholesome appearance, but didn't. Her skin was fair and pale, almost translucent, and seemed as though it had been dusted with starlight, for it glistened softly in the dim light. Her hair was no less unusual, a deep shade of auburn, thick and silky and magnificent, fairly inviting one's fingers to twine themselves in their mass. As distraught as Braldt was, the woman's beauty all but struck him numb. He stared up at her like a small, thunderstruck child.

The woman sighed, obviously used to the response, and shook her head with aggravation. "Look, do you want to get out of here?" she whispered, her brilliant eyes fixed intently on Braldt's face. He could only stare up at her and nod.

The woman studied him, her eyes bright with speculation. She nodded, more to herself than to Braldt. "All right, if I help you get out of those things, will you help me? Take me out of here when you go?"

Braldt nodded, wondering how she could free him, for even though she was tall and broad of shoulder, it seemed impossible that she could free him when even he could not.

"Promise? Give me your solemn word? Swear on your mother's head?" Again Braldt nodded his agreement.

The woman sighed again and muttered beneath her breath as she busied herself with the ever-tightening bands. ". . . world where I don't have to depend on men . . . always want something . . ." Then, much to Braldt's astonishment, the bands loosened and fell away. He took a deep breath, filled his lungs. His eyes closed as he savored the blessed relief and knew that he would never take such a simple action for granted again. Once again the woman prodded him with a sharp fingernail. "You going to sleep?"

Braldt opened his eyes and smiled at the woman. "My name is Braldt."

The woman shrugged, obviously unimpressed with Braldt

or his name. "Yes, I know who you are, I know all about you. Shall we leave, or shall we stay and exchange biographies?"

Braldt was puzzled by the woman's attitude and stung by the sharpness of her words. And how was it that she knew who he was? A sudden suspicion came to him, an echo of Septua's sad tale. "Mirna?"

The woman's full mouth quirked sharply in a wry smile. She gave a parody of a curtsy.

"What are you doing here?" Braldt asked in amazement, stunned to have found Mirna, the woman Septua had given everything he owned to possess, only to lose her to Gunnar Bakkstrom, the captain of the guards, in a plot of treachery and deceit. According to Septua, the woman had milked him of everything he had accrued in a lifetime of thievery and then betrayed him to the captain of the guards. Yet if that were true, why was she here?

For a moment Braldt considered the fact that she might have been placed here to trick him, to find out all he knew and gain access to their plans. But then he looked at the woman more closely, saw the broken and chipped nails, the filthy edges of the gossamer robes, the layer of dirt on the flawless skin, and knew that such a woman would never have agreed to such conditions.

The woman seemed to read his thoughts, for her chin raised defiantly and she stared him full in the eyes, her own eyes glittering brightly with anger and suppressed tears. "You want to know why I'm here? I can see by your eyes that you know who I am. Well, I will tell you, if that will get you moving." She was silent for a long moment. She looked away and raised her chin still higher. Her fingers drummed on her thigh and she seemed to collect herself.

"I make no apologies. None. I am a woman alone. I've been on my own since I was twelve and I learned quickly how to take care of myself. The lessons were hard. Others might have chosen to die . . . but I wanted to live, no matter what it took.

"Among the lessons I learned was the simple fact that if I do not take care of myself, no one else will. Oh, perhaps they will for a time, but it always ends and then I am alone again. I made myself a promise long ago that I would never be hungry. I would never be poor. I would never be afraid. Do you understand that?" She turned to look at him and her eyes were fierce, burning with an intensity that Braldt could not disbelieve.

She did not continue until he nodded his understanding. "At first Septua, the little one, he was no different than all the others, fair game. In fact he was easier than most because he really fell hard. He said he would do anything for me.

"When Bakkstrom first approached me, I saw a chance to win big, take everything from the dwarf and earn a commission and goodwill from the captain as well. It seemed like the chance I had been waiting for, the chance to be on my own for good, without being at the beck and call of some man. It worked just the way it was supposed to. The dwarf protested at first, was afraid to break into a Thane's apartments, but in the end I convinced him. It was easy.

"What was hard was the look he gave me when they sentenced him. I laughed and snuggled up to the captain and pretended that I did not care, but those damned eyes have haunted me every night, filled my dreams and preyed on my nerves till I thought that I would go mad. Who could have guessed that I would develop a conscience at this late date?" She laughed bitterly.

"And I worried about that damned dwarf, worried that he was getting himself killed. I was always at Gunnar, asking him if he'd heard anything from Arena, if Septua was still alive. I guess that somewhere in the back of my mind I was trying to figure out a way to get him back before he was killed.

"I tried to work on Gunnar, but now that I cared about someone, it changed me and I seemed to lose something in return. Gunnar sensed the difference, almost like a wolf scenting a sick and vulnerable creature. He cast me off as easily as I have cast off hundreds of men in my time. I was weak, soft, and no longer of any interest to him.

"Ironic isn't it? I, who have had more men in love with me, powerful men in high places, than one could easily count, falling for an ugly dwarf thief! An ugly dwarf thief whom I doubt would ever speak to me again. It's almost enough to make one believe in witches and curses!"

Braldt stared at her, wishing that he could believe her story, but it was so unlikely. Could a woman—any woman, much less a beauty such as Mirna—truly fall in love with Septua? "What is it that you like about Septua?" Braldt asked, trying to give her the benefit of the doubt, still fearing that she was the bait in an elaborate trap.

"He never lied to me. He was honest in everything he did and said." She lifted her eyes and stared at Braldt. "I guess you can't understand that. You've probably always told the truth; it's lying that would come hard to the likes of you. But Septua and I . . . we've had to fight all our lives to get what we needed and to keep what we got. Lying is our way of life, like breathing.

"For him to talk to me honestly, not lie . . . it meant something. It meant a lot. I think he was the only one who ever saw me for who and what I was and loved me anyhow. But I wasn't ready for that because it meant that I had to take a good look at myself as well and I didn't like what I saw."

"So how did you wind up here?"

"I was of no more use to Gunnar, so he got rid of me.

Free, I was a danger to him because I had learned a lot about him. I'll be executed soon; all of us will. But if you help me get out of here, I'll help you. I can be very useful.'' Mirna's voice grew soft and sensuous. She pressed her body against his and his flesh seemed to tingle where she had touched him. Her eyes promised pleasures unknown, and for a moment Braldt felt himself being sucked down, swayed by her persuasive power.

''Wait.'' He placed a hand against her chest and gently pushed her away. ''I do not require such payment as you suggest, but if I take you with me, you must promise that you will help me and not leave me for some plan of your own.''

''Do you know where the dwarf is?''

''I know where he was when I was taken. If we cannot find him, I'm quite certain that he will find us. He sticks to me like dirt to a child.''

Mirna gave him an odd, appraising look. ''You do know what's going on here, don't you?''

Braldt stared at her blankly. ''What do you mean?''

Mirna sighed and shook her head as though dealing with a stupid child. ''They are leaving here, leaving Valhalla. All those who remain behind will die. That is why Septua is staying with you, making himself useful. He knows that you will not be one of those left behind. He thinks that if he stays with you, he will be saved as well.''

''Yes, I know,'' Braldt said. ''And I suspect that our time is running out.''

16

Fortran floated quietly in the darkness of space. It wasn't really dark. When one was silent like this and spread one's aura in a manner that he was just beginning to master, there was all sorts of illumination. Thoughts came flooding in from all sides, filling his mind with information and observations he had never before experienced.

There was real light as well, the soft, beneficent radiance of other worlds, and he basked in their reflection, drawing knowledge of those far-flung worlds as easily as if he had spun a dial. This too was new and strange and yet delightful. He almost wished that he could float forever, absorbing, expanding, growing. He spread his mind and touched Zostar 411, his closest friend, he who had so often shared the same mutinous thoughts that had plagued Fortran all of his life. Zostar had followed Fortran by a mere five seconds, startling the Grand Yerk. The others had come along one at a time, but more often in pairs or larger groups, as though it took more of them to summon the courage necessary to face the Grand Yerk's displeasure.

Fortran had not remained long enough to hear how they fared, for by that time he had been sent on his way to complete the final stages of his education.

Even as he reflected upon the sudden warm golden glow of a distant star going nova, he could not help but ponder the incredible circumstances that had just transpired, which in their own way were just as explosive as that distant star.

Who would ever have imagined that they were expected—no, perhaps *expected* was too strong a word—it was *hoped* that they would be strong enough, have learned enough, to question, to reason themselves out of the limbo in which they were trapped.

Fortran could not help but wonder whether the Grand Yerk had had anything to do with their abduction and subsequent imprisonment on Rototara. Nor could he help but wonder whether or not some of his brethren would ever emerge from their self-imposed imprisonment; their minds were too narrow, their spirits too timid to question or defy authority. He wondered if they would remain on Rototara forever or if the Grand Yerk would relent and save them from themselves.

Now, what was to come next—that was the exciting and at the same time frightening thing. It had been explained to him that questioning authority was but one step along the way to final maturity. Beyond rebellion there had to be another step, constructive action of a sort that would offer a creative solution to the problem one had rebelled against.

They had nearly succeeded back on Rototara. They had seized the moment, dared to rebel in order to help their fellow prisoners overthrow their oppressors. But then, at the first word from the Grand Yerk, their courage as well as their resolve had crumbled and their rebellion died in an instant. The memory of that moment of cowardice was still painful to contemplate. He would not make that mistake again.

Fortran thought back to the ancient times his parents had told him about. In those long-distant days, children were supposed to study for long periods of time and then take—what was that word?—oh, yes, *tests*, before they could advance to the next level. In a way, that was what was happening to him now. It was a test.

Rebellion was easy, the Grand Yerk had cautioned. It was what one chose to do next that counted . . . to bring order to chaos, that was what mattered. Fortran had not been told what to do; that would have been too easy. It had been left to him to decide the whats, wheres, and whys.

Fortran did not have to think long or hard about what he wanted to do. It was difficult for him to keep the strange alien, the one known as Braldt, out of his mind for any length of time. Never had he known anyone so brave, so bold, so full of action with less regard for authority or rules!

He had learned something of Braldt's story during their time of confinement on Rototara and he could not help but wonder what had become of Braldt and his strange companions. He wondered if perhaps there was some way in which he might be of service. Fortran closed his eyes (figuratively speaking, of course), took a deep mental breath, and then slowly began to release his consciousness, allowed it to trickle outward, like tiny rivulets of water seeking the sea, reaching farther and farther, seeking the one known as Braldt among the many worlds where he might possibly be.

Fortran knew also that it might take a long time, knew that it was a dangerous thing he was attempting, for the thinner one's aura became, the easier it was to penetrate and shred. It was possible to die under such circumstances. But Fortran could feel the excitement building within him and knew that no matter how long it took, no matter how great the risk, he would not give up until he had found Braldt.

Teams of technicians had been filing aboard the *Oseberg*, the great ship of space that had been named after one of the most famous ship graves of antiquity. Barat Krol had watched them file out all morning, had hovered near the main entrance of the mountain in hopes of learning something. He did not have to wait long. Soon more and more workers were hurrying toward the ship, strapping their tool packs around their waists, worried expressions furrowing their brows. It appeared that the results of his midnight visit had come to light. He could only hope that they would not find everything.

But there was worse news still to come. The more he listened, the more agitated he became. The workers had been called out for a routine inspection, but Barat Krol learned from bits and pieces of their conversation that a launch was anticipated sometime in the near future, immediately after the king's wedding.

Barat Krol was filled with a sense of urgency as well as a sense of despair. What could he possibly do to save himself and his people? Were they all to die on Valhalla while the Scandis survived and colonized yet another planet built with the blood and effort of their Madrelli slaves?

Barat Krol pondered the problem. Uba Mintch had begged him not to use force, to find some peaceful solution. He revered the older Madrelli, respected his wishes, but in his heart he knew that there was no way they could be honored. There was not even enough room for all of the Scandis aboard the *Oseberg*; there was no way the Scandis would allow the Madrelli aboard. What was he to do?

He wandered through the huge complex pondering his options. Violence was one choice. Kill all the Scandis and take their places aboard the ship. But much as Barat Krol hated to admit it, the Madrelli needed the Scandis too much to do such a thing. What did he know about piloting a ship, and where were they to go? Even he, who had eavesdropped and spied on the Scandis in their most secret of meetings, had not learned where they intended to go. What was their destination? There were so many worlds, but so few of them fit their needs and could support an entire population.

Even if they could somehow steal the ship and force the Scandis to take them to the new world, Barat Krol had to admit that it would be difficult for them to colonize a world on their own. They needed each other. The Scandis needed the Madrelli, but since they thought of them as little more than pack animals, there was little reason for them to waste valuable space on full-grown creatures. The fertilized frozen ovum of a hundred million Madrelli filled two beakers (a loose-lipped lab worker had confided this bit of information shortly before Barat Krol forced him into that same freezer unit and allowed the door to shut).

He thumped himself on the head with the heel of his palm. How could he have been so stupid? How could it have taken him this long to find the answer when it was staring him in the face all along? He would steal the beakers! Without them, there could not be any new Madrelli. The Scandis would be forced to listen to him, for he would be holding their future hostage!

He remembered how to reach the laboratories, but the problem was that he had no business being there on his own. He was certain to be challenged. He would have to think of a way to get around the problem.

A half hour later, he was on his way. Under his arm he carried a bundle of stolen computer printouts. Normally they would be recycled, but he had other plans for them. He kept his head down, eyes on the path, and adopted a slope-shouldered, humble gait, more in keeping with his oppressed brethren and less likely to be challenged.

Soon he reached his destination, a room where newly woven garments were stored, garments woven by the nimble fingers of Madrelli women. He crumpled the paper into balls and scattered them around the room until the floor was buried. He crammed piles of the crinkly balls between the neatly stacked fabrics and draped lengths of material from stack to stack. When he had crumpled the last sheet of paper and tossed it on the pile, he lit a taper and placed it in the very center.

Barat Krol hummed beneath his breath as he exited the room, carefully shutting the door behind him. It was a pity to destroy such beautiful work, but fabric could be replaced far easier than lives. He strolled down the concourse, knowing that his handiwork would be discovered before long. He just hoped that the fire would have time to seize hold.

His wishes were granted, for he had nearly reached the bottom of the spiraling walkway before the first shouts of alarm reached his ears. He smiled and continued on his way as others rushed past him, responding to the dreaded cry.

It took him longer to find the laboratory than he had planned, even with his unusually keen memory, for it was not meant to be visited by casual passers-by and was hidden in the depths of a labyrinth of confusing passages.

Alarms had been ringing for quite some time when a secondary set of Klaxons began to sound. Barat Krol felt a deep sense of satisfaction. From this new chorus of alarms, he was able to ascertain that the fire had proved difficult to extinguish and appeared to have spread, for the Klaxons indicated a level two fire, one that was not contained and was spreading. More assistance was required than those who had responded to the first call. He received a few startled glances as white-coated technicians raced past him, reporting to their assigned posts against the possibility that sensitive materials were endangered. No one stopped to question his presence.

His luck ran out soon after he entered the first of the storage rooms. A short, blond woman with a shrill, annoying voice demanded to see his work order, demanded to know what he was doing there. Barat Krol was glad to show her his credentials, in the form of his fist. It descended upon the top of her head with a most satisfying thump and he was pleased to have stopped the dreadful sound so easily. She was not dead, merely unconscious, but by the time she revived, he would have found what he was searching for and vanished. He did not worry about being identified, for ridiculous as it seemed, it was a well-known fact that Scandis could seldom tell the Madrelli apart; supposedly they all looked alike.

The second and third rooms were devoid of people, but unfortunately they were also devoid of the precious beakers. He began to worry that he would not be able to find what he was searching for; nothing looked familiar. At that moment a harsh, ominous buzzer began to repeat itself over and over. Barat Krol knew this to be a third-level warning, an appeal for all available hands.

Barat Krol wondered what was happening, wondered if the sun had begun its final surge, the deadly flare that would precede its ultimate demise. Briefly he thought of abandoning his quest but rejected the thought even as it was formed. There was nothing he could do to help them; the only way he could help anyone was to continue what he had begun.

Barat Krol could not have know that he was responsible for the panic that had spread throughout the entire city. The fire that had begun so quietly, so neatly contained in its own little room—the fire that Barat Krol had set as a momentary diversion—had spread beyond his wildest expectations and grown into a dangerous, life-threatening beast.

The room where the material was stored was vented by a small air duct that channeled fresh air into the room. The air currents also discouraged the growth of a microscopic mold that weakened the fibers. The mold could not grow unless the air was both moist and motionless.

Unfortunately, the ductwork connected to several other chambers which also required fresh, filtered air, namely the computer room, where the massive mainframes were housed, and the operations center, where the delicate, irreplaceable communications equipment was kept. Both of these installations were filtered for fine particles that might disturb the functions of their precious equipment, but there was no way it could filter out the dense clouds of thick black smoke that poured through the vents with absolutely no warning.

Neither of the rooms was equipped with water sprinklers, for water would have been equally as devastating as fire. Fire had never been a serious consideration or threat, for the technicians were far too careful to have made even the slightest mistake. But just as no one had considered the link with the fabric room, which was just above the communications center, neither had they ever considered the possibility of smoke without fire.

The technicians went wild, for most of them were so dedicated to their machines that they thought of them more as children than as bits of metal and plastic. They shouted frantic orders which frequently contradicted one another and were soon at each other's throats, driven almost insane with the threat to their beloved machines. They who had fretted and worried over the tinest change in temperature, the smallest particle of dust carried in on the antiseptic bootie of a worker, now shrieked and wailed as they heaved at the massive machines in their attempts to move them to safety. And all the while the thick, black, viscous smoke feeding off the oily lanolin contained in the natural wool fabric continued to pour in through the efficiently functioning vents. It never occurred to anyone to shut them off.

Blissfully unaware of the chaos he had inflicted upon his enemies, Barat Krol continued to search the vast medical complex. The first and second alarms were calls for labor; the third alarm was a call for more specialized assistance, including medical.

Only as the last of the medicos with their intergalactic red cross emblazoned on their chests rushed by carrying their bags did the thought occur to Barat Krol that he might have done well to have captured one of them and persuade him to take him to the containment units.

He waited for a time, but it appeared that the last of them had passed. It worried Barat Krol that it should have taken him so long to think of capturing a medico. Such a basic thought; how could he have been so dumb? No sooner had he raised the thought than it came to him that it was not the first time he had made such a mistake. Lately, it seemed that his mind was operating more slowly, taking longer to come to obvious conclusions.

And then it hit him with a wave of certainty. The Scandis were depriving him of his daily dose of the intelligence enhancing drug, substituting a look-alike placebo! What better way to rid themselves of a troublemaking Madrelli? Soon he would sink to the same level of indifferent intelligence as his less fortunate brethren and the Scandis would be rid of the thorn in their side, bloodlessly and without implicating themselves in any way. "A failure of the drug—unfortunate, but it happens that way sometimes."

The realization was so stunning that Barat Krol sank down on his haunches and bowed his head. How close he had come to death without even knowing it, for life without intelligence was little more than death with another name.

Just then a voice intruded on his thoughts, a nagging, prissy voice, the kind of voice that belonged to one who followed every rule no matter how stupid, obeyed every sign as though it had been printed by the god of the universe and expected others to share his vision of order. "You there, what are you doing? There is no loitering allowed in these halls. Where is your permit? Show me your permit! Why are you here? Where is your keeper?" The flood of words beat around Barat Krol's head like a swarm of mosquitoes.

Third-class technician Thorvald Johannson stopped a mere

two paces from the numbed Madrelli, furious at this obvious breach of regulations. How was it that all the others had managed to pass through these same halls and not notice such a large creature on the loose? Thorvald heaved a sigh and pressed his thin lips together in a droop of martyred weariness. Why was it always he who had to clean up everyone else's messes? It was probably that lazy, no-good Erik Girstad—he never finished what he started. Why, if Thorvald hadn't decided to come along behind everyone else and check, this ignorant creature could have run amok. Thor only knows what mischief he might have caused.

Thorvald pursed his lips again and hooked a toe into the Madrelli's rib cage, a sensitive spot as he well knew, painful in the extreme. "Here! You stinking animal, up! Back in your cage!" he cried as he drove the point of his foot into the animal's rib cage for a second time, wondering if he had injured it with the force of his blow.

He had expected the Madrelli to react; a cry of pain, a crouching, posturing snivel for mercy would have been normal. Instead, a massive black furred hand shot out and grasped his ankle, hard, squeezing it hard enough to bring tears of pain to Thorvald's eyes.

He opened his mouth to scream at the Madrelli, to threaten him with punishment, when his brain finally acknowledged what his eyes had known for some time. The Madrelli was not one of those small, cowering, terrified specimens they kept caged in the labs for use in experiments.

Still gripping the technician's foot, the Madrelli stood up, raising himself to his full height, which was easily two heads taller than Thorvald Johannson. He was huge, gigantic, immensely muscled, with powerful arms and a chest and shoulders that rippled with muscles each time he moved.

Thorvald's mouth opened and closed several times, but no sound emerged. The Madrelli's mouth opened too. Thorvald stared at him in horror, his eyes opened wide. The Madrelli's lips drew back, exposing his black gums and his long, pointed canines.

The Madrelli was staring at him with a look of utter joy upon its ugly animal face. Its large dark eyes glittered insanely Without taking its eyes off the terrified technician, it yanked his leg, hard, painfully hard, drawing him closer. Thorvald Johannson took one final look—the bright eyes, the sharp teeth, the powerful muscles—and did the only logical thing left for him to do. He fainted.

17

After Braldt had been captured, Septua had wandered without aim or goal—not knowing what to do with himself. He had found himself in the labyrinth of corridors belonging to the healers and had sunk down on the seats circling the operating amphitheater to ponder his limited choice of options. When the alarms began to sound. At first he rose, fear hammering in his chest. He could hear the sounds of running feet, and yells and curses as the various workers responded to the call.

His first impulse was to run. But where would he go? He had no designated post, as did every Scandi over the age of twelve. They had not deemed him worthy of assistance in the face of danger. The old bitterness twisted in his gut, accompanied by the familiar burning anger.

He could not have honestly said whether he was sad or angry or frightened, for he was filled with currents of strong, conflicting emotions, each warring within him for dominance.

He clenched his fists and closed his eyes, trying to bring himself under control. It was then that he heard his name called. Startled, he looked up, his hand darting to his dagger even as he recognized the Madrelli—what was his name . . . Bartha Kol? But what was he doing here?

The two disparate figures, one short and barrel-chested with outsized features, the other immense and shaggy with intense, burning eyes, approached each other warily, yet with a certain amount of barely concealed eagerness. Each desperately hoping that the other, barely known, would become an ally in this place of enemies and danger.

Slowly at first, and then ever more swiftly, the words tumbling over themselves like rocks careening downstream in a flood, they told and compared stories. All the while, the Klaxon continued to blare its urgent message of alarm.

"What's 'appening? Is the world exploding?" asked Septua, looking around him fearfully.

Barat Krol barked a short, mirthless laugh. "I set the place afire. Must have done a better job than I thought!"

"Fire . . . that's good. Never would 'ave thought of fire myself," Septua said, looking up at the Madrelli with admiration. "Ought to give us some time to find the stuff what you needs."

"You'd help?" Barat Krol asked in astonishment.

"Consider it done!" Septua said, grinning broadly. "Anyone what sticks a rock in their engine 'as got me in their corner! Let's be on our way afore they comes back!"

The frozen ova were harder to find than they had anticipated, and the precious intelligence-enhancing substance no less obvious. What they did find were a wide variety of animals and Madrelli, little better than animals themselves, most of whom were in pain, all of whom were being used for Scandi experimentation.

Barat Krol went berserk when they encountered the first of these unfortunates linked to machines by various implanted wires and tubes. The creature, a doglike animal, looked up at them and seemed to cringe, although such an action would have been all but impossible considering the number of attachments controlling its body. Its eyes were large and soulful and seemed to implore them silently. A whimper of anticipated pain escaped from its muzzle.

Barat Krol destroyed every single machine that the poor

animal was linked to, in an attempt to free it. There were so many machines, it was impossible to know which one contained the link that kept the poor creature alive. When the last of the machines had crashed to the floor, the last of the bottles had broken, spilling their fluids, the piteous crying had stopped. Only then did they discover that the animal had mercifully died.

Barat Krol was shaking with rage, his eyes ringed with scarlet, the whites shot through with red. Septua had never seen such a towering rage, and despite himself he was more than a little afraid of the Madrelli. He began to edge away when Barat Krol turned to him and tried to smile, tried to bring himself under control. "I-I'm sorry. It troubles me to see creatures treated so poorly. Would they do such a thing to one of their own?"

Septua was unable to speak, remembering all too well some of the tests and experiments they had done on him as a youngster when it had first been ascertained that he was not "normal" and would never achieve his full growth. His mother had put an end to it, but Septua had never forgotten . . . or forgiven.

Together they "liberated" the rest of the animals. Those that had not been damaged beyond salvation were freed and each helped the less fortunate. Those who would never be whole again they freed as well, giving them well-deserved eternal peace and surcease from their pain.

Barat Krol and Septua were icy calm by the time they opened the last of the cages. Their earlier fury had become a steely resolve that drove them relentlessly on. Had they not been so determined to find and rescue every last creature, they might not have found the lab technician, who had done his best to squeeze himself into a tiny ball inside of a storage compartment.

A small, tight smile crooked the corner of Barat Krol's

mouth. He reached in and despite the fact that the technician scrabbled away and tried to fend him off, he seized him and pulled him out like a pile of dirty laundry.

The boy—he was no more than a youngster, really, despite his attempt at a thin, stringy mustache—began to cry and a fetid stink filled the air as he soiled himself. He covered his face with his hands and it was obvious that he thought he was going to die. Barat Krol gave him a hard shake. "Stop that noise. We have freed the only ones who had a need for tears. You had best save your breath for your prayers!" The boy wailed and cried all the louder.

Barat Krol flung him away in disgust and wrenched a leg off one of the tables. He hefted it as he walked toward the crying boy, no sign of sympathy on his face.

"Wait a minute 'ere," Septua said thoughtfully. "'E might do us better alive than dead."

Barat Krol was not easily persuaded. After all that they had seen, he felt the need to inflict pain and suffering upon one of those who had caused such agony.

"It was only a job!" wailed the boy, thinking to lend his voice to the dwarf's point. But if he had thought to plead his innocence, he had chosen the wrong argument.

"Do you not have eyes? Do you not have a heart? Could you not see their plight, feel their agony?" Barat Krol raised the chair leg, ready to club the boy, to see the blood flow. His whole body shook under the stress of his anguish.

"I couldn't stop them! Nobody would've listened to me!"

"Did you try? Did you even try?" Barat Krol was frightening to see, shivering with the need to strike out.

"'Ere now, Barat Krol, I un'erstan' 'ow you feel," Septua said appeasingly, daring to place a hand on the Madrelli's arm. "But think about it a minute, 'ere. We got us a pris'ner, eh? Don'cha see? Leave 'im live an' mebbe 'e'll just show us what we come lookin' for!

"Wot's the rest?" Septua nodded into the steaming, frosty interior of the small freezer.

"Other stuff." The boy wiped his nose with the back of his hand. "You know, other breeding stock: sheep, cows, chickens, stuff like that."

"Let's take 'em!" Septua grabbed at the handle covered with frost and cursed as he jerked his hand back, minus a patch of skin, the flesh already beading with blood. He sucked the bloody patch and glared at the boy, who raised his hands and backed up. "You have to use gloves, see! It's way below freezing in there!"

Still cursing, Septua donned the protective gloves, which were many sizes too large and came up well over his elbows, before he attempted to retrieve the remainder of the freezer cylinders.

"Now, show us the substance," directed Barat Krol in a tone that invited no argument.

The boy was clearly miserable as he slowly led the way back into the main laboratory area. He was all but dragging his feet by the time they reached the largest of the rooms, where many of the most hideous experiments had been carried out. Barat Krol had begun to realize that the boy was stalling for time when he heard the sound of footsteps and mingled voices. The workers were returning! Only then did he realize that the Klaxon had ceased its unrelenting braying. How long had it been silent?

The first of the workers entered the room and stopped, astonished expressions on their faces that might have been comical had the circumstances been less serious.

Barat Krol was the first to react. He seized the boy by the back of the neck, the fragile column dwarfed by his enormous paw. "One step, one sound, and the boy is dead!"

One of the men turned and ran. Barat Krol cursed and threw the boy aside like a rag doll, scattering the small knot of workers like dry leaves as he followed the worker down the hall. When he returned at a more leisurely pace, he wore a look of satisfaction and Septua guessed that he had finally satisfied the need to punish someone for all that he had seen.

The look on the remaining workers' faces was a bonus. If any of them had been contemplating escape, they quickly changed their minds.

"What do you want with us?" one of the braver technicians asked.

"They want the Madrelli formula," the boy answered tearfully. "I tried to keep it from them."

"Look, Stephus, they have the ova!" one of the women exclaimed, pointing with horrified recognition at the frosty containers.

"They said they'd kill me," the boy said miserably. Almost as one, the workers shot a quick glance down the hall.

"Don't worry, Tani," the one known as Stephus said. "No one will hold you to blame. Let us give them what they seek before they kill us all."

The substance was no less unusual in appearance than the ova had been. Barat Krol had been prepared for anything, a beaker of fluid, a box of pills, anything but the chunks of dry, chalky material that Stephus casually pulled out of a larger box sitting in a corner like a bit of debris.

"This is it?" Barat Krol asked, shaking the box and hearing the contents rattle dryly. "The fate of my people rests on these . . . these rocks?" He turned toward Stephus and his lips twitched, revealing his long, sharp eyeteeth.

"No, no! Uh, I mean yes!" Stephus hurried forward to take the box out of the Madrelli's hands. "Look, I can understand why you might think that something so important is worthy of more respect, but the fact of the matter is that we have so much of it on hand that, quite honestly, we don't give it its proper due. Here, here, taste a bit of it on your tongue. You'll see, it's just what I said it was!'' He thrust the box back to the Madrelli, a pleading, anxious look on his face. Clearly he recognized their danger.

The Madrelli reached out and touched his finger to the powder, flicking a tiny clump up with the end of his thick yellow fingernail. He touched it with his tongue and instantly the suspicious, distrustful look vanished, replaced by a look of sheer joy. ''This is it!'' he cried. ''We've found it!'' he thumped Stephus on the back, sending the technician stumbling forward, and when he turned, he was smiling as well. ''See, I told you the truth. Can we go now?''

''I never said you could go nowheres. I just said we wouldn't kill you, mebbe,'' Septua said with a sly grin, and over their loud protests he herded them into a large storage room with a sturdy door and bolted it behind them.

''What now?'' he asked the Madrelli.

''We must find Uba Mintch, get this to him. He will know what to do and how to do it.''

They were striding through the corridors, Septua half running to keep up with the long-legged Madrelli, when suddenly the lights blinked out with no warning and they were thrown flat.

''What the—'' exclaimed Septua, rising to his knees and feeling around for the precious canisters. ''What 'ave they done now? 'ow did they make the floor shift like that?''

''Quiet,'' Barat Krol whispered, and in the dim red glow of the emergency lights Septua could see that the Madrelli had not risen from the ground, nor was he searching for the containers. He was lying still with his head pressed flat against the floor, and Septua studied him in puzzlement, wondering if he had been injured in the fall. He hurried to the Madrelli and knelt beside him. Barat Krol waved him down and when he did not move, seized him by the hem of his robe and jerked him down and pressed his head against the stone floor. None too gently either, as Septua began to point out.

"Quiet," Barat Krol commanded. "Shut your mouth and open your ears. Listen!"

Septua did as he was told. As soon as he placed his ear against the stone, he heard it: a deep, rumbling, throaty growl, as though there were something alive inside the earth. It was an ominous sound that could mean nothing but trouble—bad, bad trouble.

Then, even as he listened, the growling sound stopped. It was as though the earth, the world, was holding its breath. And then there was a sharp, brittle snap, as though he had broken a dry branch over his knee. Yet this was no branch, but something critical inside the earth. Immediately following the sound, the floor shifted once again, throwing them hard against the far wall. This time, as the walls and ceiling began to crumble, raining down upon them, even the red lights were extinguished.

18

The vendors had barely had time to down their first cup of bland, unsatisfying herb tea and initiate conversations with tentative buyers when the earth began to move. Those who were standing felt it in the soles of their feet: an urgent, tingling vibration followed by the stiff jolt that threw them to the ground, as well as the carts and wagons and even the more sturdily built stalls.

Merchandise rained down upon vendors and customers alike as they scrambled awkwardly, trying to regain their footing. The inner cone reverberated with a cacophony of screams and shouts and the unmistakable sound of hysteria.

The ground ceased to move and slowly people began to crawl to their feet. Still, there were cries and crying, and over near the far wall a cart had caught fire and was burning briskly, adding to the confusion.

Voices were raised in an angry babble as people sought to find someone or something to blame for the catastrophe. Then, even as anger overcame fear, the ground moved again. This time it was more severe and, as they lay in a tangled jumble of arms and legs and irreplaceable merchandise, the rocks began to rain down on them from above.

Not even royalty can escape such cataclysmic events. Earthquakes, floods, fire, pestilence, all are democratic in nature and favor no one class. All men, rich or poor, peasants or kings, are afforded the same opportunity to die. And so it was in this instance.

At the time that the earth moved, Otir Vaeng, under Skirnir's insistence, had just convened the Council of Thanes for the first time in weeks. The Thanes had been grumbling among themselves, for under the terms of the law, the council was to meet on a regular basis. The Scandi nation was a monarchy, but the Thanes were historically given a large degree of input. Although it was seldom that they were so bold as to oppose the wishes of their king, in turn, it was a wise king who saw to it that he was not in opposition to his Thanes, for they were the strength behind the throne.

When the quake struck, the council had just been called to order. Everyone, from Otir Vaeng down to the lowliest page, was in attendance, for even a fool would have realized that something of importance was about to be announced. Nature, however, has no respect for the words of man and they were drowned out by the earth's voice, loud and anguished. Torn from the rocky bowels, a scream of elemental agony burst forth, a twisted, tormented wailing screech of rock grating against rock that was far more frightening than the jolt that followed.

It was the second shock that caused the most damage and the most deaths. The council chambers was one of the few places in Aasgard that reflected the Scandis' former splendor. It was a large, circular chamber with a high, vaulted ceiling. Stone panels of finely detailed bas-relief circled the room at the point where ceiling met wall. Enormous marble statues marked the positions of various families and it was the location of these statues in proximity to the throne that ordained one's standing in court.

The room itself was egg-shaped, for the floor fell in tiers from the highest (and thus the lowliest position, in their convoluted method of thinking), to the lowest level, where the innermost ring of Thanes sat clustered around the throne. The statues were not neatly placed all in rows but ranged up and down the tiers.

There was but one entrance in and out of the chamber, for the Thanes had clung to the pomp and ceremony that was all that remained of their previous glory. Flutes and tambors accompanied their entrance as the pages cried their names aloud. Sigmunds, Raggnarrsons, Andersons, Ericksons, Johansons and Rasmussens, they were all there when the ground shifted and their world changed forever.

A few of the wiser, less pompous heads among them had cautioned against the style of architecture, warned that the porous rock was not stable enough to warrant hollowing out such a great expanse without the means to support it. They had been ignored.

Those same voices had cautioned against the installation of the bas-reliefs, which told the story of the gods choosing the Scandis above all others and leading them out of the darkness that was earth and entrusting them to Valhalla—a pretty tale that grew more and more bitter and ironic to those few who still cared to lift their eyes to view it. But these voices of caution had been ignored as well. Oh, the others went so far as to add a few extra bolts to appease their fellow Thanes, but behind their backs the cautious ones were scorned and regarded as cowards.

There had been no voices raised in opposition to the statues. Perhaps the prudent Thanes had grown tired of being laughed at, or perhaps even they could see no harm in erecting the enormous vanity pieces.

It is doubtful that it would have mattered even if they had prevailed in only one issue or the other, for all three architectural elements were responsible for the horror that followed.

Even before the ground had finished its terrible dance, the

ceiling had begun to fall, huge chunks breaking off and falling upon the helpless throng below. Relatively porous and lightweight, the rock was still heavy enough to cause death and maiming when it landed on soft and vulnerable flesh.

The carved panels shook loose of their bolts in the blink of an eye and were hurled into the room by the heaving rock with much the same momentum as a stone skipping across water. Heads were lopped from shoulders, limbs sliced from bodies, and bodies themselves neatly portioned. The panels were slippery with blood, their figures coated in crimson robes when finally they came to rest.

The statues were probably responsible for causing the most deaths, for when they toppled, they crushed everything that came between them and the lowest point in the room. When the first tremor came, the statues began to rock on their pedestals. A few fell, but it was the second tremor that set them all in motion. Down they came, rolling and tumbling, falling and crushing those unfortunate enough to be in their path. Had there been many survivors, some few might have gained an ironic bit of humor out of the fact that their families were able to strike out, figuratively speaking, at those who had stood between them and the throne.

But when the earth ceased its dance of death, there were too few left alive to appreciate such irony. Those few who had lived were more concerned with escaping the chamber that was now little more than an enormous burial chamber. Here and there were moans and cries issuing from the tumbled rock, and an occasional arm or finger probed the darkness signaling for help. A few bloodied and battered survivors stumbled over the debris, ignoring or incapable of hearing the cries for help as they made their way toward the exit.

Oddly enough, as these things go, Skirnir and Otir Vaeng had both been spared, had come through the devastation with barely a scratch between them. Who was to say why such a thing had happened. Was sparing their lives a gift from the gods . . . or, as some later suggested, a punishment?

Many good men perished in that brief twitch of the earth's flank, but also many who had schemed and abetted the most evil of plans.

Skirnir had stood riveted beside the throne when the earth gave its first tentative shake. He alone seemed to comprehend instantly what was happening. A second before the ceiling began to collapse, he seized the king's arm and began to pull at his listless body, trying to get him up out of the throne and out of the chamber. But it was too late.

Perhaps realizing that he would never succeed in moving the man to whom his life was linked, he heaved Otir Vaeng out of the throne without explanation, ignoring the pain he had caused to the swollen arm and the curses that followed. With a superhuman burst of strength, he overturned the throne, which was carved out of the granite that composed so much of the planet, and shoved Otir Vaeng beneath it just as the first rocks began to fall. He himself received a painful blow on the ankle as he tucked himself into the tiny bit of remaining space, but it did not matter compared to the death and destruction that was taking place all around them.

They remained huddled in their tiny shelter, their oasis of safety, long after the final rock had fallen—Skirnir from fear, Otir Vaeng from shock and despair. He had been warned and he had ignored the warnings. He alone was responsible for the deaths that had occurred. His pain-filled mind took the next step as he realized that surely the damage and losses had not been restricted to this one chamber alone.

Closing his mind to the agony of his own body as well as the screams that surrounded him, he forced the terrified Skirnir out from under the safety of the throne. It was difficult, for the throne was surrounded and nearly mounded over by the remains of the statues which had come to rest against the throne like so many dead bodies.

Finding their way out of the dimly lit chamber was a horror in itself, for the way was clogged with fallen rock, broken statues, and, worse . . . broken bodies. Each face, bearing the wounds and terrible expressions of death come too soon, were silent accusations, blows that struck Otir Vaeng's heart and left indelible wounds. The open, lifeless, staring eyes seemed to ask him why their loyalty had brought them death. Their mouths, framing gaping, silent screams, seemed to cry out the anguish of their betrayal. Each body, each terrible recognition, was a loss that hammered at Otir Vaeng, driving nails of pain into his heart.

The dead were the faithful, the loyal cadre of men who had entrusted their lives and the lives of their families to him on the dying earth. They had cast their fate with his and had the courage to take to the stars. The way had not been smooth; it had been hard and filled with trouble and danger. There had been dissension and anger, but in the end they had always trusted in him and followed where he had led.

And this was where he had led them in the end, into death. Had the carnage been incurred in honest, open battle or even defying the odds of space, he could have borne it. But this was senseless, inexcusable death brought on by nothing so much as his own vanity.

The wise old lions such as Saxo and Brandtson had argued against the construction of the room, but he had ignored their advice and ridiculed them for their efforts. If the truth were known, Otir Vaeng enjoyed the struggles of the Thanes as they attempted to maneuver themselves closer to the throne. He enjoyed watching the changes in the statuary; he thought of it as little more than a giant game of chess. But the worst of it were the remaining reliefs, which stared down upon him, mocking him. If the gods had indeed brought them to Valhalla, it must have been Loki, for only that god of mischief would play such a trick upon them. But even though they displeased him, he had not ordered their removal, for to do so would be an admission that he had been wrong, and that was unthinkable.

Tears were streaming down his face by the time he and Skirnir reached the doorway. It too was blocked by debris. A few survivors had reached it before them and were doing their best to clear it. Blood was streaming from their wounds, and one of the men, Reynold Anderson, was working with but one good hand, his other arm hanging uselessly at his side. He had always been one of Otir Vaeng's staunchest allies and could be counted on to support his every move. But now Anderson would not even meet Otir Vaeng's eyes, did not appear to hear his voice when he was spoken to, and worked without ceasing like an automaton even though he must have been in extreme pain.

Otir Vaeng did not persist in his attempts. It was clear, even to him, where the blame lay, and no amount of self-delusion would change the facts.

The door was uncovered after a time and Otir Vaeng joined in the efforts to remove the injured. He did not leave until the last of them had been carried to the hospital, which by this time was overflowing with casualties from other areas. Only after the last of the Thanes had been gently laid on makeshift pallets did Otir Vaeng allow Skirnir to lead him away to his own quarters.

He would not permit his personal physicians to touch him, brushing them and their cries of concern off like annoying insects. In a tone of voice that was softer and less officious than any they had ever heard him use, he urged them to take themselves to the hospital and make themselves useful.

He seemed strangely removed from the circumstances, almost as though he were thinking of something else. He did not even seem aware of his own wounded arm, which had saturated the few bandages that he could bear with a stinking excrescence of pus and blood. The dark red streaks now extended the length of his arm and spidered up over his shoulder. The pain had to be excruciating, but Otir Vaeng gave no sign.

Skirnir was beside himself. Otir Vaeng paid no more attention to him than a dog pays a flea. He was a minor annoyance and no more. The shape-changers, those strange men whose violence always lay just beneath the surface ready to erupt, seemed to blame him in some way for what had happened. They paced the king's chambers, which strangely enough had suffered no damage, and cast evil glances his way. Skirnir felt that if he did not remove himself, and quickly, they would kill him, or worse, and there would be no one to stop them. They were strange, terrifying men with odd powers that not even Skirnir could understand, and he was afraid of them.

Mumbling a few words to the king, who dismissed him with a twitch of his fingers, Skirnir hurried to his own chambers, pausing nervously, casting an uneasy eye in all directions as he unlocked the multiple safety devices that he used to protect himself from his fellow man.

Despite his position, Skirnir possessed only the smallest of rooms, for he had no wife or family. The room, small and dark as it was, contained only a single narrow bed, a sturdy table, and a lamp. That was all, except for the treasure which he had so carefully amassed.

He sat on the bed amid the rumpled, unwashed bedclothes and without really seeing them ran his fingers through piles of coins and unset gemstones which he had carefully pried from their settings, all looted from the burial urns and skimmed from the treasury.

There were many such mounds in the room, each wrapped

tightly in waterproof laminates and then bound with cloth into brick-sized bundles. They were amazingly heavy for their size. This was Skirnir's treasure, his booty, his safeguard against disaster, the nameless dread fear that haunted him whether waking or sleeping. Only the heavy, solid feel of gold was able to assuage that fear.

Skirnir sat in the darkness, fondling his gold and thinking about what had happened. Even though he had not ventured into the heart of the cone, he knew from the number of casualties and from the fragments of stories he had heard that the damage and death had been widespread. It was a situation that had to be handled carefully and quickly before it escalated in the wrong direction. A wise man could turn such a disaster to his benefit, and Skirnir definitely thought of himself as such a man.

Someone or something had to be blamed for the catastrophe; it could not be allowed to pass as a meaningless occurrence. The people needed someone to blame, to fix their anger and their grief upon. Someone expendable, someone whose death would benefit Skirnir. And Skirnir knew just the man for the job.

Braldt was sitting in a corner of his cell when the quake struck, his back against the wall. Mirna had been standing beside the narrow door talking to Gunnar Bakkstrom, doing her best to charm him into adding something extra to their meager rations.

It was a game that Bakkstrom seemed to enjoy, a game with the added twist of bending to his will the proud woman who had once been his mistress, something he had never been able to accomplish when Mirna was free. Then, all too often, it had been he who had begged for her favors . . . and been refused.

Yes, Gunnar Bakkstrom was enjoying this turn of events, but still, even though she was a captive and facing certain death, the cursed woman still retained that stiff-necked, arrogant tilt to her head, a way of speaking to him with a curl to her lips and a glint in her green eyes that did not exhibit the fear and respect that he would have— The floor suddenly twisted beneath his feet.

Bakkstrom slammed against the door frame hard—hard enough to numb his arm from the shoulder all the way down to his fingertips. He stared at Mirna in amazement. How had she caused such a thing to happen? He struggled to gain his balance, to force his arm to answer his commands, but nothing happened. He was reaching for his knife when the door was thrust open, striking him a painful blow on his wrist. He staggered back under the momentum of the body that hurtled through the open door. He caught a glimpse of hate-filled eyes, lips drawn tight across teeth bared in a snarl, and then he was thrown to the floor with a strength equal to that of his own.

Gunnar Bakkstrom fought from a sense of duty, allegiance to king and throne, and also because he was a man who enjoyed inflicting pain upon others. But Braldt fought not only for his survival, which certainly hung in the balance, but also out of hatred and frustration. Gunnar Bakkstrom served quite nicely as the focus for the accumulation of anger and rage that had built within him. The Scandis had destroyed his life and his world. Even if he was able to do no more, he would have his revenge upon at least one of them.

Mirna was not a squeamish woman. She had seen more than her share of bloodshed and mayhem in her life, had indeed been the cause of much of it, but never had she seen a fight such as the one which took place before her now as Braldt and Bakkstrom fought for supremacy on the still trembling ground.

Bakkstrom soon realized that this was no normal contest of strength and wills. Nor was Braldt the usual easily vanquished, easily intimidated opponent. How had the man slipped his bonds? He felt Braldt's hands around his throat and for the first time, a cold thread of fear lanced through Gunnar's bowels as it occurred to him that it was actually possible that he might lose! Now allegiance to king and duty vanished, replaced by the much stronger allegiance to life itself.

The cells of the prison emptied around the struggling figures unnoticed, as the doors, secured by powerful magnetic bonds, broke their seals, the electric currents interrupted by the more powerful currents of the earth. The prisoners wasted no time in vacating the area, more than willing to take their chances on falling rock and the dancing ground.

They would have done better to remain in the prison, for it alone had been hewn from the rock with no embellishments, no high vaulted ceilings and loose, heavy objects that could maim and kill. Most of those who escaped soon met with death. Those who were fortunate enough to survive soon realized that there was really nowhere to escape to.

As the feeling slowly returned to Bakkstrom's arm, he used whatever came to hand to fend off the crazed Braldt. He had not been able to reach his knife before Braldt seized him, wrapping his arms around him and squeezing him in a bear hug that all but paralyzed him. He could feel the oxygen leaving his lungs. As the light began to explode in little red dots behind his eyes, he brought his head forward with incredible force, slamming it against the bridge of Braldt's nose. Blood gushed from Braldt's nostrils and he staggered back, the pressure of his arms releasing for but a moment.

It was all that was needed. Bakkstrom broke Braldt's stranglehold on his body and drove his head into Braldt's throat, pushing him back against the far wall, anticipating the peculiar cracking sound of the trachea as it was crushed, followed by the harsh, desperate gurgle, the struggle for breath that would never come.

While they were still a foot from the wall, the floor moved yet again, this time wrenching itself in the opposite direction, and the walls moved as well, seemingly torn in several different directions. Actually, there was a slight fault, a fracture in the rock, invisible to the naked eye, that ran perpendicular through the rock which had been hollowed out to form the prison. When the first tremor struck, a hairline crack raced around the room, defining the area of weakness. When the second jolt hit, the crack opened, widening visibly. With each succeeding tremblor, it ground back and forth and up and down like a massive set of hungry jaws, the crack growing larger and larger until finally it separated totally, one edge grinding against the other, overlapping like a monstrous overbite.

As the rock shifted, cracks blossomed and grew, spreading this way and that, stretching in all directions. Tiny falls of dust began to trickle down upon the combatants and went unnoticed. Mirna, however, was quick to take note and looked up to see the labyrinth of cracks widening and shaking loose the bits of stone they encompassed. She was quick to realize the implications.

It appeared that Bakkstrom was winning for the moment, but Mirna was a pragmatist and had no desire to await the outcome sitting quietly on the sidelines while the room and, for all she knew, the world crumbled around her. Fair contests had never held much fascination for her, and so without a moment's hesitation she picked up a convenient chunk of rock which had fallen near her left foot and brought it down upon the back of Bakkstrom's skull. Bakkstrom's eyes rolled up into his head and his body went limp.

Braldt staggered toward her, his eyes still clouded with a murderous rage. For a moment Mirna thought he would strike her. She stepped back warily. Braldt shook himself like an animal shedding water. Reason returned to his eyes as he looked at her and at his fallen enemy, and then, as a chunk of rock fell at their feet and shattered, he seemed to grasp what was happening around them. Without speaking, he seized Mirna by the wrist, pausing only to relieve Bakkstrom of his knife before exiting the swiftly disintegrating prison.

Outside, all was chaos. They made their way through a series of antechambers which were used for the business of the state. Reams of papers and overturned chairs and desks littered the floors. Machines with brightly lit screens and a variety of knobs and buttons hissed and crackled and buzzed. Some dangled from thick cords and others had severed their connections, which now writhed across the floor like giant deadly snakes, spitting electrical current. The dead were everywhere, crushed beneath immense rocks, electrocuted by their own machines, or trampled beneath the feet of their fellow workers. Even the stoic Mirna was visibly shaken as they passed the silent and occasionally not so silent bodies.

It was better once they reached the circular concourse, the inner artery that wound its way around the interior of the cone. Here the damage was less severe, although in places chunks of the thick railing had broken away, carrying parts of the floor with it and raining down on the central area, killing and maiming those who still remained below.

It was darker than usual and a heavy veil of dust hung in the air like a cloud across the sun, obliterating what little of the pale sunlight penetrated the broken crown of the mountain. The dim light, backlit here and there by the occasional fire, threw eerie shadows against the walls, outlining the drama that took place before it. It looked like a black and white line drawing of some ancient horror, Christians being thrown to the lions, or a slaughter of innocents—if it had not been for the screams. The sounds of death were everywhere, surrounding them in horrid intensity, impossible to escape.

As Braldt and Mirna entered the rampway, they came to an abrupt halt, stunned by the destruction that lay before them. For a moment neither of them could move. Then Mirna took hold of Braldt's arm and began to tug him to the left, upward and toward the open air. Only then did Braldt gain control of himself. He resisted Mirna's pull easily.

"Come," she urged. "We've got to go, got to get out of here before it happens again!"

"Keri." He said only the one word, but it was enough to bring Mirna to the brink of despair as she pulled on his arm, trying to stop him as he turned in the opposite direction, down, toward the heart of the destruction.

"No, don't you understand?" she said, weeping. "Can't you see, they're all dead. No one could have lived through that. It'll happen again; it's not done. We don't have to die. We can live if we get out now. Why can't you see that?"

He looked down at her tear-streaked face, her beauty marred by her extreme fear. "You go," he said gently. "I must find Keri. I cannot leave without her. Go. I wish you well."

Mirna stared after him as he turned and began to thread his way through the falls of stone and tangle of dead bodies. Her fears raged inside her. Fiercely independent as she was, she was no match for the forces that opposed her now. Man might bend to her wishes, but never nature. The thought of being alone was even more terrifying than the thought of what lay below. Sadly, fearfully, Mirna caught up with the huge man who stalked the dark corridor, and prayed that his strength and courage were greater than her own.

Keri was seldom alone these days as events moved swiftly around her. She knew that she was the focus of much of what was being said and done, but no one would tell her exactly what was happening.

Strangely, the king no longer frightened her as he had in the beginning. Rather, he seemed a sad and lonely being for all his might and power. She did not doubt for a moment that he had done many evil things in his life; you could read it in his eyes and in the deep lines carved in his face. But somehow it was gone, that evil, and all that remained was the sadness and the grief that was its legacy.

Otir Vaeng and Skirnir had taken their leave of the adjoining chambers, gone to yet another of the endless meetings. Although they had not been allowed to see as much of each other as she would have liked, by some bit of luck Uba Mintch was allowed to remain in her chambers as Skirnir escorted the king to his meeting. They were alone, save for one of the hated shape-changers, who, as always, guarded the door.

This man, who had no name that Keri knew of, frightened her badly. He bore a bright red weal across the bridge of his nose and cheekbone. His ear had also been severed and his features were curiously unbalanced. He fingered the ruined ear often and stared at her with an unblinking, glittering hatred. She avoided his gaze whenever possible.

Keri and Uba Mintch huddled together before the small fire that burned in the grate and spoke of happier times. Keri regaled him with tales of Braldt and Carn as youngsters and fondly recalled the many instances of mischief that they had gotten into. Uba Mintch spoke in turn of his long-dead mate, of her beauty and kindness. The shape-changer, crouched in the doorway, hand on the hilt of his blade, growled his displeasure at their words, or perhaps their memories of happiness.

When the ground began to shake, it was Uba Mintch who was the first to react, having experienced many such incidents at his home on the flank of the restless volcano. He pulled Keri to her feet and dragged her to the deep doorway that connected her rooms with those of the king. The shape-changer instantly leapt into the center of the room, drawing his sword as he came, certain that they were attempting to escape. He had barely taken two steps toward them when a huge section of the ceiling came crashing down without any warning, and fell directly upon the shape-changer.

Keri screamed and despite the fact that he was her enemy and frightened her beyond words, she would have rushed to his aid had Uba Mintch not wrapped his furry arms around her and prevented her from leaving the protection of the doorway. As the tremor intensified, they crouched down and

Uba Mintch used his body to shield her from the rain of rocks that pelted the room.

Only when the last tremor had faded away did he allow her to go to the man. He was pinned beneath a gigantic slab of rock, far too heavy for them to move, with only his head and shoulders and one hand protruding. He twisted his head to look up at her and the burning eyes searched her own. She extended a trembling hand to do something, stroke his brow, when the air began to ripple and shimmer. Impossibly, the man's head began to quiver, and then before her horrified eyes, it changed. It elongated, the head itself stretching out longer and thinner, and still the burning eyes held her transfixed. The air seemed to grow thicker and then the man's head grew angular and lean, and fur appeared and covered the terrible visage.

Keri shut her eyes to remove the terrifying sight and when she opened them, the transformation was complete. What had been a man was now a wolf, but in some horrible way they were one and the same. The same glittering, hate-filled eyes still glared out at her, only now they were yellow instead of brown. The scar remained, crossing the bridge of the creature's muzzle, deeper and more disfiguring than on the man. The ear was lopped in half, the remaining portion raw and festering.

The horrible creature glared at her, only at her, and its long claws scrabbled and clacked against the floor as it attempted to free itself from the huge weight. Its long red tongue lolled between sharp, glistening teeth and it snarled at her, a promise of its undying hatred, as though it blamed her in some way for the pain it was suffering.

Suddenly there was a gray blur of movement streaking past her. Beast! All but forgotten in the quake, Beast had never taken his eyes off the shape-changer. Trained not to assault humans unless commanded to do so, Beast had no such compunctions against four-footed enemies, and at the first threat to Keri, he seized his opportunity. Unburdened by human ethics, Beast had no problem in attacking a trapped enemy; what mattered was winning.

The battle was short but fierce. Despite the fact that its lower body was pinned beneath the rock, the wolf still possessed razor-sharp teeth and fearsome claws capable of disemboweling a careless opponent. But Beast was swift and had powerful jaws and claws of his own, and the battle soon began to go against the hapless wolf.

Perhaps realizing that it could not hope to win, the creature began to transform, to change back to human form. Already, even as the air began to ripple, its paw crept down to the hilt of its sword. But Beast had no intention of allowing his enemy to escape, and he lunged forward, jaws agape, and seized the throat of the wolf. A terrible howl erupted from the creature. The air ceased its shimmering and, with a final shaking wrench, Beast ripped the throat out of the wolf.

A spray of hot blood drenched Keri and spurted into the air as the life blood pumped from the fatal wound. There was a final gasping sigh as the furred head fell back upon the floor. As it died, the air wavered once again, and as it cleared there appeared the head of a man, the dead eyes still bright with hatred, the lips drawn back in a snarl. Beast threw back his head and howled in triumph. Keri sank to the floor, one hand pressed against her chest. Braldt had told her of these men who were not men, but in all truth she had not believed him.

Uba Mintch gathered her to him, cradling her head upon his huge, shaggy chest. Keri sobbed into the gray, grizzled fur, huge gulping sobs like those of a child. "I want to go home," she cried, feeling foolish at her words but no longer caring, speaking what was in her heart. "I want to go home."

Uba Mintch shushed her gently as he rocked back and forth and patted her, trying to ease her pain. "Come," he said. "We must leave this place. It is not safe."

"I want to go home," Keri repeated softly. "I want to go home."

When the earth began to shake, Carn leapt from the volva's bed, the silken sheets still tangled around his legs. For one fearful moment, he was back in the nightmare of the fiery caldron where the gods had first revealed themselves to him in all their terrible splendor.

Slowly, his senses cleared. His eyes told him that he was in the volva's bedchamber, not inside the burning mountain. But still the ground shook beneath his feet and he brushed a trembling hand across his scarred brow, tasting the oily residue that so often furred his tongue these days, and wondered if the volva had caused this to happen. She was still reclining on her silks, seemingly unconcerned with the violent movement that was destroying the room around them. Perhaps he was only imagining it. A book struck him on the shoulder and he raised a hand to fend off the tall, narrow case that had once contained it. No, he was not yet mad: It was real, it was happening.

He scrambled for his clothes among the fallen bedclothes and screamed at the woman. "Hurry, dress yourself, we must leave. We must find safety." To his amazement, the seeress merely stretched leisurely and then rose and casually strolled across the room to warm her back before the still roaring fire.

"The gods will not harm me. I know the manner of my death. They have told me how it is that I will die: by the knife, not by a trembling of the earth. Where is your courage, my little rabbit, eh?"

"You don't understand!" Carn screamed, his fear all but

overwhelming him, the memory of the fiery inferno swimming before his eyes as he looked down into the flames leaping on the hearth.

"Oh, I understand." The volva seemed amused at his frantic actions. "Come, I thought you were the chosen one, hand-picked by the gods for mighty purposes. Have you not told me this yourself? Why then are you afraid? Do you not believe in your gods?"

Her words stopped Carn cold. Only then did he realize that there was no fiery caldron, save in his mind. The earth shook, yes, but the volva was right, as she always was: He was the chosen of the gods. He must believe in them, in their promise. He could not doubt them now. The tension faded from his body; he looked down at the garment he had struggled to don seconds before and discarded it with a laugh. He joined the volva before the fire, allowing the flames to warm his still tender flesh. She looked into his eyes and a warm, ironic smile twitched at the corners of her lips. "So the rabbit becomes a lion, eh?"

"Let me show you," he replied as he drew her toward him.

Septua and Barat Krol were not as fortunate as the others. Being closer to ground level, they were thus closer to the epicenter of the quake and were among the first to suffer its devastation.

It was impossible to regain their footing even if they had wanted to do so. The jolt was accompanied by a deep, growling rumble that emanated from the depths of the earth and seemed to swell around them, reverberating in the narrow passageway till it drummed inside their heads.

Both Barat Krol and Septua huddled against the floor and covered their heads and ears with their hands and arms, trying to shut out the fearsome sound. Septua thought that he might die. He had never been so frightened in all his life. Barat Krol had experienced other quakes but never one so violent or so close; he was certain that the heart of the quake was directly beneath him. He knew that there was nothing to do but wait . . . and pray.

The corridor disintegrated around them, the sanitized white panels freeing themselves from the thin strips of metal that held them to the rock walls, the ceilings with their strips of bright halide lighting cascading down upon them in a shower of sparks and explosions. Worse was the huge pane of glass that separated them from the operating amphitheater—this parted from its moorings at the very first twitch and inflicted numerous cuts upon their bodies. One large section of glass hurled itself toward them and raked across the back of Barat Krol's arm, gouging a deep wound that immediately began to bleed. Even this did not cause them to raise their heads.

When the earth had finally ceased to move, they were all but buried beneath the wreckage. Huge chunks of rock had rained down on them as well, and only the fallen panels had prevented them from being killed outright. Septua's ankle had been crushed and several spears of bone poked through the rapidly darkening skin. Septua took one look at it when Barat Krol was at last able to free him and then passed out cold. Unconsciousness spared him the sight of the cylinder of precious Madrelliova which had been smashed flat by an immense rock, its contents already seeping into the gritty rubble.

"We're both in a bad way, my little friend," Barat Krol murmured, more to himself than to the unconscious dwarf. He looked around in despair and saw nothing but a pale blue cascade of electrical sparks somewhere in the distance. All the lights had been destroyed and everything was in darkness.

The air around him was thick with dust and acrid smoke and it was difficult to breathe. Somewhere he could hear the sound of someone crying, and then even that stopped.

Barat Krol tried to think of what he could do. He knew which way to go, but it seemed likely that the entire corridor would be filled with debris, impossible to traverse, considering the seriousness of the dwarf's injury. Barat Krol entertained the idea of leaving the dwarf behind but immediately discarded the idea. They would go together or they would not go at all.

He took advantage of the dwarf's unconscious state to bind his ankle firmly with a strip of cloth which he ripped from the dwarf's cape and strengthened with several of the thin metal strips to hold the broken joint firmly. Then, after making Septua as comfortable as possible, he began to explore.

20

It was all that Skirnir could do to persuade Otir Vaeng that he should continue with his plans for the marriage.

"How can you speak of such things now?" the king asked bleakly. "What can such a thing matter, my marriage, when so many of our people are dead or dying?"

"That is precisely the point, Majesty," Skirnir said patiently, doing his best to contain his rage and impatience, the almost physical need to shake this sick and pusillanimous fool whom fate had cast as his superior. "Kings are not mortal but are chosen by the gods to represent them and their wishes on earth. You must be married to remind the people that there is a devine destiny, that despite the disaster the gods have not abandoned us, that they are with us still."

"Oh." Otir Vaeng looked up sharply, a glint of the old fire in his eyes. He stared at his prime minister, his lips pressed into a thin taut line. "Divine destiny of the gods, eh? And what might that be? If there truly is such a thing as divine destiny, what possible purpose could these gods have had for bringing us to a dead world and then killing us off in wholesale lots? We could have remained on earth and died in our own beds had we wanted to perish."

"Majesty," Skirnir said soothingly, although his heart was pounding inside his chest. It had been a long while since the king had spoken out so sharply. Skirnir had almost forgotten what it was like to be afraid of the man who in his prime had dished out death as easily as one served up a bowl of soup. "We cannot hope to understand all of the gods' purposes, but surely this disaster has been their method of choosing from among us those who are worthy to leave, those who must make the journey to our next home."

"And where might that be, eh, Skirnir? Have the gods managed to find us a new home, or is that a mystery too?"

"No, Majesty. It is not a mystery. The gods have seen fit to spare us the planet known as K7 and even now we are readying the craft for the voyage."

Otir Vaeng lifted his head and stared at Skirnir and then half rose out of his chair before the pain in his arm caused him to wince and fall back. "K7? But we—"

"It still exists, Majesty. You see, the gods have favored us after all. You can see now why your marriage is necessary. The ceremony will serve to unite the people again."

Otir Vaeng was clearly not convinced, but now his attention seemed to drift away from Skirnir and the fire was gone from his eyes. "If you say so," he said vaguely, and cradled his injured arm as he stared into the flames.

Skirnir smiled to himself as he bowed low before the king, who no longer saw him. He exited the stifling room, which, even with its huge fires burning constantly, did not seem to warm the king.

At the last moment, Otir Vaeng seemed to rouse from his lethargy and snapped out the prime minister's name. "Skirnir, is the boat finished?"

"Yes, Majesty, all but done," Skirnir stammered, his heart racing at the steel in the man's tone. It would not do to become too sure of himself. Despite his injury, the king was still a man to be feared.

He decided then to give the people and the king what they wanted. The wedding would take place at the water's edge beside the immense high-prowed boat that the king had insisted be built. The marriage would occur in two days' time, but first there was the matter of the funeral for those killed in the quake, in its way as important as the wedding. Death and then the promise of birth. With a few surprises along the way.

Despite his determination, Braldt had been unable to reach Keri's quarters. The closer they came to the king's chambers, the heavier the guard, fully armed and fending off the flow of crazed survivors, directing them down into the interior of the cone where rescue efforts as well as teams of healers and food lines were already being established. The coolheaded ability to impose order on chaos, the hallmark of their people, had helped them respond to the crisis.

Braldt had no desire to take part in the rescue effort, his only interest was in finding Keri, Beast, and then Septua and Uba Mintch, but Mirna convinced him that the best and safest way for them to receive information, the best way to lay a successful plan, was to become one with the people.

Under her direction, they blurred their features with a mixture of spit and dust and robbed two corpses for their cloaks, concealing Mirna's bright red hair and Braldt's distinctive features. Joining the keening throngs, they made their way to the lower levels, where they were given packets of instawarm emergency rations to satisfy their immediate hungers and thirsts. In the way of all such rations, they might have satisfied the physical needs, but the esthetics such as taste and texture were sadly lacking.

They soon found themselves separated, once it had been ascertained that they were uninjured. Mirna was assigned to a crisis ward helping the healers and Braldt was singled out to help lift heavy objects off the injured. Their sad, bloody tasks kept them busy throughout the day and long into the night when most of those still alive had been found and given what limited treatment was available. There were still many areas which had not been heard from and had proved impossible to reach without heavier equipment, some of which was itself buried beneath tons of debris.

The hospital was unfortunately one of those areas still to be excavated and reaching it would be difficult because the entire concourse that led to the hospital zone had broken off, preventing access of any sort. Numerous plans were conceived and then discarded as impractical or impossible.

It was frustrating to be able to see the corridor and know that critical medicines and equipment were so close and yet so totally out of reach. Several attempts were made to climb the rough, broken rock face, but the surface was too unstable and threatened to break away at the least amount of pressure.

Braldt had seen enough hideous injuries throughout the day to know that many would die if access could not be gained to the hospital. He was studying the face of the newly formed cliff, attempting to map out a safe route, when there was a sudden intake of breath from the crowd and excited exclamations. Braldt raised his eyes to the top of the cliff and spotted a Madrelli—Barat Krol, he thought, but the distance was too great to be certain—descending the rock face with nothing more than hands and feet to aid him. Draped across his neck and shoulders was what first appeared to be a multicolored shawl, but Madrelli did not wear clothing. As he came closer, Braldt suddenly realized that what he was seeing was a person, a little person, attached to the Madrelli's broad back by torn strips of cloth. Septua! Braldt's heart leapt inside his chest and began to hammer rapidly. Was the dwarf dead? No, a hand fluttered, short stubby fingers convulsed as they neared the bottom of the rock face; the dwarf was still alive.

Braldt dashed forward to lend a hand in steadying Barat Krol as his long, flexible foot digits reached out for firm ground. Barat Krol turned at the touch, lips drawn back in an open snarl that did not fade until he recognized Braldt's features beneath the layer of dust and grime. Only then did he allow Braldt to relieve him of his heavy burden. Braldt examined Septua anxiously and found numerous cuts and bruises as well as the seriously damaged ankle joint. The crowd pressed in close, morbidly curious about anyone less fortunate than themselves.

"It's the dwarf thief," murmured one who recognized the distinctive, diminutive stature.

Anxious to head off that train of thought, Braldt shrouded his own face deeper in the folds of the cloak and spoke out, "Is such a thing of any import now? Surely the important thing is that he is hurt and needs care. There are no enemies at a time like this. We must set aside our differences and work together. Think what we have just seen. If this Madrelli can descend the cliff with such ease, we should not be thinking how different he is from us, but rather how much we require the service of those different abilities."

Braldt turned to Barat Krol and spoke to him as though they were strangers. "You are brave, good sir, to have thought of another in such a time of danger. Do the healers' quarters still stand or have they been destroyed?"

Barat Krol continued the charade with a straight face. "Much has been destroyed and the passages are filled with broken rock and debris, but I believe that a way could be cleared."

"Would you be willing to lead a party of volunteers to clear the way so that the wounded may receive proper treatment?"

Barat Krol had been tortured by the thought of what was happening to his own people throughout the long hours it took him to clear an escape route large enough to safely remove the dwarf. Many times he had been on the verge of leaving the unconscious dwarf and investigating the fate of his own kind, but always something held him back, prevented him from leaving Septua's side. He had cursed himself for a fool, but now he thought he saw a way to turn the situation to his advantage.

"I will do as you ask," he agreed, and was immediately cheered by the crowd who surrounded him. "But only," he continued, "if your healers will extend their services to those of my people who might also have suffered injuries."

A pall of quiet fell across the crowd as they pondered the outrage of his words. Excited voices battered him with cries of indignation and shock, instantly infuriated at the suggestion that a Madrelli's life might be regarded on the same level of importance as their own. They advanced toward Barat Krol with angry gestures.

"Stop!" cried Braldt, placing himself between the Madrelli and the angry crowd. "We need them. What harm can come of treating their injuries as well as our own? Is a life not a life, no matter to whom it belongs?"

It was obvious that this was not a popular thought and Braldt received many strange glances, but in the end they were forced to agree to Barat Krol's proposal. Unless they were able to traverse the dangerous stretch of ground and excavate the hospital, many who lay injured would join the list of fatalities before the night was out.

Barat Krol lost no time in making his way to the Madrelli compound, where he spoke at length to his kinfolk. At first the Madrelli were as difficult as the Scandis. They too had suffered numerous deaths and injuries, and could see no reason to further risk themselves in order to aid their masters.

It was only with great difficulty that Barat Krol was able to convince them that such an effort would work in their own best interests. Only by appealing to several females whose children had been gravely injured was he able to persuade them at last. The children were to be among the first who were healed.

* * *

The effort was launched and after the Madrelli had scaled the face of the fall and hammered home a sturdy ladder and catwalk, they were joined by teams of Scandis. It was, quite possibly, the first time such a joint effort had ever taken place, Madrelli and Scandis working shoulder to shoulder voluntarily to achieve a common goal.

Throughout the remainder of the day and into the night they worked, erecting a more permanent walkway and then clearing the clogged passageways and the operating theaters beyond. And when it was finally possible to move the first of the wounded, not one voice was raised in protest when the Madrelli young and Septua were placed at the head of the column.

Slipping away from her duties, Mirna stood beside the sedated dwarf, his leg and foot encased in a lightweight polymer cast with numerous bone filament rods extending from one side to the other. It would be a long time, if ever, before the thief did any sneaking, Mirna thought with a grin which quickly twisted into a tearful grimace. It was hard seeing the cheery, independent thief lying so still and helpless.

"Wot are you doin' 'ere? Never mind, wipe them tears off yer face or I'll smack ya."

Mirna looked up at the rusty croak of words and saw Septua regarding her through puffy, slitted lids, his homely face further distorted by numerous bruises and scrapes. Mirna's face was wreathed in a joyous smile that none of the dwarf's growls or threats were able to remove.

Exhausted but satisfied by his long day's work, Braldt wrapped himself in his cloak and settled down on one of the pallets that had been laid out for the vast horde of survivors who preferred to sleep in the open.

He had positioned himself so that he could watch the doorway to Keri's chambers. Her rooms being in such close proximity to those of the king, there was no way that he could think of to reach her. But somehow just seeing the doorway, imagining her and what she might be doing, thinking, was almost enough. Braldt closed his eyes and slept.

The blue alien known as Fortran was truly astonished—speechless, in fact, in a manner of speaking, since Fortran and the others of his kind had long ago done away with the need for spoken speech. Anything that needed to be conveyed—words, nuances, emotions—was accomplished by thought transference, which took the entire range of meaning and emotion and placed it within the being one was communicating with. It did away with such tiresome problems as language and species differences and left little room for misunderstandings. On the whole, it was a much better system than anything that had gone before.

What had astonished Fortran so completely was the second to final step in his progression, or, to use an archaic phrase, his rite of manhood. By daring to think, to question, to defy the authority which he had grown up with, he had exhibited the first necessary quality of a sentient adult, the ability to think and act on his own even when such actions were both difficult and unpopular.

This he had done, the first but thankfully not the last of his class to do so. It had all been a test, he was able to see that now, and being a natural-born troublemaker (as his mother pointed out proudly), it should have come as no surprise that he had been the first to rebel against the rigid order that had been imposed upon him and his fellow classmates.

After Fortran's emergence, others began to appear at a slow but steady rate; there were nearly a thousand of them now. More than two-thirds of their original numbers had still not emerged, however, and still remained locked in blind obedience and, it was assumed, the lowermost Rototaran dungeons.

It was to be hoped that some of them would still find their way to enlightenment, but sadly, it was not likely. The blue aliens had long ago discovered a disappointing fact: that given the choice, most would choose the safety and anonymity of blind obedience rather than the breadth and freedom of new and uncharted pathways.

While it was always grievous to lose so many, such a large percentage of their young, it was necessary. In an interesting correlation, if one was given to that sort of thing, it bore out the hypothesis of that ancient thinker, Charles Darwin. In their own way, it was the aliens' method of the advancement of their species: Only the smart survive.

The blue aliens had spent—wasted—many thousands of years attempting to pass on the lessons they had learned to their young, and found, just as countless civilizations had found before them, that the young were not interested in absorbing or embracing their parents' dictums and knowledge. The young seemed singularly disinterested in anything save their own hungers.

The odd exception to this unhappy fact came from a most unexpected quarter. It seemed that while the young rejected their parents' teachings, they would search diligently through the archives of history to involve themselves with the most esoteric and bizarre of the galaxy's theologies and philosophies.

This presented a problem, for the aliens had long known that there were no true gods other than intelligence and conscience. This, then, was the quandary: how to present and teach the important messages of life to their young without seeming to do so.

The elders conferred and decided, if their young were determined to become involved in the tangles of religion, it would be one of their own choosing. Therefore, they set themselves to the task of inventing a new religion, an interesting amalgam of all the galaxy's religions, taking this ritual from one religion, this ceremony from another, and so on until they had a fine admixture of hocus-pocus, mysticism, and romance.

The young were enlisted in a religious order rife with ritual and mystic messages. Concealed within the hokum, buried deeply, cloaked with convoluted verbiage, were the all-important words their elders wished them to absorb: Be intelligent, think for yourself, act with honor, speak with truth, be kind to others, yes, and even treat others as you would have them treat you. These and other equally simple but universal truths were planted in the young, unformed minds. Then all the parents and teachers could do was sit back and wait and hope that in time a true revelation would occur.

Now that Fortran and his comrades had taken the Great Step, there was but one final step to complete before they were permitted to take their place among the respected elders of their kind: They were to perform some act, of their own choosing, which would exemplify all that they had learned, to prove that they were indeed capable of independent, intelligent, caring thought.

This action, whatever it might be, was left to their own discretion. It could take place anywhere in the universe, as long as it did not cause damage or death to another life-form. Many of Fortran's comrades had trouble deciding upon a direction, but Fortran had no trouble at all.

The morning dawned clear and cold and, though there appeared to be numerous foggy coronas surrounding the sun, which some of the older women predicted meant disaster and death, Skirnir was determined to carry out the burials of the disaster's victims.

Everyone who was physically able accompanied the procession. The population was now so small—no more than fifteen hundred Scandis and Madrelli combined—that it was the rare individual who had not lost a family member or a friend in the disaster.

Skirnir, Carn, and the volva led the way, followed in turn by the ranks of priests, clad in ermine and sables and embroidered robes and weighted down with gold. The king was carried on a cushioned litter, his feverish eyes lifted to the surrounding peaks rather than the proceedings. With every passing moment, Skirnir felt that the king was slipping away, his body still present but his mind and heart elsewhere. He had been heavily sedated against the pain and Skirnir could only hope that it would last until he was safely returned to his chambers.

The king was followed by his two remaining shapechangers and then a phalanx of the royal guard. Next came the wailing, keening line of mourners, who trudged beside the sledges which bore the dead in their large red earthen jars.

Skirnir could not have put a name to it, but he was filled with dread, with the terrible certainty that something would go wrong and upset his carefully laid plans. For all his fears, he could do nothing more than watch and wait.

The day was bitter cold; the sun did little more than shed a thin, pale light. The odd coronas were more clearly visible and it was seen that there were four of them, each slightly larger than the last, glistening rainbows circling the sun. The sky itself was a dark, deep, ominous shade of blue that seemed to squeeze in around the sun as though it were a hungry beast nibbling at the edges before devouring it whole.

Braldt felt a deep uneasiness that had nothing to do with the cold or the color of the sky. He was fearful of what they would find when they arrived at the burial mound. All around them were signs of the devastation that had shaken their world; the mountain known as Aasgard had certainly not been singled out for destruction. Whole mountainsides were stripped of snow, naked down to the bare rock. Entire sections of mountains had broken away and fallen into the valleys below, exposing their scarred flanks to the biting wind.

The procession's path was strewn with evidence of the violence of the quake and it became more and more difficult to proceed. At length it was necessary for the guards to go ahead to break a trail through the mounds of icy snow and rock. At one point they found their way blocked by a vast sheet of ice and it was thought that they would have to turn back until one guard, braver and more daring than the rest, picked a way across the ice and chopped out a path that others might follow.

The wailing and crying ceased long before they reached their goal; each breath came harsh and painful, the icy particles in the air frosting their throats and chilling their lungs. Scarves and cloaks offered little protection against the frigid temperatures. Hands and feet and exposed skin were numb and unfeeling. Faces were mottled with frostbite despite the protective measures which had been taken. Each step was a descent into hell, without the warmth, yet they continued on.

When at last they reached the narrow defile that led to the burial ground, they were almost too exhausted and too cold to care. Only Skirnir's imprecations, like barbed goads, kept them on the path. The king had long since retreated into a mound of down-filled polyskins and was not to be seen.

The high walls of the gorge broke the vicious cut of the wind which had hounded them from the start. The silence, the absence of sound, was strange and almost eerie after the howling that had filled their ears for so long. Now they could hear the crunch of each footfall, the rasp of each painful breath as they approached the dark upright plinths that marked the gateway to the halls of the dead.

Now it was the volva's moment. She stepped forward, her hood fallen back from her face. Her cheeks were pale, devoid of color, in contrast to the bright red, wind-whipped cheeks that marked everyone else. Her eyes were bright and glistening as though fevered. Her dark hair fell in smooth waves, seemingly untouched by wind or the weight of the heavy hood. It was as though she had just stepped out of her own chambers, so little was she affected by their cruel surroundings.

A murmur of unease swept through the crowd. The seeress struck fear into their hearts, and despite her lineage—a pure, unbroken line that could be traced back into the earliest recorded Scandi history—they had never felt that she was one of them.

She threw her cape back over her shoulders, ignoring the bitter cold that lanced through insulated polyskins as though they were tissue. It could now be seen that she wore no more than her usual garb, a rough affair of skins that covered her from shoulder to mid-thigh. Skin boots, hair side out, rose to her knees. That was all she wore. Anyone else would have frozen solid, yet the seeress showed no evidence of discomfort.

About her neck, waist, and wrists were a dangle of tiny thin bones, long, glistening teeth, great hooked ivory claws, the rattle of a snake, a hooked scorpion's tail, and the vicious serrated beak of a predator bird as well as its talons. Cheap amulets of death and fear, they performed their purpose well; more than a few of the crowd averted their eyes, spat on the ground, or crossed themselves against evil.

Skirnir smiled. He had to admit that the woman performed her duties to perfection. She had the people in the palm of her hand. None would doubt her words. The only thing that troubled Skirnir was the fact that the woman seemed to actually believe what she said and did. That was not part of the plan. Skirnir shrugged. If it helped her in her job, so what? A method actress.

The man Carn was a bit of a worry too. He had fallen under the volva's spell, as Skirnir knew he would. The woman's aura of sexuality and evil were too powerful to be denied. He knew. He could only hope that when the time came for Carn to perform his allotted role, he would not balk.

The volva raised her hands and the crowd fell silent. She closed her eyes and began to recite in the old tongue, one that rang ancient yet familiar chords inside them, one whose words were familiar yet somehow unknown. The words had the feeling of rightness as though only they should be uttered in this hallowed home of the dead.

The volva finished her invocation and lowered her arms. She reached into the sack that hung from her belt and drew forth a chicken, a black cock with bright red comb and wattle. It glared at the astonished crowd with malevolent golden eyes, its scaly yellow legs clawing futilely at the air.

The volva spoke of birth and life, their brief time upon the earth. She invoked Freya's name as well as those of the gods and goddesses of life. "We are promised that if we live our lives in accordance with the wishes of the gods and do their bidding, then in death we will join them in the halls of the dead and feast with them throughout eternity. In Loki's name we call upon the gods to heed us. We live and die according to their all-seeing wisdom. Hear us, gods, we are come unto your gates and beg admittance. We knock upon your door and ask you to accept our noble dead. Accept our gift and add it to those already on the banquet table, forever renewing."

Without further words, she held the cock on high and, as though responding to her command, it began to crow loudly, its cries echoing through the narrow defile, notifying the gods as to its presence. In one swift move, the volva reached up and slit the cock's throat. Then, as dark blood spurted from its severed neck and showered down upon her uplifted face, she hurled the dying bird up and over the plinth that capped the gateway and into the darkness that lay beyond. The bird's plumage caught the rays of the sun and gleamed like polished obsidian with flashes of green and red, and then it was gone, into the place of death as well as life everlasting.

The crowd released its breath in a single exhalation as the cock disappeared into the burial ground. There were more words then, words to remind them of their mortality, words that traditionally brought them comfort and assured them of their place among the honored dead when their days were done.

Usually the words spoke of eternal joy and feasting at the tables of the gods for those who had just taken the first step on that final voyage. But those were not the words that they heard now. Instead the volva read the long list of the names of the dead. The crying began anew. When the list was finished, she stood and regarded them with flashing eyes.

"The gods are not pleased." Her words threw a pall over the crowd. The crying ceased instantly and the sobbing of the wind could be heard as it keened over their heads. "The gods are not pleased," she repeated, fixing them with her unblinking stare. "These dead will not seat themselves alongside the heroes in Valhalla. Nor will they lift goblets of ale to their lips or sing the songs of victory everlasting. Their spirits will forever roam unclaimed; they will know no peace. They will writhe in torment forevermore."

A great moan went up from the crowd. "Why?" came the question, more a wail than a word.

It was what the volva had been waiting for. "They are not pleased, the gods. They have shown their displeasure; it was but a sign. More deaths, more desolation, more ruin will follow if we do not heed them!"

Her voice had risen to a shriek and the mass of mourners flinched as though they had been struck, and indeed the thought of their dead being deprived of eternal reward, as well as the fear of further disaster, was almost too much to be borne. They were not a weak people, but the volva's threat was as terrible a threat as excommunication or damnation had been to Christians in an earlier age.

"Walter! Walter!" a woman screamed, tears wetting her withered cheeks as she clutched her heart and collapsed on the downtrodden snow.

"Stop! Do not touch her!" the volva's voice rang out, a sharp command not to be ignored. "She is the next but will not be the last."

Those standing nearest the woman saw that her chest no longer rose and fell; it was as though the volva had smitten her dead with her words. A space cleared around her fallen form as the people drew back in fear.

Suddenly the volva's eyes rolled back in her skull. Only the whites were visible. She staggered and nearly fell. Her head fell forward until her chin struck her chest and it lolled as though without strength or control. She swayed and her hands dangled limply at her sides, the bloody knife dripping on the snow. Then slowly she stiffened, her head raised, looked out upon the horrified throng with sightless eyes. Her mouth opened and she began to speak. But her voice was not her own, and the words were formed by one unfamiliar with the tongue.

"Kill the intruders! Kill those who are responsible for the deaths of your kin. Do not allow these deaths to go unpunished. Revenge! Vengeance! Death to the unbelievers!"

The words were loud and booming and masculine and issued from the volva's wooden lips in stentorian tones. The final words were not spoken but screamed, and when they faded away the volva tottered and then collapsed on the snow.

Only Carn and Skirnir knelt to aide her. The others would rather have died themselves than to have touched her. But movement of any sort appeared to be impossible, for they were locked in the grip of total fear, still mesmerized by the volva's words. Or were they her words?

"It was Thor," muttered one of the women. "What did he mean?"

"He meant that we have to kill the unbelievers. That's what he said," said a voice from the depths of the crowd.

"What unbelievers?" asked another.

"The Madrelli!" shouted a small man who stood on the sidelines, and he drew his sword and tried to push his way through the crowd.

"Those who come from other worlds!" added another voice. "We have to kill them all or we'll die too!"

Braldt, who had taken his place with Barat Krol and the Madrelli, had watched the entire performance with interest. Perhaps because they were not his gods, not his heritage, it was easier to doubt, to see the sham, the performance created by the volva. That it was a sham he had no doubt. He did not know how it had been done. Perhaps the volva had learned to deepen her voice, to make herself sound like a man.

Or perhaps, Braldt thought with sudden certainty, it had been Carn, who had been standing behind the volva throughout the entire proceedings. Even as Braldt pondered the purpose of the volva's trick, the clash of steel ringing against scabbards, the sight of knives being drawn and hostile eyes turning against the Madrelli told him what her purpose was. She sought a means to drive the separate groups apart, to cause hatred and dissension and death. He drew his own blade and stood before the unarmed Madrelli, prepared to inflict as much damage as possible.

The crowd began to advance toward them. Behind him, Braldt could all but feel the rise of the Madrelli rage, that terrible madness that came upon them in times of battle. A few of the females sought to calm the males, but their fury was very nearly a physical force and once it was set in motion it was not easy to regain control.

A great voice interrupted the action, a huge, booming roll of laughter that rolled over the crowd. "Who dares to speak for the gods? What puny mortal is so foolish as to put words in Loki's mouth?"

"Stupid children," sighed a second ghostly voice, pitying rather than angered.

"Children who play at dangerous games!" roared the first voice, sending the mass of mourners stumbling backward in fear, Scandis pressed against Madrelli, forgetting their earlier animosity, forgetting that only minutes earlier they had been ready to fight to the death. "Who are they to dare to speak for the gods? This pitiful twitch of the earth was nothing beside our true wrath."

"Listen, fools!" commanded the voice, and there were none who would have dared to do otherwise. Only Braldt dared to suspect who was responsible for this "voice" of the gods, and he was not about to say or do anything to deflate the ploy.

"The souls of your dead are already seated beside their glorious ancestors. The sweetness of mead flows down their throats; nevermore will they thirst. The flesh of the cock fills their stomachs; nevermore will they hunger. The heat of the fires warms their flesh; nevermore will they feel the bite of the cold. They are wrapped in the fellowship of those who have gone before them and the love of the gods. Now go, and do not displease us with such mockery again or your souls will wander the void forever."

And then, miraculously, a cock, its black plumage gleaming red and green in the rays of the sun, flew through the gateway and landed on the trampled snow where its life's blood had flowed only moments before. It threw back its head and crowed and there was no doubt that it was alive.

Braldt would dearly have loved to explore the darkness beyond the gates, to discover the secret of the voices and the living bird. But there was no way that he could have done so. Already the entire crowd had turned en masse and was rushing back the way they had come as fast as their feet could carry them. The laughter of the "gods" echoed through the narrow gorge and spurred them on their way. Braldt grinned wryly and then set out after the terror-stricken procession.

21

Braldt was seated beside Septua, who was propped up on a vast pile of pillows. Mirna constantly fussed with the coverlets and pillows, plumping and rearranging them as though by doing so she might earn a kind word from the dwarf, who displayed only irritation and disdain toward her.

"I'm certain it was Brandtson and Saxo," Braldt said in a low tone, having just related the entire tale of the morning's amazing events. "At least they're alive."

"What a gag. Whisht I'd been there to see it!" That woman, tho', what mischief be she up to? An' that there Carn, 'e may be yer brother an' all, but it don't sound like 'e's playin' on the same side!"

"I know," Braldt said solemnly, turning to Barat Krol, who was there at the dwarf's insistence. "What do you make of it?"

"It's simple," the Madrelli replied bitterly. "She is trying to kill us off."

"Ayuh," agreed the dwarf, " 'an everyone else she can get rid of."

"But why?" asked Braldt.

"Because there are too many of us to leave this place," answered Barat Krol. "She wants to whittle the numbers down."

"Where is there to go?" asked Braldt, perplexed.

Barat Krol and Septua exchanged a glance.

"What?" Braldt demanded, realizing that they possessed some bit of information that was unknown to him.

"Our world," Uba Mintch said at length. "The world they call K7. It is not destroyed, but exists still."

Braldt could do nothing but stare at him. He felt his eyes fill with moisture and his hands trembled. "It exists?" he whispered huskily. "How can you know this? How can it be true?"

"We have had certain access to information from the observatory," Barat Krol said as he examined the backs of his hands, the smooth fur suddenly requiring his intense concentration. "It seems that the explosion did not succeed in destroying the world, but merely rearranged it, you might say."

"Mirim, Auslic!" Braldt said, half rising. "I must find a way to tell Keri that her parents are still alive!"

"No!" Barat Krol and Septua both spoke at once. Septua grimaced as his still tender flesh tugged against the bone filaments and then sank back upon his pillows, nodding to Barat Krol to continue.

"It would be cruel to tell her anything, even if you could get to her, which I doubt. No one knows how much of the world remains. There is too much cloud cover to see."

"Then how do they know it still exists?"

Barat Krol shrugged. "They have machines, computers, measuring devices that tell them such things. But the machines cannot tell us what we really want to know: whether our loved ones are still alive."

"But that means . . . if the world still exists, no matter how badly it might be damaged, that we can leave here and go there!"

Barat Krol and Septua exchanged yet another of the meaningful glances.

"Uh, no, not really," said the dwarf, rubbing his whiskery chin with his callused hand.

"Why not?" challenged Braldt. "Oh, I know the argument. The sun flares disrupt the transporter and there are too many of us to fit in the spacecraft. But still, there must be a way!"

"Uh, it's a little more complicated than that," muttered Septua.

"What my small friend here is trying to say is that no one who enters the spacecraft will arrive at their destination," Barat Krol stated in quiet tones. "I have long known that they would not take us, the Madrelli, anywhere with them, no matter what world they found. What would be the purpose of taking up valuable space with our large, furry carcasses when they can take but a single container which holds all the Madrelli clones they will ever need? No, I knew they would not include us in their plans. They would leave us here to die, to freeze alone in the darkness. So, I decided, if we Madrelli cannot go, they cannot leave either. We will all die together."

Minra gasped. Braldt looked at the Madrelli with sharp eyes. "What have you done?" he demanded.

"I have fixed the ship so that its course cannot be controlled."

"Surely it can be fixed!"

"Perhaps, in time," Barat Krol said pleasantly, "but only if they knew about it."

"I will tell them!"

"No, my friend, you will not," Barat Krol said quietly. "Unless you give me your word, you will never leave this place alive. You will slip and fall, I think, and tragically break your neck. I would not like for this accident to happen, but you must understand I cannot allow my people to be sacrificed, discarded like something that has absolutely no value. If we die, so do they."

"What if a way could be found to take all of us back to our world? What then?"

"Then I would ask you what I could do to help," said Barat Krol. "And my heart would be happy that you were spared such an untimely death."

Barat Krol and Braldt looked into each other's eyes and smiled. They were cold, knowing smiles that acknowledged the other's stand. Neither Braldt nor Barat Krol were afraid of the other; in fact, they were well matched physically and any attempt on Braldt's life would have thrown the Madrelli's into question. But it was not a contest that either of them wished to enter, for despite their vast differences, they were friends.

"That be all well an' good," Septua interrupted. "But we still gots time to work that one out. What I wants to know is, what be you gonna do about this 'ere wedding?"

"What wedding?" asked Braldt.

Septua looked at him with exasperation. "I been in a turrible accident, buried up to my neck in rocks, operated on, stuck 'ere on my bed o' pain, an' I still knows ten times as much as you. Ain't you sumpin'!"

"What wedding?" Braldt asked, glaring at the little man.

"The wedding termorrow 'tween Keri an' the king!"

Braldt stared at the dwarf, thunderstruck.

"When and where is this to happen?"

"I tole you, termorrow mornin', down at the water, on the king's boat what he 'ad made special."

Braldt's face was hard, as though chiseled from stone, as he rose and strode away.

"Wait, come back 'ere! Wotta ya gonna do?" But Braldt did not even slow his pace, much less respond to the dwarf's question, and then he was gone.

"Well, wotta ya make a' that?" asked the dwarf.

"I think there's not going to be a wedding," said Mirna.

* * *

The volva paced back and forth in her chambers, ignoring Carn, who sat beside the bed watching her restless figure. He had tried to calm her, tried to reason with her, to tell her that she was wrong, that her importance had not been diminished by what had occurred that morning. But she had struck at him, and from the dark fury that he saw in her eyes he knew that she would not hesitate to kill him if he troubled her further.

He had not told her the truth. In fact, he thought that what happened that morning had caused her irreparable damage. He had not been fooled by the voices of the gods, recognizing, as Braldt had done, that they were but voices that had been projected, a trick they had mastered early in their young years. But it had served to fool the mass of mourners, sunk so deep in their own grief that they were easy to manipulate.

By rejecting the sacrificed cock and returning it alive, a trick which he had yet to figure out, the voices had turned the tables on the volva, using her own ploy against her so that it appeared that the gods rejected her and the theories she espoused.

But Carn had more serious matters on his mind than the volva's emotional state. Tomorrow was the day Keri was to wed the king. Such a joining was well and proper for one of royal birth such as his sister. Normally he would have been pleased for her success, despite the fact that Otir Vaeng was so very much older than Keri and held no attraction for her. But that too was the least of his problems, for this was to be no normal wedding.

According to the plan that had been conceived by the volva and the prime minister, immediately following the wedding ceremony, Keri was to be sacrificed to the gods, an act of propitiation and supposedly an ancient custom of their people to gain favor with their gods.

Carn stared into the flames that burned on the hearth and wondered if he would be able to do it. Keri was his sister, he had loved her all his life, but she had turned her back on him and on their gods, choosing to love Braldt and casting aside Mother Moon and the other deities they had worshiped, simply because Braldt had done so.

She had actually dared to laugh at him, to chide him for his beliefs after he had been shown the miracle at the heart of the fiery mountain, a miracle which had scarred and hideously disfigured him. By laughing at him, she scorned their gods as well. Carn's heart had ached at her laughter; he had trembled under her casual dismissal of that which they had held holy all their lives.

He had waited for the gods to strike her down for her impertinence and when they did not, he knew that it was his commandment to punish her for her sins. He grieved under the heavy penalty, but never once did he question the rightness of the action. Keri must die, and by his own hand. There was no other way.

Keri stood tall and proud under the busy fingers of the seamstresses. The dress, more lovely than any she had ever possessed, brought her no joy. The purest of white silks, it fell from her shoulders in soft gathers, gently draping the swell of her breasts and then cinched at the waist with a wide belt which was worked with gilt embroidery in a pattern of flowers and leaves. The blossoms and buds of the flowers were gemstones, pale blue, soft pinks, and glowing reds. The skirt was full and fell to her ankles in heavy folds. The hem was worked in gilt and precious gems as well and was heavy and awkward to walk in, swinging around her legs like a great bell.

Her hair had been lathered and rinsed and perfumed with a flowery attar before it was pinned to her head in a mass of dark curls which framed her face and hung down over the nape of her neck. She wore around her brow a gold diadem set with a single large moonstone that reflected the firelight in its milky depths, seeming to burn with a life of its own.

Her ears were hung with tiny chains of gold and around her neck was clasped a wide gold band, nearly the width of her hand, from which a second enormous moonstone was suspended, easily the size of an egg which rested between her breasts. Her arms and wrists and fingers were heavy with gold and silver and precious gems as well. She caught a reflection of her image in the mirror and had it been Braldt she was marrying, she would have taken joy and delight in her appearance. As it was, she barely noticed.

Keri could not understand why it was happening. Why would Otir Vaeng want to marry her? It made no sense. He was old and sick and perhaps even dying, thanks to the wound that Beast had inflicted on him. By all rights, he should hate her, not want to marry her.

It did not really seem as though he wanted to marry her. He seemed curiously devoid of any desires other than sitting before the fire and looking into the dancing flames as though they held some secret message, some vision that only he could see or hear.

The wedding had to be the idea of Skirnir, that disgusting worm of a man. Keri felt her temper begin to rise at the thought of the man. She hated him far more than she hated Otir Vaeng. The king elicited her sympathy despite the evil he had caused in his life, but Skirnir . . . she wished she could step on him as one might squash a poisonous bug. He was that loathsome.

She could not expect any help from Otir Vaeng, who seemed to lack the energy necessary to take a stand, any stand. Nor could she expect any help from Skirnir, who she suspected was at the bottom of this ill-conceived marriage. But what about Carn, and most of all, what about Braldt?

Her brother's actions puzzled her. It was clear that his mind had been severely affected by his ordeal at the heart of the volcano. He had come away damaged, not only in the flesh, but also in the mind. He had babbled some nonsense about Mother Moon revealing herself to him.

She had tried to reason with him, tried to convince him that their entire religion was a sham, put in place long ago by the Scandis to prevent them from straying into lands which they were using for their own purposes. But Carn had reacted violently to her words and refused to listen.

Since that day he had looked through her whenever they met and refused to speak to her. It almost seemed as though he hated her. And the volva—Keri shuddered. That terrible woman had a hold on Carn that Keri knew would be difficult to break.

Braldt. Keri's heart lurched sickeningly when she thought of Braldt. Was he still alive? She had had no word of him since he had first disappeared. Skirnir had told her that he was dead, but she tended to disbelieve whatever Skirnir told her. Braldt could not be dead; something inside her would know it if he ceased to exist. But if he was still alive, why had he not come for her? Had he stopped loving her? Keri could not believe that that was so either; something in her would have known that as well, had it been true. But if he was alive, where was he and why had he not come to her aid?

It was time. She could hear the women coming. A wave of desperation swept over her. What was she to do? Was there no one to help her? Even Uba Mintch was gone, taken away by the guards. Only Beast remained, and he only because it would have been necessary to kill him in order to separate him from her. Not knowing what to do, at the last second

Keri snatched up a small knife, a tiny thing with a blade no more than three inches long, its hilt the head and neck of a horse worked in gold. It was a woman's knife, one of the seamstresses', unlikely to cause serious damage, but it possessed a keen blade and would serve to slice her wrists. She would not be wed to Otir Vaeng if Braldt still lived. If he did not come, if he did not rescue her from this marriage, she would do whatever was necessary to free herself.

She stood tall and proud as the women flitted around her, commenting like foolish, twittering sparrows about her beauty and how happy and honored she should be. Nonsense, all nonsense. They led her to the door and then escorted her out of her chambers with Beast slinking at her heels, growling and snarling. They gave him a wide berth but still circled her completely. Once outside the chambers, standing on the broad concourse, she could see for the first time the incredible damage that had occurred.

Her view was short-lived, for almost immediately a large platoon of heavily armed guards took up positions surrounding the bevy of handmaidens, and the entire party made its way slowly down the winding concourse.

Here and there Keri saw eyes gawking at her, children clinging to pillars and calling down excitedly to report what they saw, but she herself could see nothing and no one. Braldt himself might have been standing there and she would never know. Her heart wept inside her, despite the fact that her face was stony and set in a rigid mask. She would never let them know how she felt. They might force her to do their will, but her thoughts and her feelings were her own.

The procession paused before the great doors that led to the outer world. The musicians, who had joined them at the same time as the guards, increased the tempo of their music—horns blared and cymbals and drums tinkled and thumped. A sense of gaiety prevailed, even though Keri doubted that any among them truly shared that emotion.

She was draped with a heavy fur-lined cloak and high furred boots were placed on her feet over the thin golden slippers. She felt like a large doll, dressed and prettied for another's pleasure.

The blast of intensely cold air that rushed in as soon as the second set of doors were opened brought the first sense of reality to the unnatural scene. She felt her eyes water and sting with the bitter cold, but it felt good. She welcomed its frigid touch.

She was not allowed to walk, but was placed upon a litter and swaddled in furs and polyskins. Beast trotted beneath the litter, growling and snapping at ankles that dared to come too close to his fearsome teeth. From her vantage point, Keri could see a second litter ahead of her which she guessed held the king, whom she had not seen for several days.

For a time there was nothing to be seen but the cold snow-covered peaks which surrounded them. Then a sharp scent came to her, borne on a wind which seemed more moist and temperate than it had been only moments before. She lifted her face to the wind. Yes, it was so! There was definitely a tang of salt on the wind and moisture in the air.

The procession rounded the flank of a mountain and as they began to descend the foothills down to the plains, she saw it: a vast body of water, perhaps a lake, but most probably an ocean, for the taste of salt was heavy on the air. It stretched as far as the eye could see. Its surface was dotted with ice and snow, some small clumps that bumped together on the lift of the waves, other drifts of ice the size of houses which bobbed atop the gray waters like ships.

They appeared to be making for a small bay, and tied to the shore was an immense ship, unlike anything Keri had ever seen before. Its prow was high, nearly as high as its masts, as was its stern. Both prow and stern had been carved in the likeness of a fierce beast, not serpent, not lizard, but a combination of both. Its head was proud and arrogant, its eyes hard and cold. Its jaws were agape and a forked tongue and carved flames emerged between the cruel fangs. This hideous creature was carved in wood, as was the entire ship, but was painted so realistically that Keri would not have been surprised if it had turned its head around to glare at her. It was a frightening apparition and she was glad that it was not alive.

The rest of the ship was no less curious. Long and narrow, it was widest at the middle point, and here the gunwales appeared to spread themselves as though some giant had reached down out of the sky, seized the prow and stern, and squeezed slightly, forcing the middle outward. All along the sides of the ship were shields, each bearing an emblem in its center. These were emblems that Keri had seen before: the head of a horse, an eagle with widespread wings gripping a pennant in its claws, the head of a wolf, and that one there, a lightning bolt, a brilliant silver against a dark blue background. She knew without being told that these were the shields, the emblems, of the various houses or clans who served the king.

The pace increased, as well as the wind, which streamed off the water bearing pennons of salty spume. Because of the angle of their descent, Keri could see that the musicians led the procession, followed by a phalanx of guards, then the volva and Carn, both of whom were dressed in skins and primitive amulets. Keri felt a moment's unease at the sight of her brother, who now even dressed like the fearsome woman who had him in her thrall. Could he not feel the emanations of evil that all but dripped from her?

The king's litter was next, guarded on all sides by his own

personal batallion as well as two slouching figures of the shape-changers, who presented the single largest danger to Beast, for they matched him in size and ferocity and there were two of them to his one.

Her own litter followed that of the king, and behind her came representatives of the various houses, preceded by their flags, although it seemed to Keri that their numbers were greatly reduced, and many of those who trailed behind their flags were bandaged and bruised and wore grim expressions.

Behind the clans came the mass of common people who belonged to no house but were separated into noisome groups of artisans. Only these people, necessary for their skills and bound by few social restraints, exhibited any of the joy normally associated with such an occasion. Many, it seemed obvious by their gay demeanor, had already partaken of some form of liquid happiness. She wished that she could feel some of their enthusiasm, even as her eyes searched the crowd for one who might be Braldt. But of him there was no sign.

She wished that the journey could have taken longer, wished that it was but the first leg of a longer voyage. But such was not the case and all too soon they arrived at the shoreline at the base of the great ship, which rose and fell on the waves. It was easy to believe that it was a live creature. Keri could feel its baleful yellow eyes glaring down at her, could almost feel its hot breath on her shoulders, feel the touch of its flames on the nape of her neck. She dared not look up lest the strength of her fears somehow bring it to life.

A small boat was tied to the shore, anchored by a rock, and Keri and Otir Vaeng took their places on narrow seats while Carn, Skirnir, and the volva seated themselves in the stern. Beast whined and paced at the foam-flecked shore, obviously afraid of the water, but as the boat began to pull away, rowed by four strong oarsmen, Keri cried out to him—"Beaasst!"—her voice betraying the depth of her fear and despair, and forgetting his own fear, Beast leapt into the water and swam to the boat, pulling himself inside and dropping to Keri's feet. Pools of icy water dripped onto Skirnir's feet and he pulled a dagger that hung at his side as though to strike at Beast.

Otir Vaeng roused himself from the deep mood of contemplation that enveloped him and placed his good hand upon Skirnir's arm. Nothing was said. There was no need; the look that passed between them was more than enough. Skirnir sheathed his blade and seemed to shrink inside himself, but his eyes, which flicked at Keri like the tongue of a serpent, were filled with dark hate.

She felt a surge of gratitude, even caring and concern, for Otir Vaeng at that moment. She studied the face of the man who was soon to be her husband. It was a noble face, the brow high and wide, the cheekbones cleanly etched, the nose slender and straight. His mouth was turned down with exhaustion and pain, but it was shapely and well formed. His jaw and chin were clean and noble. Even though she knew that his apparent youth was a falsehood, his life artificially extended by the healers, Keri felt her heart stir for this man. He had power, he had wealth, both beyond measure, he had led a long and busy life and had controlled the lives of a nation and now a world. But for all that, what had it come to? A marriage to a woman who did not love him, surrounded by a people he could not trust, who would kill him in a second if they could attain his power.

Though she knew that he had caused much grief and bloodshed during his lifetime, and was in fact responsible for the death of her own world, Keri could no longer hate Otir Vaeng. As she stared at him, she felt the last of her hatred fade away, to be replaced by sorrow for his sad and empty life.

As though reading her thoughts, Otir Vaeng opened his eyes, looked at her, and smiled gently. His eyes were soft and warm and rested upon her with love. Keri returned his gaze with a tremulous smile of her own. He looked at her so clearly, as though he actually saw her, with none of the absentminded air that had accompanied him so long. It almost seemed as though he were trying to reassure her. She stared at him, bewildered. What was it that was happening? A hard knock interrupted her thoughts. They had reached the ship.

22

The moment had come, the moment which Carn had dreaded. The priests had droned on and on in the old Scandi tongue, which Carn suspected none of them understood. There were three of them, draped in gilt and satins with high-domed hats and long, swishing robes. They carried miters and curved staffs as well as psalm books. Their voices had intermingled, at times reciting the same lines, at others oddly at variance with each other. There had been other languages as well: Latin, a harmonious if pompous-sounding tongue, and common Scandi, which all of the various clans and tribes spoke.

The ceremony had dragged on forever, the priests commanding Keri and the king to recite first this bit of nonsense and then that bit of rhetoric, none of which seemed to have any meaning under the present circumstances. Keri had knelt and dipped in obeisance, been anointed, draped with circlets of gold and flowers, and finally a large signet ring was placed upon her finger. It was done; she was wed to the king. Keri was now the queen of the Scandi nation. But still, it was not done.

Carn could see the tears glinting in her eyes as she turned to look at him. Her chin was tilted proudly, perhaps even defiantly, but her lower lip trembled as it always had whenever the two of them had been forced to face the consequences of their mischief as youngsters.

Suddenly Carn felt the years drop away: He and Keri were standing side by side, awaiting punishment for the breakage of a valuable vase, an accident which he alone had been responsible for. But Keri had spoken out and accepted half the blame, even though she had no part in the incident. Her lower lip had trembled exactly so then, afraid of her father's wrath, for the vase had been important to their mother. She had stared at him defiantly then too, commanding his silence even though she was younger by several years.

She had borne her share of the punishment without comment or complaint and had silenced him with a look when he had haltingly tried to stammer out his thanks. He had never understood why she had done it, but now he thought that perhaps he did. It occurred to him for perhaps the very first time that his sister loved him.

It was a simple thought, perhaps even an obvious one, the acknowledgment of an emotion that bound most family members together. But things had not been simple for Carn for a long time. Jealousy of Braldt had colored everything, including the knowledge that his sister loved him despite the fact that he had turned his back on her.

Even as he admitted to himself that he had been wrong, had treated her unfairly, a wind seemed to blow through his mind, as cold and chilling as the wind that swept across the deck of the ship. It was as though a curtain had been pulled aside, revealing truths to him that he had long sought to hide from himself. Braldt was not his enemy. Keri had not betrayed him. It was he who had been wrong, it was he who had betrayed them both in his heart and in his deeds.

Carn touched his brow with his fingers, feeling an ache behind his eyes that was echoed in his heart. Where had it all gone wrong, and most of all, how was he to put it right?

Dimly, through the tumult that was occurring in his mind, he heard the volva speaking. Her voice was like a knife cutting through the festering wound of his sickness, lancing the poison that had corrupted his thoughts. He turned to her and seemed to see her for the first time. He was repulsed by the sight of her. Her long, dark hair, whipped by the wind, no longer invited his fingers to tangle themselves in their strands. Instead they reminded him of a nest of vipers, their heads questing, tongues flicking, anxiously searching for their next victim. Her eyes were crazed, her vision focused inward on some private goal that he now knew he served as the pawn for. Her teeth were small and white like those of a child, but were filed into points that could and did draw blood. How easily she had drawn him into her spell. He had been so willing. The promise of power and her sexuality was all that it had taken. He had been pathetically simple. Shame swept over him in a hot wave.

Words began to filter through, come to him, punctuating his self-loathing. Her arms were lifted to the cold heavens, which were filled with thunderous dark clouds. She shrieked her words into the force of the winds, which were increasing in velocity, her cloak billowing out stiffly behind her. She seemed to be calling upon Thor, calling him down, inviting him to join them, to accept their offering.

Once the ceremony was completed, Otir Vaeng collapsed in a carved wooden chair which had been provided for him, his arm cushioned by soft pillows, his body wrapped in furs and polyskins to hold in the heat. He seemed drained by the long ceremony and paid little attention to the volva's imprecations, staring out across the cold horizon as though his thoughts were a million miles away; and perhaps they were, seeing some other horizon, remembering some other, distant, happier time.

At Otir Vaeng's feet there rose a tall pile of timber freshly cut at his direction, perfuming the air with the sharp, clean scent of dripping sap. Skirnir had attempted to question the order, but the king had not replied and Skirnir was not foolish enough to countermand the king's wishes.

Skirnir scanned the deck, attempting to see what it was that the king stared at so fixedly. But there was nothing to be seen other than the pile of wood and the tiny cabin at the prow of the boat where a navigator might have stood in ancient days.

Skirnir might have objected to the added detail, but he had not, for he had begun to suspect what the king had in mind. He scarcely dared to believe that he could be right. Nothing was that simple. Perhaps he was wrong; Otir Vaeng had delighted in proving him wrong many times in the past, for the man was wily and his mind moved in convoluted patterns.

Skirnir dragged his attention away from the king. It didn't really matter what the man was planning; he was dying, that much was easy to see. The damned lupebeast had actually done Skirnir a favor by biting the king. Skirnir had seen many wounds during the course of his life and knew the miracles the healers could perform, but there was only so much they could do and this wound had progressed far beyond their ability to reverse the damage. All he had to do was watch and wait, and soon he, Skirnir Rolgvald, son of commoners, would be king of the Scandis.

The moment had come. The volva had reached a feverish pitch, calling upon the gods, importuning them to accept the gift and return their beneficence to the land.

Her words were met with a howl of wind that swept down from the roiling clouds, their swollen underbellies black and heavy with the threat of rain or snow. She turned to Carn and her eyes drilled into his, attempting to overwhelm his fragile sanity with the sheer force of her maddened mind.

She snatched a dagger from her belt and forced his fingers around the hilt, a bone, polished to a rich gleam by the caress of centuries of reverent hands. The blade was long and thin, honed to a state of near transparency over the ages.

Her fingers locked around his, clenching them tight till the knobs of the bone handle pressed painfully into his flesh. Her touch was feverishly hot, her eyes burning into his, commanding him wordlessly to do her bidding. He felt drugged, his mind numbed, his will slipping away from him like the storm tide pulling away from the shore. His fingers wrapped around the bone shaft of their own volition and he felt himself turn toward Keri, his feet devoid of sensation as though they obeyed another mind, supported another's body. A part of him remained isolated from the factotum that obeyed the volva's will, seemed to view himself from afar and yet was powerless to rebel or intervene.

He turned to Keri and they looked into each other's eyes. She was aware of the knife in his hand but never lowered her eyes as another might have done. It was clear from the way she raised her chin that she knew what he intended to do. He saw the tiny knife she held clenched in her hand yet knew that all she would have to do was speak and he would be powerless to harm her.

That portion of him which remained free of the volva's grip screamed silently for her to speak, cried for her to say the words that might break the spell. But she remained silent, holding his eyes with her own, a link as hypnotic as that of the volva's. It seemed to draw him toward her and the knife came up, his nerveless fingers meeting his shoulder, his taut muscles trembling with the need to unleash the waited action.

The screaming wind seemed to echo the torment of his soul and his anguished mind. Carn felt as though he were going mad. The volva was screaming again, her words indistinguishable from the violence of the rising storm. He felt as though she too were an implacable force of nature, one that he could not dare to stand up against, one whose power was far greater than his own frail will.

Tears fell from Carn's scarred eyes, fell unnoticed upon the twisted flesh of his face, and he took a step toward Keri, hating himself, hating what he had become, praying that she would use the knife she held. But still she did not move, only stared at him with love and fear and steadfast courage in her eyes.

And then he was beside her and as he raised the knife for the killing blow, the ship was slammed sideways by a massive wave. He stumbled sideways, off balance, and out of the corner of his eye he saw a blur of movement. Keri was thrown off balance as well and the connection between them was severed. Carn's arm struck the side of the king's chair and the knife was dislodged, knocked from his grip, and went clattering along the deck. The spell was broken. He made no attempt to retrieve the blade, but stared at it, drained of all emotion as well as strength.

The volva seemed to realize instantly that she had lost her hold on him. She screamed in fury, a wild, inhuman sound that was snatched away by the howling wind. She dived for the knife. Carn knew what she was going to do. He threw himself forward, reaching the blade a brief instant before her fingers closed around it. He raised the knife and smiled at her gently. She sagged briefly, believing that she had regained her hold upon his body as well as his soul. Even as he smiled to reassure her, he brought the knife down, not upon Keri, who was sprawled helplessly beside him, but into the volva's body, straight down into the soft flesh of her breast. The knife passed through the woman's flesh as easily as through paper. Her eyes opened wide in disbelief and her mouth opened wide. A gout of blood stained her teeth and colored the lips crimson before dripping down her chin and falling upon the blade that had stolen her life. She reached for him with shaking, nerveless fingers and he moved back so that she could not touch him, for he feared her still.

She died with the disbelief still written in her eyes, the unspoken curse still on her lips, the knife lodged firmly in her chest. Carn stared down at her as she stared up with unseeing eyes into the ominous sky. He was chilled. Cold, so very, very cold. He tugged the knife free of the flesh he had known so intimately and stared at the dripping blade.

He looked then at Keri, who was attempting to rise from the heaving deck. Her eyes were filled with confusion as well as compassion. She reached for him as though forgiving him, urging him silently to take her hand. Carn smiled at her softly, her forgiveness a deeper pain than he had ever known. He knew the depth of his betrayal, knew that even if she could forgive him, he could never forgive himself. He had been willing to sacrifice his sister, Braldt, those who had loved him, for his own warped ambitions.

He heard her call his name as he turned the blade upon himself, an act of courage greater than any he had ever known before. He was surprised to feel the lance of icy pain that pierced him. It was cold, yet burning at the same time; it was not what he had expected. It seemed a foolish thought. Keri was screaming. Her voice seemed to come from far away. He looked up at her, surprised to note that he was lying on the deck. He did not recall having fallen. He tried to smile at her, to tell her that it was all right, but no words came to his lips.

A great calmness descended upon him. He could see the wind tearing at the naked masts, see the ropes straining under the force of the rising gale, sense the rise and fall of the deck beneath him, but he could feel nothing. He wished that he could comfort Keri, could tell her that it was the right thing to have done. Perhaps she would know it in time.

Through the dim and distant light, he saw Braldt and Skirnir struggling over Keri and then Beast was there and an eerie howling was echoing in his ears. It was curious that he could not feel any emotion other than relief. He felt as though he had completed a long and difficult journey and if he only closed his eyes, Mother would be there to welcome him home.

Otir Vaeng watched the proceedings with a sense of weariness that matched Carn's. He had spent his life maneuvering others, manipulating them to his will to attain, achieve and protect his power, and now none of it seemed to matter.

Even before Carn closed his eyes, his blood mingling with that of the volva's and spreading in dark pools across the deck, Otir Vaeng had bent forward and touched the fire starter to the pile of dry kindling that formed a dense layer under the mountain of wood. He no longer felt the pain of his arm, which had by now filled his body with deadly poisons.

He knew that he had come to the end of his life, and strangely, it no longer mattered. He had known it was done as soon as the Beast had bitten him. It seemed oddly fitting that that should be the method of his death, a creature from a world that he had caused to die for his own gain.

He had spent much time reviewing the events of his life during the course of the last weeks and knew that it had all been foolishness based on pride and greed. He had done much that was good, but little that would be remembered if any of his people survived the coming catastrophe.

He had never thought of himself as a coward, and in choosing the time and manner of his death, he thought that he could meet it bravely. He had no desire to rot away, suppurating with approaching death and whining for release.

He had never believed in gods or an afterlife either, despite the fact that he had imposed such beliefs upon his people with an iron will. Now, as death drew near, he found himself welcoming it, wishing for it with the fervor he had once held for his only loves. He wondered if there truly were gods and whether the spirits of those he had once loved, those few who had truly loved him, would be there.

He had thought the voyage to the stars, the founding of a new world, to be the greatest adventure he had ever undertaken, ever hoped to experience, but now he knew that this was a far greater adventure that he was about to embark upon, death.

The fire had seized hold now. Flames rose, crackling and snarling around him. The heat felt good upon his chilled and aching body. But there were other sounds as well. He dragged himself back from the gathering clouds and forced himself to concentrate on what was happening around him. He resented the intrusion, the need to return, but there was still something holding him, something he had to do.

Keri, the girl. Otir Vaeng stared at Keri, attempting to comprehend what it was that he was seeing. His mind was still occupied with thoughts of what was to come and it was difficult to resolve the images he was seeing. Braldt—that was the man's name. He had thought that he was dead, but here he was struggling with Keri, trying to pull her away from Carn's body. The flames were perilously close.

Braldt heaved her to her feet and then suddenly she was clinging to him! Otir Vaeng looked down upon her tear-streaked face and saw with amazement that some of her tears, some of her grief, were for him! He had little strength, precious little to spare, but he forced his lips into a smile and raised his fingers to touch her face. It was all the time that he was granted. Braldt seized her and clutched her to his chest. For a brief moment, his eyes met those of the king, and Otir Vaeng read compassion, understanding, and, even more importantly, respect in Braldt's eyes. Braldt nodded to Otir

Vaeng, the benediction of one king to another, and then he was gone, with Beast at his heels.

The shape-changers were all that remained. Otir Vaeng nodded to one of them and the dour, dark creature understood his unspoken command. Stepping to the stern of the boat, he brought a great ax down upon the thick hawser which held the ship to the shore. It parted with a twang and the ship leapt forward, its prow slicing through the waves, headed for the dark horizon.

Braldt and Beast struggled through the pounding surf which crashed upon the stony shore. Ahead of them, Skirnir, wet and dripping, his robes clinging to his skinny legs, fought his way through the raging water. Anxious hands reached out to grab Braldt and Keri, to pull them to safety out of the grip of the undertow that sucked at their legs and threatened to devour them in the icy gray waters. No one hurried to Skirnir's aid and it was by sheer determination that he managed to reach the shore.

They were wrapped in polyskin cloaks and Keri's sodden finery was stripped from her as water turned to ice upon contact with the bitterly cold winds. But Keri seemed unaware of the ministrations and concern that were being lavished on her. Her eyes followed the rapidly vanishing ship as it rose and fell upon the storm-tossed waves. The fierce forbidding visage of the monster carved upon the prow looked back at her until it disappeared in a drift of smoke.

The sky was black and terrible, the clouds churning and rolling with fearsome turbulence. Everything was darkness, one could scarcely tell where the clouds left off and the dark seas began. Only the bright spot of crimson gold flames served as the ship's beacon.

Then an amazing thing happened. The skies parted as though separated by hands and a clear blue patch of sky emerged. Sunlight, warm and golden such as they had not felt since leaving their own worlds, streamed down upon the blazing ship—beams of light that Carn and Keri had always called God Rays—enveloping the burning ship. Then, in the empty sky, as barren of life as the planet, two winged figures were seen. A cry went up from the crowd as disbelieving eyes fixed upon the sight. A third winged figure joined the two, and then one more. Higher and higher they circled above the blazing ship, their joyous cries echoing across the thin, cold air. They were bathed in the rays of light, their broad, strong wings outspread, catching the sun and the wind. Higher and higher they circled until they were no more than specks in the bright light.

Then, as they entered the hole in the clouds, the clouds closed around them, shutting out the light, and then they were gone. Only the ship remained. There was a brief burst of flames which flared against the dark, seething sea and then it was gone and a hard, cold rain began to fall.

23

The insanity began almost upon the instant that the clouds came together. A terrible, cold rain began to fall, pelting down upon them with a vengeance. As soon as it touched them, it turned to ice which coated flesh as well as clothing. Every step, every motion, was accompanied by the tinkling of ice breaking and falling to the ground. The rain turned to sleet and struck them like tiny pellets that stung painfully when they landed on exposed flesh. Not even their clothing was adequate protection from the constant bombardment.

The musicians threw down their instruments, the guards tossed aside their weapons, even the priests abandoned their accoutrements of office, and as one, regardless of rank, the crowd raced for shelter.

There was no shelter to be found close to the shore, which was exposed to the full brunt of the wind and the elements. As they hurried toward the path which would lead them into the foothills and thence through the mountains, it seemed to Braldt that the ground felt uncertain beneath his feet. It was solid, that was not the problem, but somehow it seemed not to be where it should be when his feet came down. He felt as though he were walking on a quaking swamp. But that could not be, for the ground was frozen solid. He became aware of other people having similar difficulties around him. Everywhere people were stumbling and falling off balance. Braldt halted his flight and clutched Keri close to his chest. Beast hung at his heels and crouched low, growling and snapping his jaws, searching for the source of the danger which he too sensed.

Once they were still, the danger was immediately apparent. It was the ground itself which appeared to be trembling, vibrating just enough to cause the earth to move underfoot.

The advance wave of the crowd had reached the top of the first of the foothills, a small rise from which it was possible to see the spread of mountains that lay beyond. They began to scream. Many of them covered their eyes; some of the women began to cry. Braldt hurried forward, his heart hammering in his chest, suddenly afraid of what he would find.

It was an impossible sight, one which his mind and eyes had difficulty accepting. The mountains were moving. As far as the eye could see, the mountains appeared to be shaking from side to side as well as moving up and down. The entire landscape was in a state of upheaval. As Braldt watched in disbelief, the entire side of a mountain seemed to break away and fall into the valley below with a roar that was clearly audible despite the distance that separated them. That was merely the opening salvo. A peak that was much closer to them seemed to tear itself in half, one section falling slowly toward them, the other vanishing in a cloud of dust.

The remainder of the crowd had joined them on the small summit and together they watched as the entire mountain range crumbled and shook itself into ruin. It was no longer possible to stand. The violence beneath their feet was too great. The great mass of people, all that remained of the once mighty Scandi empire, huddled together and watched their world destroy itself. There was no longer any thought of returning to the mountain they had named Aasgard. Even if they could have reached it without losing their lives, there was no longer any point in doing so. Anyone who had been inside the mountain when the quake struck was no longer alive.

They could not remain where they were; they would freeze to death before the quake could kill them if they did not find shelter. Braldt covered Keri's face with a corner of his polyskin cloak, shielding her from the wind and sleet as well as the horrible sight and wracked his brain for a place of safety. And then it came to him: the great sky craft, the ship that flew through the heavens! Barat Krol had damaged it, prevented it from rising. It might never sail the skies again but it might provide some form of safety from the elements.

He voiced his thoughts to Uba Mintch and Barat Krol, who had made their way through the crowd and crouched at Braldt's side. Braldt never knew what ignited the crowd. Perhaps he had spoken too loudly; perhaps he was not the only one who thought of the great ship. Whatever the reason, almost immediately the entire mob reversed itself, flowing down the foothill like a surge of tidewater, and raced along the shore toward the plain where the spacecraft was moored.

Carrying Keri, who hung limp and uncaring in his arms, Braldt was overtaken and passed by the majority of the panic-stricken crowd. Only Barat Krol and Uba Mintch stayed at his side. Barat Krol gave him a lopsided grin. "Do you think they will attempt to fly the ship?"

"How could they?" asked Braldt, stumbling along the ice-coated rocks. "You have made certain that it will not fly true."

"They do not know this," Barat Krol pointed out.

"They cannot fly it; they do not possess the necessary skills. Nor is there enough room. Surely they would not attempt to leave if all could not go."

Barat Krol shook his head and grinned at Braldt wryly. "Ah, my friend, I am glad that I do not have the same dumb trust that you enjoy. I would have been a rug before some Scandi's fireplace had I been so naïve.''

Braldt was unable to concentrate on discussions of man's nature. Other thoughts were demanding to be heard.

''What about Septua and Mirna and the old ones, Brandtson and Saxo? Do you think that they might have gotten out?''

Barat Krol shook his head. ''Septua and Mirna, perhaps. Those two are survivors; if there was a way, they would find it. But Saxo and Brandtson . . .'' Barat Krol shook his head. ''I do not see how, my friend. Those mountains . . .''

They were making their way along the shore. Talk became impossible as the footing became more treacherous. The rocks were tilted at awkward angles and coated with ice and moved continuously in jittery, unpredictable ways. Braldt was consumed with worry for himself and Keri, and with grief for those who had died. He felt numbed by the painful memory of Carn's death. Even the treachery he had committed could not erase the love that had bound them together for so many years. To Braldt, he would always be a brother. Braldt could easily understand the depth of Keri's grief. But now it was necessary for them to concentrate on their own problems, their own lives, or they would be joining the dead themselves.

Braldt stopped for a moment to catch his breath as well as his footing before attempting a dangerous stretch of broken shoreline. Beast whined and pressed himself against Braldt. Braldt looked up and his breath caught in his throat. Coming in from the sea, heading directly for the shore, was an immense, towering wave, far taller than any normal wave, a solid wall of icy gray water.

Braldt yelled out a warning, but no one could hear him—his voice was lost in the tumult of wind, rain, sleet, and waves. Far ahead of him, the mass of people and Madrelli clawed their way along the storm-wracked shore. Chivalry and nobility were foreign concepts now; it was every man, woman, child, and beast for himself. They fought and shoved and hurled each other aside to gain mere inches. None of them seemed aware of the giant wave that was moving toward them at a terrifying rate of speed.

Braldt and the Madrelli took shelter, such as it was, behind an upthrust slab of granite. Braldt wedged Keri up against the rock and dragged Beast in as close as he could go. Beast needed no urging and wormed forward, wriggling into a tiny space at Keri's feet. He was panting and his amber eyes were wide and ringed with white. The animal was clearly terrified. Braldt was no less frightened. Never had he seen such a thing. He chanced one last look and was held in a deadly fascination, watching the vast mountain of water as it slid over the crest of other, lesser waves, absorbing them, growing larger still as it moved majestically toward the land. A huge paw grabbed the back of his neck and forced his head down, pushed him into a crouch on top of Keri and beast. He could smell the wet fur of the Madrelli and felt the heavy bulk of the others pressing him painfully against the rock.

Then it was on them. There was a curious hush in the air as though the moving water had pushed a wave of air ahead of itself to announce its passage. The wind and rain and sleet were blotted out, gone. The air was almost calm, though filled with a sense of expectancy. He could even hear the tiny lappings of water upon the edge of the shore, hear the most minute sands and stones grating against one another. It was an eerie experience and the tension was almost overwhelming.

They did not have long to wait. The wave struck them with such force that the huge rock they had chosen to protect them moved in the ground, shifted like a loose tooth. For a moment Braldt was afraid that the rock would fall back upon them, crushing them with its great weight, but it did not give way. The water surged around and over it, pounding down upon them with a force that could not be believed. The water was frigid, filled with bits of ice, and it sluiced into every crevice of their bodies and took hold with an icy grasp as it tried to wrench them free.

Braldt felt the water lift him up, tug at his fingers, pull at his clothes. He felt Keri and Beast dragged against his legs and dug his heels into the shifting sands, searching for a firm hold. The water streamed through his hair and stung his eyes, plucked at his nostrils and mouth, attempting to gain access to his body.

He did not know how long the wave lasted, how long they were submerged. It felt like a lifetime. Two lifetimes. As the water began to recede, it was even worse than the influx. Their lungs were already straining, burning from lack of oxygen, and now the water was forcing against them in the opposite direction, trying to drag them out to sea.

When it passed, surging around their ankles as though unwilling to admit defeat, they were battered and drenched to the skin. And Uba Mintch was gone.

None of them had felt him go. Barat Krol was wild with grief, beating himself upon the chest and running along the streaming shore, crying out the old Madrelli's name. Braldt wrapped his arms around him, restraining him, although the Madrelli's strength was much greater than his own, for he feared at one point that Barat Krol meant to fling himself into the sea and swim out in search of his lost leader.

Braldt tried to reason with him. "You are chief now. You must lead them. What will become of them if you die too?" But it did not seem as though the Madrelli heard his words. His great brown eyes were filled with tears and his huge frame shook as he stared out to sea.

The great wave was gone, but, familiar with the nature of waves, Braldt knew that it would return. He must see to it that the survivors too were gone before it returned. They would not live through a second such inundation.

Keri was breathing but appeared to be in shock. Her lips were blue and her skin was mottled with pasty white patches and veins of red lines. Beast was shivering and miserable, but he was alive.

The shore ahead of them was devoid of life. Exposed and defenseless as the others were, the wave had carried them all away.

It was late afternoon before they reached the plain where the ship was moored. There no longer seemed to be the same driving force to get there. A numb, unthinking, mechanical type of mentality had taken over. They were cold, colder than they had ever been. Only the action of walking saved them from freezing, and even so, their extremities were numb and unfeeling. Their hair and Barat Krol's fur were caked with tangles of icicles, and Beast's tail clinked as he walked.

When the ship came into sight, its bright silver nose cone reflecting dully in the sheets of endless lightning that lit up the nightmare sky, they were astonished to discover that they were not the only survivors. A large number of others had reached the ship as well. Perhaps they had been out of reach of the wave or, like Braldt and his companions, had managed to hold on to something and save themselves.

As they hurried toward the ship, overjoyed to find that they were not alone, they slowly realized that some sort of conflict was taking place at the base of the great ship. Alarms began to go off in Braldt's head and he held out an arm to stop Barat Krol from going any farther. The Madrelli looked up at him with dull, grief-stricken eyes, uncomprehending of anything except his own pain, all too willing to allow him to take the lead.

"Something's wrong," Braldt muttered, staring at the scene more closely. There was fighting at the base and sides of the ship. Many had already fallen, their bodies trod upon by others as they attempted to heave themselves up the gantry.

Others—the king's guards, primarily—appeared to be holding them off, using swords and whatever weapons were available to them. One of the guards appeared to be dismantling bits of the gantry network and hurling it down upon those who were attempting to gain access.

Braldt could not understand what he was seeing. Why was there such conflict? There was more than enough room for all of them to shelter inside the ship, for the majority of their numbers had been killed in the desperate flight to reach the plain.

But logic did not appear to have any part of the fray and as his eyes traveled up the length of the gleaming vessel, Braldt saw Skirnir perched in the open doorway, gesticulating wildly, giving frantic instructions to the captain of the guards. The man nodded, touched his head in recognition of Skirnir's right of power, and clambered down the gantry to carry out his orders. Skirnir paused in the open door, looked out across the desolate plain, and seemed to savor what he saw. His eyes met Braldt's and despite the distance, Braldt saw the jolt of recognition that came into the man's eyes as he recognized Braldt and his companions. There was fear in those eyes, as well as malevolence and hatred. The eyes held for a long moment, and then Skirnir stepped inside and slammed the door shut behind him.

The thin screech of the metal as it was dogged shut rang out like a shot in the thin, cold air, echoed in hundreds of desperate ears as the crowd realized instantly what the sound signified. They flung themselves at the ship with renewed desperation, attempting to reverse the action before it was too late.

But it was already too late. Keri sagged against Braldt, hugged tight inside the curve of his arm as a great whoosh burst from the base of the ship, increasing in volume and pitch until it became necessary to cover one's ears against the sound. The sound was accompanied by fury as well, a blast of white-hot exhaust that thrust against the frozen earth and melted the basework of the gantry, instantly killing all of those who clung to it and those in the immediate vicinity.

White flames beat at the ground and licked up the sides of the ship itself. Horns and Klaxons blared and those few who were able staggered away from the ship, putting as much distance between it and themselves as possible, knowing what was to come.

Barat Krol began to laugh, his red-rimmed eyes squeezed tightly shut, his long arms and huge black-palmed paws resting upon his knees, his body bent nearly double under the force of his laughter.

Braldt, who knew what would happen to those in the ship, found Barat Krol's laughter strangely unsettling. But what Skirnir had done, shutting them out and leaving them all behind to die . . . was that any better? Braldt realized that the entire question was pointless. The assignation of blame no longer mattered. People were dying, more people would likely soon die if they did not find shelter, and eventually, sooner rather than later, all of them who remained would die as well.

Braldt dragged Barat Krol back from the widening circle of flames. The heat was sufficient to melt the ice that clung to them and dry their clothes and hair in less time than it took to reach the perimeter of safety.

There they, along with those who had survived the quake, the towering wave, the swords of the guards, and the fiery blast of the ship's engines, watched as the huge ship freed itself of the gantry and slowly, excruciatingly slowly, heaved its bulk free of the earth and then flung itself headlong into the heavens.

24

They milled around aimlessly within the small shelter that had once protected the guards from the weather. They had found supplies, medical necessities and foodstuffs adequate for their needs in the attached blockhouse.

The mood was oppressive. Few of them had failed to grasp the seriousness of their position, even those who did not know of Barat Krol's sabotage.

The ground had finally ceased its incessant rumblings and many among them were proposing an expedition back to Aasgard to search for survivors and supplies. Although the situation looked hopeless, few of them had surrendered hope. Many wild and impossible plans had been suggested, and even though they were just that—wild and impossible—Braldt was glad that the people were thinking and acting at all. Perhaps somehow they would discover a way to save themselves yet.

It was decided that an expedition, a group of twenty-five Scandis and Madrelli, would leave in the morning and attempt to reach Aasgard. The others—247 in all—would remain behind. Braldt and Barat Krol would be among those who led the expedition. They settled themselves down for the night, but few of them slept, lost in their thoughts and personal grieving for those who had died during the disastrous day's events.

Keri had maintained her silence, but now she slept in

Braldt's embrace. He felt her slight weight resting in his arms and was filled with the need to protect her and keep her safe always. If there was a way to return to their world, he would find it and spend the rest of his life at her side.

Braldt opened his eyes and stared up at the stone ceiling, failing for the moment to recognize where he was. Then it all came back. He sighed, stiff and sore and aching in every limb. His arm was asleep where Keri had lain upon it all night. He was beset with despair. How could anyone have survived the quake? No one could possibly be alive. The mountain had certainly collapsed in upon itself. It was surely a fool's mission; they would find nothing of value and most likely kill themselves in the bargain.

Many of the others woke with the same thoughts, but Barat Krol would not allow them to retreat into gloom and depression, and soon they found themselves setting forth on the first step of the journey.

The going was difficult, for the snow was deep and it was impossible to know where it was safe and where it was not. They had found six sets of skis in the blockhouse and the most adept members of their group were using them to break a trail. Braldt and Barat Krol, having had no experience with the strange objects, followed behind, leading the rest of the party.

They were negotiating a wide expanse of mixed snow and slippery stone when suddenly they heard excited shouts from those who had gone ahead. Their first thought was of disaster, some falling snow or unstable ground that had given way. But they soon realized that the sounds were joyous and not the sounds of disaster.

They crossed the slope as quickly as possible and as they rounded a large outcrop of boulders and ice, they were confronted with an almost unbelievable sight: their own party of six, totally surrounded by a group of more than two hundred Scandis and Madrelli!

It was an odd group, extremely odd, for these were the majority of those who had been injured in the first quake and had been left behind during the wedding. Their caretakers and healers were with them, and loved ones who had regarded them as being more important than the king's wedding. Septua was there as was Mirna, and, most happily, Braldt found Brandtson and Saxo, with Thunder still riding on his shoulder, among their numbers.

They had arrived on an odd assortment of sleds pulled by whatever animals were large enough and strong enough to pull them: sheep; small, long-haired arctic cattle with wide thick horns and placid temperament; and even a few pigs. The rest of the sleds were powered by Scandis and Madrelli who had shouldered the burdens willingly. Any and all caste divisions had vanished in the mutual threat. If they did not help each other, they would die.

Their story was simple. They had felt the ground begin to rumble and shake soon after the wedding party departed. Fearing another quake, they had been quick to remove themselves from the interior of the mountain, seizing whatever they could lay their hands on to make good their escape. They were bundled in numerous layers of clothing and polyskins, knowing that it would be freezing outside. They had grabbed whatever foodstuffs were available and their sleds were piled high with bundles of booty.

They had managed to reach a plateau that fortunately was spared the worst of the destruction. There they had spent the day and the night watching their world destroy itself, and had seen the ship's departure and realized that it could not have taken everyone aboard. For lack of a better plan—or any other plan at all, for that matter—they had come to investigate in the hopes that they were not alone.

Saxo and Brandtson had been found along the way, having hastily taken their leave of their sanctuary, which, of course, was no longer safe.

They returned to the plain by midday and those in the blockhouse heard their glad cries and came running out. There were many happy reunions, and there were many whose worst fears were realized.

Unwilling to return to the confining walls of the stone blockhouse, the survivors of Valhalla, earth, and the planet known as K7, huddled together on the snowy plain beneath the gray and lowering sky.

It was Barat Krol who started it, it was later remembered: a joining of hands, a great circle, Madrelli, Scandis, misfits all, one people, with no home in the universe. It was a prayer, it was a song, it was thanksgiving, it was sorrow—it was all of those things and more. And as they stood there beneath the dark sky, someone chanced to look up—a child, perhaps—and was the first to see it.

At first they thought the sun had returned, for the sky was blue—as far as the eye could see, blue. But then the sky, the blueness, drew nearer, and those among them who were fearful began to cry, for it seemed that the sky was indeed falling. Then those who were braver, or perhaps had simply ceased to fear, pointed upward and exclaimed that what they were seeing was not the sky at all, but numerous squares of blue—much like small carpets, some later said—floating down from the sky to land beside them.